PENGUIN BOOKS

FOR THE PEOPLE'S GLORY

Lee Jeong-Ho is an International Relations lecturer at Korea University and Ulsan University, and serves as a non-resident James A. Kelly research fellow at the Pacific Forum. He has an extensive background in journalism, having worked at *Radio Free Asia*, *Bloomberg News*, the *South China Morning Post,* and *News1 Korea in Seoul*, Hong Kong, and Washington D.C. He holds the belief that the free flow of information is vital to democracy, as it equips citizens with knowledge and empowers them.

With academic experiences spanning South Korea, Australia, and the UK, and a stint in the South Korean Air Force, he has successfully transitioned from military service to journalism and research. He is also the co-author of the novel, *Two Sides of A Lie*.

Elaine Chan is a journalist and writer covering Asia and Greater China. She was the Shanghai bureau chief of *Bloomberg News* and has written and edited for the likes of the *South China Morning Post* and the *Associated Press*.

While growing up in her native Singapore, she also trained in Western art and painting. But realizing she'd never be a van Gogh, she decided to pursue journalism, which she believes is the society's conscience. She is also the co-author of the novel *Two Sides of a Lie*.

Also by Lee Jeong-Ho and Elaine Chan

Two Sides of a Lie (2021)

For the People's Glory

Lee Jeong-Ho and Elaine Chan

PENGUIN BOOKS

An imprint of Penguin Random House

PENGUIN BOOKS

Penguin Books is part of the Penguin Random House group of companies
whose addresses can be found at global.penguinrandomhouse.com

Published by Penguin Random House SEA Pte Ltd
40 Penjuru Lane, #03-12, Block 2
Singapore 609216

First published in Penguin Books by Penguin Random House SEA 2024

Copyright © Lee Jeong-Ho and Elaine Chan 2024

ISBN 9789815233124

Typeset in Garamond by MAP Systems, Bengaluru, India

www.penguin.sg

Contents

Part I

The Alchemy of Honour

Prologue

Ding-dong. Bang! Bang! Bang!

The loud thuds jolted Cai Yiping from his deep slumber. He groaned, twitched, and finally turned to the side of the bed, struggling to balance and sit up.

'What's going on?' his wife asked, half asleep as she burrowed herself deeper into the covers to cancel out the noise.

'Don't know, probably a drunk neighbour getting his unit wrong,' he grunted. 'Unbelievable, at such an ungodly hour.' He rummaged for his light woollen cardigan at the edge of the bed as he told his wife to go back to sleep.

He hurriedly tugged a plump arm through the armhole of the sweater, which pulled up and rumpled the sleeve of his pyjamas. He trod, barefoot, past the bathroom and across the living room towards the front door. The marble floor was icy cold, as it was already past mid-autumn and late October.

'Who is this?' he growled, opening the front door slowly—the other sleeve of the cardigan dangling off slightly from the shoulder.

Two men in dark jackets stood before him. They had poker faces, but apart from that, Yiping couldn't make out much. The corridor lights were out except for a pathetic flickering bulb at the end of the long passageway near the lift. 'Damn the building management!' he cursed under his breath.

'We would like you to come with us, Mr Cai,' one said, flashing his badge. In the semi-darkness, Yiping caught sight of an ID photo above printed characters, but they appeared blurry to him without his reading glasses.

'At 4 a.m., are you nuts? What right do you have? Who are you people?' He unconsciously raised his voice.

'Mr Cai, it's just for a conversation at this point,' the second man said flatly, before murmuring, in an even lower voice, his official status. Struggling to awaken his senses, Yiping couldn't make out what the inaudible comment was. He didn't get a chance to clarify because his visitor, apparently anxious to brush over his questions, in a normal tone, said, 'If I were you, I wouldn't wake the neighbours.' But he thought he'd heard 'the Bureau of State Security'.

'Er . . . give me ten minutes,' he muttered. 'I'll wash up and tell my wife.' He turned his back, shut the door, and headed to the bathroom. The sleepiness had all but left him. His heart was sinking, he knew this wasn't good. There were only a few departments in this country, Utopia, that would haul people out from their homes at such an ungodly hour—catch you when you were most vulnerable—and most would never make it back.

* * *

Tian Li had lost some sleep. Fatigue bracketed her eyes. It had been more than a week since the black-suited men escorted her husband away early that morning. She couldn't see their faces clearly, as she stood behind him at the door, their bodies half-turned, ready to leave. They looked hostile, certainly not people you could mess with.

'Which department are you from?' She had asked the men as Yiping slipped into his sneakers. But her words echoed hollowly into the darkness of the unlit sky, evaporating into the crisp autumn air. The men didn't even bother to look at her.

Yiping had phoned just once on the second day. It was an unknown number. The call was so brief that it ended before it really began.

'I'm assisting in an investigation,' he had whispered.

'Are you all right? Do you . . .?' she had asked anxiously.

'I'm all right, no cause for worry,' he had said firmly, cutting her off before the line went dead.

Somehow, Tian Li hadn't been assured. Like Yiping, she was also a researcher at the state-owned United Front Institute (UFI), in a different department and several ranks below her husband who ran the semiconductor R&D laboratory tasked by the central government to develop the nation's superchip. Yiping's stakes were much higher, for the superchip was *the* key to transformative technologies that would change the country's fortune and international status to that of a tech superpower.

Tian Li's relationship with her husband was not exactly great. They had drifted over the years and were, as of late, going through a rough patch. She was disturbed but not terribly worried, as she believed twenty-five years or so of marriage would tide them over any bumps. She wouldn't say there was a passion in the relationship, but there certainly was love, the kind you'd have for a family member. At a practical level, they shared some common interests and a twenty-two-year-old daughter. Whatever her feelings were right now, he was family after all.

At work, her colleagues avoided talking about Yiping in her presence, but she knew that they gossiped about his 'disappearance' behind her back. Those whom she counted as friends in her department shied away from contacting her, as did the few she knew from her husband's lab, cutting off the already limited avenues there were to seek information within UFI.

As word that her husband had been taken away slowly spread over the days, she felt a layer of biting cold prematurely descend around her even though the trees were just changing colours outside UFI. The mood was unusually tense, particularly on the two floors that were dedicated to the superchip project. Since the decision to transform the nation into a tech superpower had been written into the Party doctrine almost ten years ago, the atmosphere of UFI or, for that matter, in Unitas, the capital city, even the entire country, had changed.

She concealed her emotions—fear and anxiety—as much as she could to be on the safe side. Every corner she turned there was a surveillance camera—she began to not know who she could trust.

Nonetheless, she made a request to see the director of UFI the third day after Yiping had gone with the men. The director was the most senior Party official, a person who had little contact with researchers at her level, and someone she wouldn't normally have access to. All the same, she gave it a try, because the truth was, she was at her wit's end, like the sole person left in the dark.

Three days later, she secured a meeting with the director. More than securing it, she thought it was the institution being ready to state its position. Whatever it was, it would be her first opportunity to get some information.

'*Xiao* Cai is being asked to assist in providing information on a very important issue, which is classified,' said the director flatly from his desk, as she entered his office and walked towards the heavy wooden table. He promptly stood up, though not to usher her towards the sofa up front for a seated discussion, but more to signal that this exercise had been undertaken to inform and nothing else. She hated it when her hunch was right.

The director, who was a few years into his retirement, had been Yiping's teacher at the university since the latter's undergraduate days, and always referred to his student in a way that would be seen as an affectionate address, one that was used for another younger person or a friend. In this instance, Tian Li thought it clearly distinguished the hierarchical gap between the two men. The director's cold voice was also unusual for someone with his boisterous character—animated, as he was, in his words and body language. Everyone at UFI knew Yiping was the protégé who, until ten years ago, had been one of the hundreds of minions with little chance of shining. The director, who rose up the Party ranks, remembered his star student, and when he was appointed the deputy of the UFI, he recruited his mentee. 'He plucked me from obscurity,' the student told his wife. The director also embraced Tian Li like a distant family member. But today, the elderly, rotund man was being distant.

While she had psyched herself to not raise her expectations before the meeting, she was still taken aback by his abnormal behaviour and, more worryingly so, at his attempt to build a wall between him and them. Quickly shuffling aside her bafflement, she returned her focus on getting answers.

'What is the issue? Is he incriminated?' She felt her frustration rising.

Ignoring her questions, the director responded, 'Don't say or do anything hasty that you'll regret.' He stretched out his arm in the direction of the door and nodded his head. The meeting was over.

As a long-time employee of the state institution, Tian Li understood, and had become resigned to, a rigid system, where asking questions yielded more trouble than answers. Her personal justification for such acceptance was a chance at a stable life. Her hope and desire for more was solely reserved for their only daughter, who was in her final year at an American university. She was not ambitious herself, but she knew that a blemish in the family records could spell disaster for her daughter. Yiping's detention was upending that, and she was secretly indignant that the state was not keeping its side of the bargain. She struggled to stay calm as she left the director's office. She was too preoccupied with her own thoughts and speculations about what could befall her family to consider the director's motivation to keep her at arm's length.

Tian Li needed information so that she could prepare to protect the family's interests, especially when she was oblivious to Yiping's engagements outside the home.

In fact, being unaware of the specifics of Yiping's challenges at work, there wasn't much she could ask. Nonetheless, she had long sensed that his professional challenges were somewhat mounting. All she knew was that there had been progress and piecemeal achievements, like memory chips, but no breakthrough at levels of parity with the world's leading semiconductor giants. The stakes were naturally high for Yiping. Tian Li had seen her husband age, gradually at first, but it quickly picked up pace. His interest in her and their daughter also waned somewhat, she thought, but she wasn't completely certain. Because there would be occasions when he would be in a joyful mood and he'd bring home some desserts or new additions to the household, like a new television or other home appliances. She assumed that they were celebratory tokens for when the lab managed tiny breakthroughs in their innovation.

'What are we celebrating?' she tried asking her husband when he had bought a new television home one time.

'You know I can't talk about my work. It's a state secret.' That had been the end of the conversation.

Though she was trained, as a scientist, to pick up on the slightest sign and indication, she tried to remove complex thinking from her home life. Whether it was conscious or not, Tian Li slowly lost interest in Yiping too.

His detention made her realize how little she had come to know of her husband in the last ten years—only familiar with his daily routine between the lab and home. There had been some business trips overseas and around the country, but the travel dates were all she knew or cared about. Outside the work routine, she assumed that his Saturdays were spent playing chess with his university buddy Shan Hongbing, who headed the country's leading semiconductor foreign joint venture (JV), and browsing at the bookstore. Her own weekend usually revolved around cleaning their 150-square metre flat and grocery shopping. The family would dine together on Sundays at a neighbouring restaurant, but conversation was usually minimal.

'What would you like to eat?' Yiping would ask his wife and daughter when the latter was still living at home. Each would name a dish and those would probably be all the words spoken during the meal. They would mostly eat in silence.

Tian Li also knew Hongbing from the university, where she had been a year behind the men. Hongbing was an optimist by nature and fiercely loyal to the Party. All three had been Party members for more than two decades—since they were undergraduates. She and Yiping also supported the Party because, after all, they worked in a state organization and lived in a government-assigned flat until economic reforms allowed them to buy over the property at a subsidized price. They also saw faults in the Party unlike Hongbing, who staunchly believed that the Party could do no wrong. When they were younger, the couple used to hang out with Hongbing and his wife. The women were never close, but they were cordial to each other. Over time, however, Tian Li saw less of the couple, not only because she spent less time with her husband and his friends but also because she found Hongbing's wife, who had succeeded as a real estate businesswoman, to be overly flashy for her liking.

Yiping and Hongbing were also loosely connected on the work front. The UFI was affiliated with the state-owned enterprise that owned a 51 per cent stake in the JV firm, which Hongbing oversaw.

Tian Li felt hopeless after the meeting with the director. She struggled with the idea of publicizing what had happened to Yiping, which may— or may not—pressure the authorities into divulging more. She had heard about bureaucrats being detained, but they were usually friends of friends or someone that others knew, never a direct acquaintance. She had also heard, through the grapevine, about how some family members made a din, which then usually quickly—and suspiciously—subsided. There were others who hired human rights lawyers, who themselves ended up in detention too. She was convinced most kept mum and simply prayed.

Failing to get any information at UFI, Tian Li rang Hongbing on his mobile.

'Tian Li, what a pleasant surprise! How have you been? I keep telling Yiping that our families should have dinner together soon. How about next weekend?' An upbeat Hongbing came on. 'We can—'

'Hongbing, dinner can wait,' she cut him off. 'I'm calling about an important matter. Can we meet tomorrow night? It's urgent.'

'Er, sure . . .' he paused, 'I'll get Sara as well . . .'

'No, please,' she said firmly, 'just come alone and tell no one.' She told him where to meet.

* * *

At 7.55 p.m. the following day, Tian Li arrived at a tiny teahouse tucked away in one of the myriad narrow alleys that framed a local, grassroots district in the south-west of the capital city. Since the city was flooded with surveillance cameras—under the auspices of the

Party's magnanimity to steer its people away from harm's way—she was as vigilant as she could be. She didn't know what she was dealing with. *Too much is unknown,* she thought.

She settled into a corner table behind a traditional bamboo screen. Two other tables were in front of the screen—a more open, spacious area that made up two-thirds of the teahouse. It was run by an old high school friend, a discrete woman she trusted.

Hongbing stepped into the teahouse on the dot at seven. Tian Li waved him to the table behind the screen.

'Long time no see,' he said, taking his jacket off. 'Where's Yiping?' He turned his head to look around.

She didn't respond. Instead, she looked right into his eyes and placed her index finger lightly over her mouth, indicating that he should dial down. He heeded the cue and slid onto the wooden chair quietly. Her cheeks were sunken, eyes hollowed with pronounced dark circles under them. Hongbing didn't remember her being so thin and worn out. Something was amiss. His own face turned solemn.

'It's Yiping,' she leaned forward, 'they took him a week ago.'

'What do you mean "took him"?'

'They came to the house, two men in dark jackets. They wouldn't say where they were from. I think it was state security.'

Hongbing felt his brain slipping away from him, his heart racing. He opened his mouth to respond but no sound came out. His throat went dry, and he tried to gulp down his own saliva. He stared at her in disbelief as Tian Li gave him time to process.

'What have you found out?' He finally found his voice.

'Nothing. The director only informed me Yiping's assisting in the investigation of a very important matter. I couldn't get anything else out of him. I was hoping you might have heard something from your headquarters.'

Hongbing shook his head violently. He lost his words once more as he tried to digest the news.

'It's been more than a week, Hongbing,' she said, 'I'm feeling really scared and lost. I'm not sure what to do. Perhaps, I should call this out, go to the media to build them some pressure.'

'No, don't do that!' He unconsciously raised his voice, horrified by her suggestion. 'I'm sure he will be all right. The Party takes care of us.'

He softened his face and looked at her sympathetically. She looked unconvinced.

'Don't worry, I'll do whatever I can to find out more,' he reassured her. 'Yiping is like my brother. Maybe it's just as the director said.' Hongbing felt he was reassuring himself as well.

He left the teahouse with a heavier heart, but always one with a glass-half-full attitude, he was sure this would resolve itself. The Party only had their best interests at heart, he believed.

Chapter 1

The Mission

Monday mornings were almost sacred for Hongbing. It was the start of the week and the end of the much-loathed weekend. He always seemed to have twice the energy on Mondays. Grabbing his good old brown leather shoulder bag that had been sitting idly in the corner of his room for the last two days, he left his sleek, new house with brazen joy and pride, humming. His grey overcoat blew away with the wind as he grinned at the overhead surveillance cameras outside his house—there to ensure his safety and well-being, of course. 'Another great day,' he reminded himself and whistled gleefully—his daily ritual before going to work—breathing in the fresh autumn air.

Being a part of the Party's journey to build the New Utopia had been a thrilling, life-changing experience for Hongbing. It made work exhilarating and his off-duty weekends unbearably tedious, making him feel like he was imprisoned in his own home. His weekends were uneventful except for the routine chess game with his long-time friend Yiping every other Saturday. There had been no games in the past two weekends. When he was not playing chess, he barely did anything but read the Party's official history book and dream of his contribution—as a loyal Party worker—to make Utopia the most powerful state on earth.

His wife, though, seemed to have understood less about this great cause. She sometimes pestered him to go shopping with her or to go have meals with her friends. He mostly refused, finding the activities frivolous, despising his wife for her shallowness. Nothing gave him more satisfaction and happiness than settling into his favourite armchair to read the Party history or any literature that perpetuated the ideology responsible for transforming the country into the world's second-largest economy. And to think that he was part of that history.

The musky smell of the red, decades-old Party history book pierced his brain, tickling his senses, and fostering his sense of pride as he visualized the accomplishments of the Party for its people. He could read the book over and over again and, each time, he felt his understanding and gratification deepen. *How fortunate I am*, he thought. The Party was almighty and irreproachable, the very essence of the nation itself. Hongbing often boasted of the remarkable journey that Utopia had undertaken across every part of this great nation, encompassing everything from the economy to society. He vividly remembered how his grandparents had struggled economically, barely managing to have a full, proper meal each day. Absolute poverty and hunger were constant companions for the people just four decades ago. The newborns now could hardly relate to any of these stories. The country now enjoyed the biggest market in the world, and everyone lived comfortably. One of the most memorable accounts he had was when he had gathered with his best friends, including Yiping, and drunk a fine French wine to celebrate Utopia's total GDP surpassing that of Japan—its biggest rival in Asia since decades. To him, that was far more than just some number in the economic data book. It was a representation of his hard work and the people's resilience in achieving the common goal set by the Party and a testament to its effective ideology.

Hongbing could hardly remember having to skip a meal due to poverty—a stark contrast to the generation before him. The days of him seeking favours from foreign officials for diplomatic and economic concessions were gone—another stark contrast to the previous generations. This was a luxury that stemmed from the strong groundwork laid by the officials who had served before him. But there remained the nagging few in the West who just didn't get the greatness of the Party's ideology. *Bah!* With a dismissive snort at their 'sacred democratic ideals', he now no longer hid his disgust at their failure to see the greatness of the Party's path.

It was now his turn to serve, his turn to lay even more robust groundwork and pass this priceless glory onto the next generation.

There was never a doubt in his mind that he was contributing to the good of his people, who represented a significant portion of humanity. Nothing would stand between him and his calling. It was a deeply inherited belief that the Party's supreme leadership had brought about the great transformation in his beloved Utopia. In the corridors of power, Hongbing witnessed the Party's ultimate guidance in implementing a control policy favouring state-owned-enterprises (SOEs) over private businesses. To him, the Party's full grip over its resource allocation and technology was far from a political manoeuvre. It was, instead, a necessary step for economic efficiency. A step towards making this proud nation a self-sufficient and strong state. There were some critics, of course, although they were a rare breed in Utopia. Hongbing remembered having a conversation with them to hear them out but found nothing of credence—they were unable to make a good point and, thus, their voices were naturally marginalized. They were eventually silenced as the Party's leadership proved their success and as it became undeniable that the quality of people's lives was indisputably improving. As the people living in this great nation understood, some sacrifices were inevitable on the path towards greatness. The stories of those who had been working in private businesses losing jobs were pitiful and sympathetic, but they were a necessary toll on the road to Utopia's hegemony. The same train of thought resonated with the people around him.

The Party had been highly ambitious from the outset and that ambition always resonated with Hongbing. He grew up hearing tales from his grandparents about Utopia's early days when the state was ravaged by a civil war. But now, thanks to the Party's unwavering dedication—with it pouring infinite resources into advancing its technological prowess—he was living in a state that would soon become the next superpower.

He had long admired and followed the Party's strategy to make a strong Utopia, especially its strategy to partner with foreign tech giants. He saw this as a clever play in the international chess game. The Party lured foreign high-tech firms—especially the ones involved in manufacturing semiconductors and artificial intelligence development—with its market size, encouraging them to build factories and data centres in the country. In exchange for access, foreign partners needed to impart advanced technology to the JVs they set up with the SOEs. In his eyes, this wasn't any kind of exploitation, they weren't deceiving other states. Each step was a personal victory of the people of Utopia, a brilliant manoeuvre to establish the nation's technological supremacy. As Hongbing witnessed the rise of his country due to technological advancement, he just couldn't help but feel a stronger and deeper connection with the Party, as its every decision was propelling Utopia forward.

As an SOE representative at UF-Clanta—a semiconductor manufacturing JV with South Korea's Clanta Corporation—Hongbing's job was to transfer the foreign firm's classified data to Utopia's relevant authorities. The job was stressful, but it wasn't impossible, given that some documents and information on Clanta were accessible via his various surveillance channels. The almighty Party called him a Collector, and with pride, he fulfilled his duty by feeding crucial tech data to the relevant authorities, thereby strengthening Utopia.

High-spirited and humming the soundtrack of the latest patriotic drama that was currently streaming, Hongbing walked into the Link—a dedicated subway transporting Party workers who worked at JVs and foreign corporations. As a senior-level manager, he was entitled to a chauffeured company car, but he opted to use the subway because it was the right 'Utopian spirit' to have—to be an equal among his comrades. The Link was a state-of-the-art system built with the necessary infrastructure for the Collectors to have access to whatever resources they needed on the go. It was also designed, as an unspoken rule, to segregate Party workers from non-Party members so that the workers would not get distracted from their missions. Foreign ideas and thoughts, especially the myth surrounding the concept of 'freedom', were considered common tools used by adversaries to taint Utopia's ideological purity, thwarting the nation's progression. No expenses were spared to minimize the risk.

The soft, synthetic scent of scilla flowers dispensed from the ceiling grazed Hongbing's nostrils as he walked into the Link. Plastic clusters of the flower, which symbolized loyalty and constancy, filled the subway station. Their sight and smell reminded each worker to never forget their loyalty to the cause.

Another step towards the New Utopia. The thought came as naturally as his breathing. He stepped onto an inclined travelator that sucked him deeper into the Link. He liked the reflection he saw in the mirrored wall on the left side of the travelator—a 1.74 metre, clean-cut looking professional wearing close-cropped hair and a confident look. His dark and steely eyes were sometimes cold, usually when he was exerting his authority in the Party hierarchy. The travelator—connecting the station hall to the train platforms at the lower levels—glided through the 'Great Hall of Glory', where homegrown 3D holographic technology rendered the story of the Party's milestones over eight decades. Hongbing's favourite segment showed mobilizing tanks and ammunition, and Utopian people's bloodshed during the fight against the Western imperialists in the 1950s. It went on to depict the opening up of the economy and Utopia's transformation from a manufacturing powerhouse to a high-tech nation in which prosperity was brought to every citizen. He had watched and listened to the story daily for the past ten years, yet never tired of the narrative that always made his heart pound. It was the perfect way to start his workday. *I, too, must play my part,* he vowed again, as he hopped off the travelator and headed towards the Scanner, with a row of identification optical readers.

'Subject 4201. Collector at UF-Clanta. Access granted for Platform 8.'

A baritone voice boomed from a speaker, verifying Hongbing's identity as the camera in one of the scanners scanned his face. A green light flashed on the surface of the vertical post of the turnstile, with a holographic image of him floating mid-air as the swing glass gates opened.

He never questioned what 'green' was supposed to mean, assuming it was simply a Party classification for bureaucratic purposes. He walked through another round of face scans before entering Platform 8, where a few other UF-Clanta Collectors waited for their ride, which sent them directly to the basement of the JV's office building on the outskirts of Unitas.

'Next train arriving in twenty-four minutes,' Hongbing's smartwatch beamed, in sync with the baritone voice broadcast through the public announcement system. As though on cue, the giant screens on the platform lit up with the latest internal news gathered overnight by the Party's United Front Intelligence Agency.

'Today's intel.' A female hologram sprang from the screen, accompanied by a simple and diatonic melody. 'The chairwoman of South Korea's Clanta Corporation, Jacinta Lee, will be visiting Unitas, the capital city next month, according to our dearest foreign workers in Seoul,' said the AI presenter whose mouth moved while her eyes remained expressionless. 'Collectors are encouraged to gather as much information about her trip as well as any intel on Clanta's latest tech of 1.4-nanometre chip production.'

The holographic presenter faded into the dark background to give way to a chart tracking share prices of all Clanta stocks over the past month—traded in different foreign stock exchanges—displayed on one side of the screen, with reels of already-aired news of the company on the other side. The screen then turned dark before a ceremonial drum roll burst in with a spectacular display of fireworks that segued into a music video worshipping the sacrifices the current Party Leader made for Utopian people and celebrating the communal economic prosperity that he realized for the state. The segment ended at the twenty-third minute.

Shifting his attention from the screen, Hongbing caught sight of his colleague Jane Hu, whom he had known for many years, a few metres away from him.

'Morning, Jane,' he said brightly.

'Morning,' she mumbled lethargically, pulling her hair back into a ponytail. She looked frazzled, but Hongbing only noticed her unironed white shirt, with one shirt tail peeping out of the waistband of her equally crumpled black pencil skirt. He frowned and thought, *This is in no way befitting Utopian workplace.*

Out loud, he said, 'One step towards the New Utopia. How's everything going with your duty?'

'Er . . . been all right,' she hesitated, forcing a smile. Then, momentarily, with a seeming change of heart, she blurted out, 'Actually . . . not too well, to be honest.'

Shite! I shouldn't have asked, he regretted his question immediately. He then chided himself for this. *Why so negative? Surely, she's not showing disloyalty?* If so, it would really complicate his day, as he was obliged to report any waywardness to the higher-ups to minimize ideological impurity that may damage the Party's grand plan. But he could tell that whatever the pressure was, it was eating her up.

'Don't know how much longer I can do this,' she continued feebly. She was relieved to confide in him, oblivious to the horror that was slowly writing its way on her friend's face.

By then, Hongbing desperately wanted to cover her mouth and make her stop. She was now a dangerous, vindictive witch. He was almost certain that whatever she was going to say next wouldn't be positive—which threatened to jeopardize his day and career. Clearly, what one said and did were important metrics, but who you associated with could be as much of an advantage as it was a risk. When those around you were proven to be ideologically contaminated, you had little chance of climbing up the Party ladder.

'Whatever the problem is, I'm sure it's nothing that you can't overcome,' he told her matter-of-factly. He was trying his best to remove himself from the exchange.

'I got low grades from my supervising Controllers for the last three months, and I'm starting to get worried,' the witch went on.

'Don't worry, you'll be fine,' Hongbing muttered, turning his head in various directions to avoid eye contact.

'You just don't get it,' Jane said, her voice rising mildly. 'I've gotten Ds in the last six meetings. What if this costs me my chance to serve the Party? I can't disappoint them.'

It was then that Hongbing breathed a sigh of relief. Reassured that Jane's loyalty towards the Party was still intact, he returned his gaze to her, this time with a bit of sympathy. *Actually, what she's going through is quite natural,* he thought. The work of Collectors was highly stressful, as they were usually thrown in the middle of nowhere and were expected to collect as much intel as they could via their team of assets. They met with their supervising controllers every fortnight, where they were assessed on the value of intel collected. These meetings contributed to their annual appraisals, making the pressure perpetual. Everyone followed the process as any loyal public servant working for the progression of Utopia would. Being conscious and anxious about their performance was natural but speaking about it, even among Collectors, was a customary taboo. The Collectors themselves were also convinced that any discussion would only amplify their concerns, and excessive anxiety would exacerbate their poor performance, ultimately compromising their chance to become a part of the Party's journey in realizing the New Utopia.

'What did they say in the reports?' Hongbing became curious. Now that the sense of risk had subsided, he wanted information. It would also help him to prepare. *You know, just in case.*

'They're saying my team isn't doing as much and that what we do gather is often incomplete, needing more work. I mean . . . what else am I supposed to do, you know? I'm pretty burnt out as it is. Seriously, what more do they want from—'

'No, Jane,' Hongbing interjected. *That was enough.* He had just painstakingly contained potential damage and couldn't risk letting her continue her spiel—which he was being made party to—that, by now, sounded blasphemous. 'The Party is always right and benevolent,' he stated, with a tone of finality.

'Trust the Party and stick with its guidance when waves roll over,' he quoted from the Collector's handbook, staring straight into her eyes. For a brief moment, he wasn't quite sure whether this was aimed at comforting Jane or himself.

'But it's still . . . somewhat annoying, you know. They also said our team underperformed because we were slow in flagging materials to them.'

'Well . . . were you?'

'Not true, of course,' Jane said, looking frustrated. 'But there's nothing I can do. If you do question the supervisors, it is treated as mutiny under the Party constitution, right?'

Ding.

He was spared responding as a red, sleek train pulled into the platform precisely at the twenty-fourth minute, dispersing the awkward air between them. *Thank God.* Jane also didn't press on. *Think I might now have to distance myself from her. No need to put myself in a difficult position, or have my ideals contaminated by her personal anxiety.* Hongbing jumped onto the train as fear replaced his curiosity. Both were quiet, losing themselves in their own thoughts, throughout the forty-minute ride to UF-Clanta.

* * *

'Let's head off for another great day,' Hongbing broke the heavy silence between him and Jane as the train hit the UF-Clanta building. With his beloved workplace before him, he was compelled to revive some positivity, to cleanse off any impurity that had arisen from his earlier conversation with Jane.

'Another great day indeed,' she echoed flatly. The deepened wrinkles of anxiety on her forehead had smoothened out. Her face was now emotionless.

Hongbing and Jane marched, with scores of others, through a marble corridor at the UF-Clanta basement and towards the changing room.

Uniformity Is Diversity
Conformity Is Harmony
Prosperity Is Freedom

The mini holographic Party slogans popped up from his locker door as he scanned his face into the camera attached. Party workers were constantly reminded of what was expected of them at workplaces and, of course, elsewhere as well.

Hongbing had always reflected on the importance of having uniform behaviour, the bare minimum that all citizens needed to put into practice to conform to the Party ideology. The intent of this principle of uniformity was not to impose excessive control over people but to safeguard the Party's internal solidarity, crucial to unifying the sixty ethnic minorities; most of whom spoke different languages. Hongbing often witnessed the challenges this posed through the state media, which showed the violent movements of some separatists revolting for independence from the regions annexed by Utopia. With the undercurrent of resistance haunting the mainstream Utopian people, demonstrating uniform behaviour was the basic obligation of all responsible citizens.

It's the cleverest idea, Hongbing thought, *that the Party forces the minorities to speak UniTongue*—the standard language officially permitted in the nation—*to weed out even the slightest possibility of independence movements*. Yes, it did curb some cultural expression of the minorities, but some sacrifices were inevitable for the greater good. It wasn't a total cultural crackdown anyway. These minority groups could still retain their unique cultures within the boundaries of the Party, with the benevolent Party approving their cultural dance choreographies and music scores to see if they adhered to Utopia's official narratives.

Dereliction had dire consequences and those defecting would be labelled as rebels. These rebels were then shipped off to one of the numerous detention centres scattered throughout the annexed territories for 're-education'—a fate that Hongbing believed was essential for maintaining law and order in his country.

Straightening his back—as if straightening his mind for work—Hongbing read the three slogans with renewed energy. The locker opened with a tiny creak. Inside hung his UniDress—an army-like uniform consisting of a burgundy-coloured shirt and jacket, grey trousers, and a pair of black leather lace-up shoes. His security code number was printed on his shirt and jacket while a location chip was inserted in the soles of his shoes so the Controllers could track all his activities within the UF-Clanta grounds. The Party required all employees working in large corporations—including foreign JVs—to wear the UniDress for uniformity. *When in Utopia, do as Utopians do.* Most foreigners felt indifferent. The experience of having lived and worked in Utopia was fascinating, even priceless, when they returned to their democratic countries. Few would want to stand out. And their goal, anyway, was only to make money. The uniform also made it easy for the Party security division to differentiate between the visitors and the outliers. The UniDress was made of the Party's latest technology of smart fabric that could detect the wearer's emotions. Microsensors embedded in the shirts exposed biodata—including the person's pulse rate, hormone levels, and neuron signals—that were then collected for evaluating the subject's overall state of mind.

Hongbing draped the UniDress shirt over his shoulders and stuck his arms through the sleeves. Buttoning up, his torso rubbed against the silky and buttery smart fabric, which now felt like an extension of his skin. Dressed and ready, he stepped onto another moving pathway to the Kilgate—a 300-metre tunnel that the Collectors called the Gate of Truth.

Clink.

Mild warmth wrapped around Hongbing's body as the smart fabric released heat, stimulating his blood circulation. It felt like being whisked into a warm milk bath. The Kilgate activated the sensors of the smart fabric to examine his emotional status, and hence his ability to conform to the Party's guideline of uniformity. The emotion-detection technology ascertained his feelings for the day in order to deduce his political attitude towards the Party. Excited for work, Hongbing picked up his pace on the walkway, darting into the Kilgate tunnel where random images of the Party were displayed. Dozens of small surveillance cameras, which closely watched his facial expressions, were laced through the tunnel walls. Their job was to detect Hongbing's immediate and instantaneous reactions—which were extremely hard to mask even for trained agents—to measure his loyalty and obedience.

Benevolent images of the Party Leader—dressed in a light-coloured suit—working in his office after working hours bombarded Hongbing. In one video, he looked tired and was noticeably thinner, but he still didn't stop reviewing documents and meting out orders on the phone. Footage of him staging a military parade followed. Standing on the gold-coated Supreme Balcony of the Party Headquarters in the capital city, he fixed his gaze on the thousands of goose-stepping Utopian soldiers marching across the United Square to the south—waving and smiling. The visuals spiked his dopamine levels. There was no need to fake or control any emotion as the army of surveillance cameras silently filmed Hongbing's smug face. The facial recognition data was then combined with his biometric identification—his pulse and blood flow patterns—that was also being simultaneously monitored. The authorities spared no effort in constantly advancing their technologies to sharpen their accuracy in detecting the complexity of human emotions, a key to building a flawless control system. At lightning speed, the Kilgate also cross-checked his latest biodata with archived records before it ultimately arrived at an overall emotional status for the day.

Hongbing had witnessed the development of the Kilgate from the very early stages—the Party's most sophisticated technology programme to date that was used to learn people's emotional and political attitudes by collating the gazillion facial expressions captured by the millions of surveillance cameras throughout Utopia. He was fully aware of, and fully understood, the Party's need for such comprehensive surveillance. It was to maintain uniformity, which was important for keeping order and stability in Utopia. To realize this, Hongbing saw that an average of five surveillance cameras were assigned per person in the bustling top-tier cities. Surveillance became a part of the daily lives of the people. The scale of such data infrastructure was a point of pride for him, a feat he knew no other nations could even dare to match. It gave Hongbing a sense of superiority when he thought of the authorities of other states, who could only dream of the insurmountable effort required to collect such data without resistance from its citizens for infringement of privacy or without being confined by legal and bureaucratic restrictions. Companies could also refuse the authorities' demands for data, a scenario that would never happen in Utopia. In contrast, the biggest Utopian tech firms and corporations shared data with the Party. *Now, that is patriotism and that is the power of Utopian people*, Hongbing thought, boastfully.

At the heart of Utopia's new societal framework for greater uniformity was the Social Credit System—a concept that had been concocted and implemented about ten years ago when Hongbing was in his thirties. Now, with the system in its twentieth edition, Hongbing saw that it had developed into one of the Party's most advanced and powerful tools to manage social behaviours and pre-empt harmful acts, even crimes. The system promised a safer environment for all—a pledge Hongbing firmly believed in. He felt far more safe and secure knowing that every facet of the people's lives was being watched for efficient social security under this system. *Looking out for the 'contaminants' of the society before any crimes occurred is what all states are required to do*, he thought. The contaminants or outliers who posed a threat needed to be eliminated in advance so that the rest of the population stayed clean and focused on the Party's blueprint for the New Utopia. Those who fought against it were nothing but *Quislings*, tainted by foreign thoughts and influences aimed at impeding Utopia's progression. Hongbing had heard of his colleagues talking about some individuals who dared to vocalize and politicize their protests against the system. A few days later, he overheard his colleagues say that these individuals had disappeared from the community. *Great!* Hongbing thought. *The Party did what was necessary.* Unspeakable as it might seem to the outside world, it was simply a norm for Utopian people.

'The Social Credit System will ensure total safety for you and your loved ones,' Hongbing vividly remembered how he had felt when he first heard this news on TV during a work meeting. It took him a good ten seconds to fully digest what the Party had created for the people—the ultimate protection for him and his family. He was ecstatic. *Finally, an answer to the years of agony suffered!*

A few years earlier, his most cherished belonging—a university graduation ring made of gold and ruby—had been stolen when his home was burglarized. The burglar, who later claimed that he had to steal because he didn't have money for food, broke into his flat and took the ring along with other valuables, including his wedding ring. But nothing mattered to him except the graduation ring. He fumed in anger for weeks and even entered a cold war with his wife. She was tired of his moaning over a ring when she had lost half of the jewellery from her dowry. He installed a few personal security cameras throughout the flat afterwards but gained no comfort. As a graduate of the country's most prestigious educational institution—the University of Unity—he held the ring as the first badge of honour and acknowledgement from the Party. The police later caught the burglar, but the ring was forever lost, sold to the thriving black market. When he learned of it from the police, Hongbing, trembling in fury, dashed down to the police station where the burglar was being held. Flashing his Party official ID, he slapped his hands on the police front counter and barked his demand for a meeting with the criminal. Before the rookie officer behind the counter could react, he charged behind the counter towards the door that led to the lockup.

'You cursed trash,' he had bellowed, kicking the red iron bars that divided him and the accused.

'Where's my graduation ring?' Seized with rage and despair, he had continued punching the bars with his fists, even as two burly policemen tried to pull him away. His extraordinary outburst stunned even the nastiest crooks in the cell, and there were a few of them, alongside the burglar, who appeared amused. Intrigued by Hongbing's behaviour, he inched forward but was careful to keep an arm's length from the bars. He whispered with a slight snigger, 'Good afternoon, such rage is bad for your health.' The insidious greeting was enough to send Hongbing into another wave of fury and he would have torn the cell down if he wasn't being held back by the two policemen, one on each side. *How dare this lowlife speak to me in this manner? Where is that confidence even coming from?*

'Damn it, I asked, where's my ring?'

'Get off your high horse. You think I keep track of all the junk I snatch?' the burglar had said calmly, as though he was speaking to a child.

'Watch what you say! That ring means more to me than you could ever comprehend.'

'You really are a piece of work, ain't ya? Maybe check under your ego, huh?' mocked the burglar, this time looking a little irritated. Frowning, he had deepened the wrinkles in his forehead, and tarted, 'You think you're a player in this system?'

'Cut the crap and answer my question! Where is my ring?' Hongbing had continued his interrogation.

'My God, you're totally brainwashed,' the burglar had rolled his eyes and looked away.

'I said where's my ring?'

As Hongbing had raised his voice and kicked the bar dividing the two, a young police officer moved towards them to intervene.

'Get out,' Hongbing had ordered. 'I'm handling this.' He had little patience for lower-ranked people meddling in his affairs. It was completely against his principles.

Looking at Hongbing's behaviour, the burglar had shaken his head in disbelief and chuckled slyly. 'The Party must be so special for you. All high and mighty, lecturing me about the system when you've got no idea how it works on the streets. Sorry . . . I sold 'em all in the black market for food.' He cocked his head and shrugged his shoulders.

'You what?' Hongbing had felt another rush of blood to his head, which was now throbbing violently. 'You . . . you had no right to . . .'

'And you have no right to sit in your office and look down on us, but you do anyway. Wake up, bureaucrat, you are not a real player here. You may think you're a bishop on the chessboard, but you're just one of the numerous pawns.

'The sad thing here is . . . that you'll never really get it until the system hits you,' the burglar had continued, pounding him, ironically, from the moral high ground. 'As a citizen, you should've fought against the system to protect our rights, but you never did, as it was *yet* to affect *you*. Instead, you were swooned by the officialdom and whatever petty power they gave you. A bystander. A traitor. A puppet in the grand scheme of things, a tool used by the system, too blinded by your false sense of superiority to see the real world. The system will one day hit you too and sooner than you think. No one will help you then, just like you show no compassion now. And when that happens, I'll watch, and I'll laugh.

'Oh, wait. I know how people like you operate,' the burglar had continued, a spark igniting in his eyes. 'When you feel abandoned by the system, you'll probably fight back, acting like some kind of newfound hero. But the moment you see an opportunity to rejoin the system, you'll drop everything and jump back into the game. I'm familiar with your breed.'

Hongbing had been seething so badly by then that he could find no words to refute it. *How dare this petty criminal try to lecture me? Hopeless. These crooks deserve total segregation from the rest and thank God for the Party and its tireless effort to advance the system to contain these cancer-like contaminants!*

'God I hate all these idiots,' yelled the burglar, as though he had just read Hongbing's mind.

'Well, the feeling's mutual!' Hongbing had snapped back curtly.

He had stayed and cursed for another good ten minutes before he left. 'I will demand that you get capital punishment,' he fired his final words.

Since the Social Credit System had been rolled out across the country, Hongbing thought it had done wonders to prevent catastrophes like the theft of his ring and overall crimes. He couldn't understand how any fellow Utopian would not love the system as much as he did.

His co-workers who were in the meeting when the TV news came on with a segment on how the Social Credit System had improved the lives of the citizens were walking examples.

'No more fear and insecurity,' said the AI presenter. The moment he heard that, the sip of hot coffee he had drained from his mug tasted like chocolate. He felt the thrill in his veins from every part of his body. He unwittingly raised his mug in joy but was surprised and dismayed to see his rather apathetic colleagues who weren't displaying even half his enthusiasm. It only showed one thing—they weren't as loyal as him, which was why he was the leader of this team.

'The System would take us closer to economic hegemony, as it would enable our SOEs to make fully informed business decisions. Social Credit Scores provide an indicator about whether an individual or an institution can be trusted,' the presenter said, a line that the state media had been drumming up for the past five years. It was effective. Resistance was minimal, and the Party practically faced zero opposition in widening the coverage and deepening the implementation of the System.

The Party cannily used a small city called Warc as its test bed before a complete rollout throughout Utopia's first- and second-tier cities. It took less than three months to implement the necessary technologies; including surveillance cameras, facial recognition systems, and AI data processors. Hongbing had been fully captivated by these initiatives and harboured a desire to be part of the Warc Social Credit Task Force. Dreaming of becoming a crime preventer, he had even applied for a job transfer. His application was unsuccessful, but he unquestioningly accepted the decision, as it was made by the Party, which undoubtedly had a good reason for rejecting him. To satiate his interest, Hongbing turned to following a TV reality show called *Crime-Zero City* and thus fulfilled his yearning to take down criminals. The show, broadcast weekly via state-owned online and traditional media platforms, followed the avatars of Warc residents who earned and lost their Credit points through their activities in a simulated city. The 300,000 residents were each given 100 points to start with. Hongbing watched it intently as points were deducted for any wrongdoings as minor as jaywalking to more severe offences like subversion. His favourite part was that residents were also awarded points for showing exemplary behaviour, such as donating to the Party, working overtime at the factories, and voluntarily polishing the life-sized bronze statues of the Party Leader scattered throughout the city. For Hongbing, it was fascinating to see that all behaviours were closely monitored by state-of-the-art cameras that generated a real-time scoreboard on the internet, showing how residents fared by Credit points. He just couldn't take his eyes away from this scoreboard that was updated by the millisecond, showing the scores of the entirety of the 300,000 people of Warc. For him, this wasn't another piece of the Party's marvellous technology. It symbolized the Party's vision, *his* vision, for an organized, controlled, and thereby safer, society. As he watched the show, he often imagined how he could have participated in this endeavour if his transfer had been authorized. The show fulfilled his aspiration to be on the front line of shaping Utopia's future. Humanity's future.

What made Hongbing dive further into this show was the Party's decision to add an underground betting pool to its format. Bets could be placed on each week's top and bottom ten scorers, adding an unprecedented thrill for Hongbing, who had long yearned to be part of the game. He made a bet and watched the show with a mix of fascination and disapproval as the top fifty scorers were nationally lauded on the show. The show's emcees also ardently offered commentaries on who overtook whom—like a horse racing programme. This was Hongbing's favourite part. As Hongbing got fully addicted to the show, so did others. A dedicated fandom for the show developed and Hongbing noticed that people around him all had their favourite *players* that they supported. The entirety of Utopia, including Hongbing, of course, went fanatic when the Social Credit Scores were linked up with a SOE-developed dating mobile application, where in the top fifty were given rights to choose their state-selected dating partners—a twist that Hongbing found both intriguing and unsettling. Those who were picked, had no option to reject the date unless they themselves had scored higher. Hongbing cracked himself up, laughing when a seventy-year-old man continuously picked a pretty university freshwoman as his partner.

He just loved the show and appreciated that it even demonstrated the value of humour and entertainment. Whether it was through the underground pool or casual bets among colleagues about the weekly top fifty, the excitement was palpable.

Like Hongbing, the entire nation got addicted to the show, and it naturally embedded the benefits of the Party's Social Credit System in the social psyche. It depicted people with lower scores to be more inclined to commit crimes, thus tying Social Credit Scores to the character and trustworthiness of each individual.

Hongbing saw the Party swiftly jump on the public fervour, creating a blacklist of individuals based on their low scores. Those with poor scores were usually ostracized at work or failed to secure work and were barred from eating at restaurants and even buying necessities in supermarkets, which cornered them into stealing, or committing crimes. But their backstories or the causal factors were never made public, and Hongbing didn't really care to find out. *After all, a crime is a crime*, Hongbing thought. Thanks to the show, the Party received an overwhelming 96 per cent approval for the System in a survey it conducted. With the crime rate rapidly declining in Warc, a growing number of municipalities called to be used as the next test bed for the System. As Hongbing watched these developments, he once again felt a strong pride in the System's efficacy.

Buoyed by their efficiency and success in Warc, the Party quickly expanded the implementation in other big cities. Hongbing watched with a particular interest as those classified as 'first-class citizens'—those with the top 5 per cent of Social Credit Scores—were rewarded a myriad social and bureaucratic benefits. These included the privilege to use the express line when queuing and using public transportation, priority in booking restaurants, discounted prices for visiting tourist attractions, and even reduced taxes. On the business front, entrepreneurs enjoyed fewer inspections and audits from the United Front Inspectors, and fast-track approvals for state approbation of their business projects.

On the other hand, penalties were ruthless. Low-scoring parents, for instance, were denied from enrolling their child in a primary school. The divide extended further into everyday life. Only the loyalists to the system could use and enjoy Utopia's social facilities like public sports parks, maternity homes, hospitals, pharmacies, grocery stores, and community centres. The sanction applied to anyone who failed to maintain sixty points. Citizens were banned from applying for government and SOE jobs as well as those at foreign firms in the country. Businesses that didn't toe the line incited more frequent state auditing and inspections. Indeed, it was unthinkable that any CEO or business leader would let their Credit points slide below sixty, as this would be catastrophic to the business. If that were to be the case, the entire company would face immediate scrutiny and more audits or government inspections, which would pressure the board to either sack the individual or use peer pressure to force a resignation.

As Hongbing observed the Party's brilliant scheme, ensuring the people's safety, he just couldn't help but feel a renewed admiration for the System's effectiveness. What he particularly liked was the Party's ruthless measures against those whose score fell below fifty. That's when one's basic lifestyle was turned upside down. Failure to keep the midpoint score meant citizens were banned from travelling to other cities—a pre-emptive measure to prevent them from becoming fugitives. When the person's IDs were scanned at any airports and train stations—a procedural behaviour in Utopia when buying tickets for cross-country travel—the system would show that the person was unqualified for the purchase. At the forty-point mark or lower, citizens were stripped of access to almost all public services and goods including local buses, subways, trams, and automated taxis, as well as the right to rent a car. Other social benefits were also cut off, ranging from the use of maternity homes and community centres to the extreme end of the right to call for an ambulance and fire services during emergencies. The Party called them the 'untrustworthys'.

'Get away, you *untrustworthy*,' Hongbing had once told a person attempting to rent a car, despite having a low score in the Social Credit System. 'If you don't comply, you'll pay the price,' he said firmly, nudging the individual out of the queue. Ultimately, Hongbing firmly believed that it was the responsibility of each individual to completely ostracize these contaminants.

* * *

Clink.

Hongbing reached the end of the tunnel, marking the end of the minute-long emotion assessment. He jumped out from the Kilgate with confidence.

A green, smiley face appeared on Hongbing's right sleeve cuff, which was simultaneously projected as a floating hologram from a silver-coated machine at the end of the tunnel. The end of the tunnel opened out to the lift lobby.

'Subject 4201. Sound,' came an accompanying announcement from the machine.

I hope Jane's okay. Hongbing's conscience nudged him a bit, but he didn't feel safe turning his head around to take a peek at her just behind him. Pulling his bag tightly towards his body, he made a beeline for his office on the twelfth floor. Keeping some distance from Jane was essential.

'Subject 2412. Requiring medical attention.' He heard the mechanical voice from the machine announcing Jane's emotional status as he waited for the elevator. Frozen, he kept his back to the tunnel and her while glancing up and down between his feet and the lift landing indicator panel above the elevator doors to calm his nerves. Somehow, the lift was descending slower than it usually did this morning.

'Possible neurodegenerative disease detected,' the mechanical voice continued. The additional information flustered him more but his worry for Jane also grew. *Is she sick? What on earth is a neurodegenerative disease?* He couldn't resist, at this point, turning his head around slightly. For all the years that he had passed through the emotion tunnel, he had never heard of such an assessment; it was Greek to him.

He caught a glimpse of a holographic flat-faced emoji being projected from the machine in a sickly shade of green. His earlier exchange with her replayed in his head, making him nauseous. Still, it was green and not red, which presumably was a good sign. Green must mean that she was not a threat to the Party, but he was still bothered by her health. When the subjects were sick, they were usually taken to hospital immediately and returned to work after weeks of treatment. He sighed in relief when he saw medical staff appear instantaneously, taking Jane away. Jane looked at Hongbing imploringly, as if seeking help. He quickly turned his head away, avoiding eye contact. There was nothing he could do nor should he worry about it. She was being taken care of by the Party.

Ding.

The lift came, finally. A strong scent of scilla slithered out as the doors opened. As he stepped into the glass lift, the display panel came to life with holographic images of information from the weather to the latest Party achievements on both the political and technological fronts. But, oddly, unlike his usual self, he seldom paid attention to the material confronting him in the lift. He always looked out of the glass planes to the vast field in front of the company building as the lift ascended. He savoured the ascent, as if it was levitating him upwards in the Party hierarchy. It was one of his favourite moments of the day. It took him decades to arrive at the corner office he now occupied. Whenever he rode the lift with lower-ranking colleagues, it reminded him of the hard times he had persevered through to be who he was today. He felt a sense of superiority that he had conquered others, and a feeling of triumphant success had eked its way into his life.

'Level twelve,' said the voice announcement system.

After scanning his face at a security checkpoint, he walked briskly towards his office, which looked out at the open office floor where his subordinates worked. The walls were lined with display panels showing state TV news as well as the production floors of the adjacent chip fabrication plants churning out the latest chips. Optimized with the Party's latest technology, the AI analyzed the behavioural patterns of the Clanta counterparts, which his office studied to come up with strategies to engage. Most of his team was already buried at their desks working, with a few walking back and forth clutching some confidential files in their hands. They nodded and greeted him. He simply gazed back, flexing his position and authority.

Hongbing opened the door and entered his large, high-ceilinged office at the end of the open workspace. One side was a stretch of windows that looked out at the stunning mountains where the colours were changing as autumn beckoned. His heavy wooden desk was next to the windowed wall. A floor-to-ceiling bookcase filled with books by generations of Party elders and leaders on Utopia, world politics, and Party ideologies covered another wall across his desk, towering over a wooden meeting table. Cameras were built into the bookshelves that hooked back at an automated recording room on the other side of the wall; they captured some of the meetings he chaired with his reporting Controllers. In the middle of the room, an Italian leather sofa set with matching armchairs framed an oval-shaped glass coffee table with a potted scilla plant. Behind his desk was a pair of pictures—a portrait photo of the Party Leader and an illustration of the Party emblem.

'I want my assets in my room,' Hongbing said tartly, as he touched a button on the panel embedded in his desk.

'They'll be there shortly, sir,' his executive assistant sitting outside the room answered.

He'd had a good week the past week, and today was the time for him to finalize and sign the documents that would set the course of the JV for the next few years. He was looking at expansion plans for one of the plants to manufacture a new generation of chips. It had taken five years of haggling with his Clanta counterparts to get this in ink. Oddly, he liked his South Korean partners and considered the JV relationship in the past two decades to be successful. It had been a win-win. Clanta executives, aware of Utopians' propensity to steal their technology, agreed only to manufacture what was a *relatively* new generation of semiconductors in exchange for access to the world's largest market. Utopians were satisfied for the most part, as their own technological expertise was extremely backward to begin with. But the tide was changing. Utopia was rising in the world, and it demanded tech that was more advanced, and Clanta would provide them with this if it wanted to enjoy the same level of market accessibility.

Hongbing threw himself onto one of the ergonomic chairs at the head of the meeting table. He took a sip of coffee from the mug his assistant had placed on the table. The coffee warmed both his throat and mind.

Ding.

Placing his mug on the coffee table in front of him, he pressed a button on the side of his armchair to answer the call.

'Your division heads are ready for the briefing, sir.'

'Let them in.'

The division heads piled in. Each was a trained Party agent charged with tracking the activities of Clanta officials to gather intel.

'Please,' he said without looking up, eyes remaining on his tablet. 'Have a seat.'

He put aside his device once the six had sat down, three on each long side of the table.

'Let's start. What's coming our way?'

'Reporting from the House Division, sir,' the House Division Head, surnamed Wen began. Wen also ran the badger game, a scheme that tracked the moral behaviour of employees at the JV, including foreigners. On the surface, it safeguarded the integrity of the company but, in reality, they gathered intel-like information on extramarital affairs. This gave the Utopians additional bargaining power against any wayward staff, which made the South Korean staff vulnerable to blackmail. Under Wen, there were around twenty agents dispatched to the homes of senior Clanta executives seconded from Seoul to the JV—integrated into their households as housekeepers and chauffeurs under fabricated names with meticulously prepared supporting documents vouching for their backgrounds.

The postings were positioned as a goodwill gesture by the Utopian partners, but the expenses were incorporated into the JV's financial books. The agents were also the finest graduates of the Party's United Front Academy of Tactical Operation, trained for espionage—using all means necessary to achieve their ends. Their main mission was to seduce the top Clanta officials and get relevant classified information such as Clanta's business plan, which could be used as a guideline for the Party's own tech advancement programme. One of the most commonly adopted tactics was the 'honey trap', using romantic relationships to solicit confidential information. Female housekeepers would focus on collecting every piece of information they could lay their hands on, from the executives' daily habits, preferences, and schedules—both business and personal—to social networks including connections with local politicians back home. With this information, the female agent would begin to charm the Clanta executive to engage in an illicit relationship. The relationship would open doors for her to make inroads into Clanta's inner circle of power and their political connections in South Korea, ultimately finding out, if not influencing, decisions in Utopia's favour.

Another axis of the mission was to retain evidence of such illicit affairs to use as ransom when needed. These affairs often took place in cars, a preferred setting where recordings were conveniently made by the vehicle's black box that the authorities could easily access. A second, widely used, more direct tactic was to steal commercially sensitive data from the homes of these officials, whose cellular and communication devices were monitored and tapped regularly. In other words, the Party knew their every move.

'No exceptional new development to report from our division, and the deal will go ahead as planned, sir,' Wen said, loud and fast.

'So . . . no one's opposing the deal?' pressed Hongbing.

'I was getting there, sir,' she said, raising her left eyebrow with a slight irritation.

'Executive director Robert Choe has been opposing the deal for weeks.'

'How exactly?'

'He called the Clanta CEO in Seoul directly last night using a secure line and urged her to scrap, or at least delay, the deal today.'

Wen pulled out a Ziploc bag, containing a unique five-centimetre by five-centimetre salt cellar. This was a cutting-edge tech device designed by the Party, ingeniously embedded with a microscopic camera. Slipping on a pair of surgical gloves, she fished the salt cellar out and placed it on the table. In a jiff, the smart table was optimized with the jar—a voice and video recorder—decrypting the data into a hologram.

The footage, taken from between the ventilation vents, showed a flustered Choe on his mobile phone, pacing irritably up and down the dining room.

'Lovely patterns,' Hongbing commented mockingly. The division heads were silent as they listened closely.

'We just can't sign this deal,' Choe urged in frustration. 'Yes, yes . . . I do understand what we're giving isn't really new tech, I get that

. . . But these barbarians will first get us to invest so that we're stuck, then they'll urge for the change of our facility design to produce newer versions of chips. When we don't comply, they'll just seize our assets here. They'll hold the plants hostage until we back down. We've seen this happen in the past.'

A pause followed as Choe listened to the party on the other end.

'Market size? We're losing our market share here anyway. And that's not because we've been uncooperative but because these guys are stealing our know-how, and the tech gap is narrowing. They are playing us, that's what it is! And before we know it, they'll surpass us . . . unless we stop this deal.'

'Okay, that's enough,' Hongbing interrupted, halting the playback. 'Can we confirm that the deal will go ahead today?'

'Yes, sir. We double-checked with our operatives in Seoul ten minutes ago. It will go ahead as planned.'

'Good. The semiconductor plant expansion plan has long been the centre of the Party's major projects. We must get them to manufacture their new generation of chips on our soil so that our people and firms can *learn*.

'We do need to eliminate this guy though. Seems like a cancer cell. Any plans?'

'If authorized, we can offer him a job in our think tank at three times his current salary.'

'What would that be?'

'2 million People's dollars (PD).'

'That's a penny. Double that. The bait needs to be sexy when you lure a tiger. He seems to know how we operate, so he may not bite. Unless the offer is irresistible.'

'Contract period, sir? We usually offer three years.'

'Make it five.'

Hongbing took a gulp of his coffee to hide a smirk.

'And if he refuses? We've got no leverage on him . . . yet.'

'Have *his* housekeeper double down efforts—do what she needs to get the damn leverage.'

Sensing his annoyance, a few members of his team looked down at their feet, or tablets and notebooks.

'Next,' Hongbing said coldly, turning to the head of the Office Division.

The Office Division was responsible for gathering intel from Clanta's 'secure offices', where the Koreans amplified their security against Utopia's espionage and surveillance activities. While most of Clanta personnel were attached to the JV, the Korean tech behemoth maintained a separate company wholly-owned by them—Clanta East—in the country where several of its top officials were based, overseeing the offices that stored classified data such as design layout options for its new manufacturing plants. Clanta East also operated ten research and development centres as part of the agreement for it to produce and sell chips in Utopia. The company's primary purpose—among other, lesser responsibilities—was lobbying work with UFITC and Utopian bureaucrats and, to a lesser extent, with UF-Clanta, to meet Clanta's short- and long-term and goals in Utopian market.

The Party was never able to plant microcameras in these 'secure offices', as the Clanta officials were highly vigilant, sometimes borderline paranoid, about possible surveillance and espionage. Every morning, they swept the offices, wary of cameras and eavesdropping equipment. They also used satellite phones when contacting the Clanta headquarters before making any major decisions, complicating the intel-gathering process for Hongbing and his team. He could only resort to old-school tactics like the ones in the spy movies he'd seen decades ago. Or rely on luck, which sometimes struck.

'Sir, it seems like Choe's not the only one opposing the deal,' began the Office Division Head, an ambitious-looking man who came across, on many occasions, as too aggressive for Hongbing's liking. He could be a 'loose cannon', but he was highly competent.

'Interesting ... sounds like you got some more work to do,' Hongbing remarked with a tinge of sarcasm.

The Office Division Head was indifferent, accustomed to his superior's occasional snide remarks. He pulled out a USB flash drive and plugged it into a socket on the table, which then projected recorded footage of a meeting between the Clanta executives with the visiting deputy CEO from Seoul. The meeting had taken place in one of the secure offices a day ago, and the executives could be seen deliberating about the deal to be signed the next day.

The Office Division had managed to plant a microcamera in the Clanta logo lapel pin worn by one of the officials from the secure offices. The pawn was fifty-three-year-old Kwon, a Clanta veteran, but a newbie to Utopia, who was deployed several months ago. Per usual, the Party watched him closely from the moment he landed on its soil but, so far, it had obtained nothing of significance—nothing particularly juicy at least. Kwon was quite a . . . solitary figure. He was single and didn't like to mingle, even among his Korean colleagues, and was not likely to even make friends, let alone have an affair with anybody. Neither did he have any hobbies nor did he go out in the evenings and on weekends. He led a routine life and poured all his time and energy into his work.

In short, Kwon was a boring workaholic. So, the division turned its attention to his personal habits. And what stood out was Kwon's sensitivity to heat. In the summer, he complained endlessly of the weak air-conditioning. With the autumn months turning chilly, some offices in the capital city used to turn on the heating. The heated offices would become unbearable for him, and he would habitually remove his suit jacket, even in formal meetings, and would carelessly leave it around the premises of Clanta East. His absent-mindedness presented the Office Division the chance to engage in an old-school espionage tactic. Firstly, the team recruited his personal assistant as an asset. That inroad led to access to Kwon's work calendar and meeting schedule. Just two days before the crucial meeting with the visiting Clanta deputy CEO, the assistant swapped Kwon's corporate lapel pin—which he always pinned on his jacket—with one that was 'enhanced' with a hidden camera. Ironically, despite being unknowingly used in the espionage effort, Kwon turned out to be the second antagonist in this scenario. 'Seems like we've got two black sheep opposing the deal from this video,' the Office Division asset said as the holographic meeting popped up.

A group of eight men and women sat around a long table. The meeting kicked off with a superficial round of pleasantries among the Clanta executives. It then sank into an awkward silence, probably due to the political stakes of the deal.

'This deal must go ahead as planned,' a woman executive, Kim, eventually broke the silence, 'because more than 60 per cent of our semiconductor exports come from this country, and no other market can replace that output.'

She looked around at her colleagues who neither affirmed her nor disagreed with her, but two other women in the group made eye contact with the remotest sign of respect for her courage to speak out.

Egged on, she carried on, 'We can't just give up this market because some other country thinks we should. They don't govern us. Will they compensate for our, no wait, our country's losses? When politics comes before the economy, we fall. At the end of the day, we are doing business here, not playing bloody politics.'

She was clearly referring to a meeting that had happened in Washington DC a week earlier, one that Hongbing, too, had paid particular interest to. In that meeting, the US Secretary of State urged the South Korean foreign minister to slow its technological investments and halt the sales of semiconductors to Utopia. The request put the Koreans in a bind. Ignoring the US's directive would mean they would likely end up facing sanctions in the American market, which was Clanta's one of the biggest revenue sources and one it couldn't afford to risk. Hongbing knew that for that reason, the South Korean tech giant had been lobbying for months—for an exception or at least a delay—before the US imposed the sale restriction. It was revolting to see, though, how the US was adamant about penalizing Utopians for their thievery of technology over the past decades. For the US, making an exception for South Korea was not an option, as it would undermine their efforts to contain Utopia's rise in global power dynamics.

Clever punks, Hongbing tarted. It seemed like Washington was also well aware that semiconductors were the fundamental chess piece in this complex geopolitical game. In fact, the cutting-edge technology was required for manufacturing both military and consumer goods, indispensable in the age of the internet, as they were in all devices—from smartphones to washing machines to the most advanced fighter jets. It, therefore, was Hongbing's duty to collect as much information as possible for Utopia to attain its technological supremacy. For Utopians, this was not just a matter of technological advancement. It was about reshaping the global order—a prospect that excited Hongbing, fuelling his fervour day and night.

And what the woman was saying in the hologram just further bolstered his sense of Utopian pride.

'Just look at Utopian market size,' the brave woman in the meeting room went on. 'It's the largest market in the world, more than quadruple that of the US. If we were to take sides, isn't it obvious where we should stand?

'Let's face it, if we scrap this deal, Utopians will retaliate, possibly shutting down our existing production facilities here. These guys are capable of doing anything, and we all know that. Our plants here account for more than 25 per cent of our entire global production. On the contrary, the Americans won't shut us down because the US has the rule of law. Frankly, it's less damaging to mess with democratic countries than with totalitarian ones.'

'No,' a bespectacled man with thick, salt-and-pepper hair refuted, shaking his head. 'We must prepare for the worst-case scenario. This tech war is unavoidable and fence-sitting, which might be ideal on the surface, is not a realistic option and it might even actually be riskier.

'We're losing market share here anyway. Improving our cooperation with the Americans is the only option we have to maintain our technological edge. It's the only way we can survive. At least the US doesn't steal our technology. They play fair in the market—well, at least they try to—and in that way, we have a chance to continue being a leader in this field.' The man gritted his teeth and paused. Then, he continued.

'Besides, our market share here is falling, and that's because the local Utopian chip makers are mimicking our technology, no thanks to the Party's spying efforts.' He pointed his finger at the window where a faraway and faint view of the Party's liaison office building could be seen. 'If we let these guys continue to steal our know-how, they'll surpass us before we know it. Besides, the playing field is increasingly uneven, with Utopian policies blatantly favouring domestic manufacturers and cutting off foreign companies, not to mention surging labour costs.

There is absolutely no guarantee for stable corporate activities in the long-term.'

'I agree,' Kwon chimed in, nodding to the male colleague across the table from him. He clasped his hands under his chin, leaned forward and said in a penetrating voice, 'We mustn't bend backwards for them every time, especially when they are not giving us full and fair market access. We must at least secure our interests. Abandoning the deal after the signing could lead to an even greater crisis, don't you think? We can still proceed with the expansion plan, but we should seriously think of this as our last.'

At this point, Hongbing interjected, 'I've seen enough, turn it off.' His eyes narrowed, and his spine stiffened. 'We need to do something about those two. Apply the same approach as Choe for those two but prepare for a plan B in case they don't bite. I want the House Division to report everything on them—down to their tiniest habits. Understood?'

'Yes, sir,' Wen, the House Division Head said.

'Also, any updates on Jacinta Lee's visit to the city? It's disturbing that the first I'm hearing about this is from the Link this morning. What's been going on with you all?' He shot a reprimanding look around the table.

'Nothing on that so far,' the Office Division Head responded softly, shoulders sagging.

'Impossible! There must be something. Access their data from whatever you can lay hands on—laptops, desktops, phones, emails and so on—I want to know with certainty everything about Lee's visit and what she's up to on this trip. I want intel from my people, not from the Link. Got that?'

'Yes, sir.'

'Good. Let's move on.'

'Reporting from the HR Division,' said the Human Resources Division Head seated furthest away from Hongbing.

'We've managed to inject three more Party members as senior researchers into Clanta East's R&D centres over the last month. That would make a total of thirty-two of our people in their labs.'

'Isn't that still under 5 per cent of their total researchers there?' Hongbing hissed. 'Anyways . . . what have we achieved so far?'

'Each of them was given the mission to get Clanta's latest chip technology during the development process—so we can see how they are developing the tech and hopefully get a head start to produce them ourselves.'

'And . . . the output? I don't recall hearing anything from you over the last few months.'

'Well . . .' the Division Head mumbled in a defeatist tone. 'Our agents have struggled to get access to classified data, which is restrictively granted only to an exclusive pool of South Korean researchers. So, we're now trying to work on these researchers to gain access indirectly.'

'Are you just changing tack now?' Hongbing torpedoed the Division Head, rolling his eyes. The air in the room was heavy as he continued. 'One of the biggest advantages of competing with these democratic countries is that we can exploit their system, their freedom of expression, to sway public opinion, and hence, even their top-level decisions.'

No one responded. The division heads were focused on staying calm and not allowing their facial expressions to betray their thoughts. After a moment of silence, they heard Hongbing raising his voice, which usually meant an *order* was in place.

'While your researchers continue to cozy up to the Korean researchers at the R&D centres, reach out to our agents in South Korea and connect with local advocacy groups there. Bribe and encourage these groups to rally and demand anti-discriminatory and fair treatment for all Clanta employees regardless of nationality. Then, get our media puppets overseas to report and be all over the issue. It will pressure Clanta a little, as its reputation will be at stake.'

'I'm afraid that won't guarantee any access, sir,' the HR Division Head wrung out his last drop of courage. 'Besides, we've never actually succeeded in bribing any of them.'

'Just keep trying. Unless you have a better idea.'

'Yes, sir.'

Suddenly, Hongbing's eyes lit up. 'Speaking of which, we need to broaden our scope to also target research labs in universities and leverage the Party's global partnership scheme with foreign universities. Why take the bumpy road, when we have the motorway?'

The partnership scheme was built on a talent-recruitment programme with a dual track of planting Utopian scholars and researchers in foreign universities, and simultaneously wooing foreign academics and experts in these institutions with generous research grants to do the Party's bidding—obtain and transfer the latest proprietary technology. The scale of the scheme was beyond imagination. Around 3,000 PhD degree holders were sent overseas every year with specific missions. The universities were perfect, easy targets, as they often collaborated directly with global tech companies in developing commercializable cutting-edge technologies, and these R&D institutes and labs did not necessarily maintain the high level of security that tech companies or government agencies did. The idea of 'restricted access' was anathema to many academics whose work was built on the pursuit of truth and knowledge. The principle of the free movement of ideas, independent of governmental influence, was the foundation on which academic institutions were built. Academic freedom in a democratic system presented a vast playground for Utopia's talent-recruitment programme to flourish. The scholars used their status in universities to acquire relevant technologies under the guise of 'academic purposes'. The espionage went beyond university campuses to government agencies and companies whenever possible and was also widened to different industries that were crucial to Utopia's objective of reaching hegemony.

'I'll request the Party to send more of our brainees to South Korean universities as well as increase partnership activities with these institutions. We need to be all over this. Flood the scholars with emails,' Hongbing told his team.

'The scholars don't read those emails any more, sir. They've been warned by their governments.'

'Just keep sending them. One nincompoop is all we need.'

At that moment, his mobile phone vibrated.

'I have to take this. Give me a report next week. And I want results. You're all dismissed.' He watched his team file out before he swiped his phone to pick up the call. It was Tian Li. She wouldn't say much on the phone but was insistent they meet that night.

* * *

The crisp autumn weather was pleasant as Hongbing stepped out of the teahouse, but he couldn't shake off the chill that wrapped his body as he walked towards the Link after parting ways with Tian Li.

Chapter 2

Ideology and Entitlement

In the handbook for the Party's model worker, self-doubt was frowned upon but doubting the Party, however fleeting the moment, was a cardinal sin, and the first step towards the point of no return. By Hongbing's yardstick, it was an act deserving the harshest punishment. Sure, he would do what he could to find out about Yiping, but his work remained his priority. After the previous day's meeting with his direct reports, the pressure had mounted. Although he was pretty certain that the few antagonists of the JV's expansion plan would not be enough to thwart the deal, the broader antipathy towards Utopia was disturbing and not to be taken lightly. As the saying goes, 'There would be no waves without wind.' It was pressing that he stay focused on his work at this critical juncture. Besides, work would kill two birds with one stone by eliminating any pervasive negative thoughts about the Party's detention of his friend.

The truth was he found it inconceivable that Yiping would err at such a fundamental level. The superchip project was Utopia's future, it was expected to bring honour and glory to the Party and the people. His friend was an even keel and wouldn't jeopardize his own future. He thought logically, wasn't easily ruffled, and was certainly almost never impulsive. Even his loyalty to the Party was expressed measuredly, unlike Hongbing who could be gushing and explicitly emotional. It was more likely a transient circumstance and the air would be cleared very soon. *Unless the Party has found some kind of hold on Yiping. No! That's impossible!* He shook his head violently, somewhat ashamed by his moment of doubt for his friend. His mind drifted in and out of thoughts of Yiping over the next few weeks.

Hongbing's memory of the time when both Yiping and he had secured their dream jobs was vivid, in spite of the passage of more than twenty years since. Yiping had decided to take the path of becoming a scientist while Hongbing would contribute to Utopia's technological advancement as a party official overlooking its business sector. Yiping's goal was the UFI and Hongbing's the United Front Industry and Technology Corporation (UFITC). By virtue of their names, the two organizations are related, and at the beginning of the twenty-first century, they were also leaders in their respective fields in Utopia. Hongbing and Yiping had competed with millions of young graduates for a much smaller number of openings at UFI and UFITC. The competition was cut-throat, but the two young men had no doubt they would overcome the three stringent rounds of interviews. The arrogance of youth, perhaps, but it didn't cross their minds at the time that it was unwise to put all their eggs in one basket. The economy was booming as the Party reinforced its ambition to be a tech supremo, opening the Utopian market guardedly to more foreign tech players. Everyone was fighting for the best talents with top money. Both Hongbing and Yiping were top graduates who were scouted by some of the biggest multinational companies and private Utopian firms. Still, they were stubbornly focused on their targets, and confident that they would get what they wanted.

The UF interview process took about one-and-a-half months, broken into three rounds of interviews. Even for the brightest, it was a stressful experience, because the subliminal test for recruits was political—the best talents must also be the most politically correct. The United Front name was not just the eponym for Utopia's most important organizations, it also embodied the Party's political strategy to greatness. Hongbing's grasp of the strategy was fuzzy then, but as time went on, and with his own rise within the Party rank, the picture became clear—the UF strategy was a network of individuals, businesses, and organizations around the world that influenced outcomes in Utopia's favour. For a young Hongbing, the words of his professor from the university etched themselves in his brain.

'Only when you're within the system, can you contribute to the Utopian cause, towards change for the better,' his mentor Li Wei had said to him.

His parents, who were regular state workers, had been puzzled when Hongbing turned down lofty job offers from foreign companies and instead, agonized if an offer would come from UFITC, weeks after the final round of interviews. He had convinced himself he needed to be in the UF universe to realize his dream. He believed Yiping was of the same view.

The good news had arrived eventually, and the young idealists were ecstatic.

'I will develop the most advanced and powerful chip,' declared Yiping. 'It will crush the world's top tech superpower and leave them chasing our tail for many, many years to come!'

'And I will make sure this chip conquers the global markets and eliminates all our rivals!' Hongbing added.

The UFITC had been a sizeable SOE with countless subsidiaries and with a not-bad-payroll when Hongbing first stepped foot into the organization. He needed half a month just to figure out the physical company grounds that consisted of multiple office buildings and manufacturing facilities spread out over an entire district on the outskirts of Unitas, the capital city. Unveiling the organizational structure was a bigger task and he took about a month to learn of all the divisions and their responsibilities as well as the divisions that his unit—the Strategic Planning Division—had direct dealings with. Idealistic and ambitious, there were times he felt deflated that he might never be able to climb the ladder. There was simply too much deadwood at the senior management level.

But the tides had changed in his favour. Technology was developing at lightning speed and the UFITC deadwood who failed to adjust had to go because the SOE was also losing money. Hongbing, the staunch Party member, on the other hand, was a rising star. At the end of his third year, he convinced his supervisor to let him revamp a small production team that constantly failed to meet output targets and budget. Hongbing's plan was to automate more of the manufacturing process. By automating an important part of the workflow, he steered production output back on track, and brought profitability back to that team within a year. What impressed his supervisor most was that no one was made redundant as Hongbing reallocated manpower to newly created tasks needed for technological transformation. The small success led to bigger enhancement tasks. Hongbing became known as not just a troubleshooter, but as the visionary operator adept at rescuing any faltering business with innovation, the same basis on which UFITC developed state-of-the-art technologies for civilian use.

Bit by bit, Hongbing had built his credibility within Utopia's bureaucracy. In his tenth year at UFITC, the SOE was pretty much devoid of bleeding units, an outcome in which he and his team could take credit and pride in. A stronger UFITC drew more foreign tech companies, like bees to honey, desiring to form JVs to enter the vast Utopian consumer market. The Strategic Planning Division, which Hongbing was now heading as a director, established different partnerships with multiple foreign companies to develop similar technologies in order to acquire tech that would produce the state's own advanced semiconductors. The competing foreign companies resented the conflict of interest in such simultaneous arrangements, but they were not in a position to bargain.

Among the numerous JVs that he helped broker, UF-Clanta— formed when Utopia's relations with South Korea were at its best— was the most notable. Hongbing was also, at the time, overseeing the operations of a subsidiary firm producing low-end semiconductors, which he then revamped, successfully doubling its sales in two years. He witnessed, and was acutely troubled by, the severe laggard that Utopia's chip technology was. In contrast, Clanta boasted of the latest know-how that would effectively bridge the gap. He asked for a transfer to the JV. His bosses agreed in a heartbeat. What's there to object to? Besides, it was planting one of the best and most loyal talents in a foreign firm with the technology that Utopia coveted. From UF-Clanta, Hongbing forged a new chapter for himself and Utopia. After seventeen years at the JV, he was assigned to oversee the overall operation, sharing the privilege with his Korean counterpart Jay Kang.

Hongbing had become a made man, holding the senoir position for two years, running a smooth operation. Sometimes, subordinates would fail to deliver, but their missteps were inconsequential. *Their fundamental flaw is that they have not embraced the Party wholeheartedly and followed its path*, he thought. He constantly thanked the Party for what he had. He had no doubt whatever was up with Yiping would resolve itself quickly. But Hongbing was still curious, and he planned to ask around during his next meeting at the headquarters—to prove that the Party was just, and he wasn't wrong.

Every Wednesday, Hongbing dutifully made the mandatory visit to the UFITC headquarters. It would take up the entire morning, during which he would meet the heads of various departments to report on UF-Clanta's operations and all significant activities surrounding his foreign colleagues. The routine included a regular meeting with the director of the UFI, Yiping's boss. The Wednesday schedule was to safeguard Utopia's national security and Hongbing couldn't be more agreeable to the intention.

His first stop this morning was, as always, his immediate supervisor, UFITC's head of foreign partnerships and the Party-Secretary of technology for national security, Lan Tao, a towering figure—literally and figuratively—who rarely displayed his emotions. The Party propagated an egalitarian society in Utopia, but somehow, there was always, without fail, a first among equals. Because he was the Party-Secretary for the Party's most important areas, he inevitably felt more important than his peers and Hongbing knew that well. Lan was also a deputy director of the United Front Intelligence Agency—a secretive outfit that gathered technological intelligence—a national state security office in its field.

'Morning, sir,' Hongbing bowed slightly at the door as his nostrils grew accustomed to the thick cigarette smoke hanging in Party-Secretary Lan's office. The Party had banned smoking in public areas and workplaces twenty years ago. However, old habits die hard, and not everyone complied. Lan had a hard face and smoked like a chimney. The deep lines etched on his face testified to a life that hadn't always been easy. He was from a generation before his subordinate, whose university education was disrupted by an internal revolution to eliminate the ills of the bourgeoisie society and make way for Utopia. For all that he had suffered, he harboured a sense of entitlement and was harsh to his subordinates, many of whom he thought knew not of hardship like he did. It was true enough. Hongbing had only known life in a country that was only growing stronger and more prosperous, an exhilarating experience that the Party masterfully used to unify citizens and harness nationalism.

'Hongbing, good to see you. Come, sit down.' He motioned towards the sofa in the middle of the spacious office. For someone who rarely smiled, he forced an awkward one on his wrinkled and aged face. He liked Hongbing, whom he categorized as a loyal and accommodating subordinate, one who got the job done, whatever the circumstances.

'What do you have for me this morning?'

'Quite a bit, sir.'

'Good, just what I like to hear.' The more intel collected, the better. 'Fire away.'

'Well, first of all . . .'

He used fifteen minutes to run down the more routine items on the list before coming to the final and most important one for the week.

'Jacinta Lee is visiting soon. The official line is that it's her routine biannual visit to Clanta East and UF-Clanta. But there's a chance that she's here to meet the president of Red Crescent to set up a JV. As you know Red Crescent has been expanding rapidly in the semiconductor sector, and they have got the backing of certain factions of the Party.'

Lan did not appear the least bit surprised. Why would he be? You didn't climb to that level of power without a formidable network of assets and, of course, superior intel. His eyes blinked slowly behind his semi-rimmed glasses as he thought deeply.

'I've heard rumblings.' One corner of his lips curled up, raising an eyebrow followed by a light snort. 'Red Crescent, ha!'

Hongbing wasn't sure which way his boss was swaying. He kept quiet and patiently observed.

Red Crescent was hardly a traditional SOE. It had no history. In Utopia, despite the constant harping about building a brand-new society and world order where everyone had a fair shot, history and who was related to who mattered deeply. *So much for Utopia!* But the quasi-government linked company—backed by a minor ministry—had a very charismatic president, an Ivy League alumnus, who spent twenty years on Wall Street and brokered the biggest cross-border deals between Utopia and its arch rival, the US. He had been accused multiple times of commercial espionage through the transactions he underwrote, but the American authorities failed to find evidence that could back these claims. After the eighth allegation, he had enough and returned home to help build his motherland further. The descendant of a first-generation senior Party leader, he had the backing of certain senior officials, who also happened to be foes of the Party Leader.

Red Crescent aspired to give UFITC a run for its money, but it had yet to make a dent in the SOE. Lan and his bosses were unperturbed. Still, its presence was annoying, like a fly that won't go away.

'The Party encourages fair play because our common interest is achieving Utopia 2030,' Lan stressed, referring to a Party-project aimed at transforming Utopia into a globally dominant high-tech manufacturing power and weaning off its dependence on foreign technologies. It was always important to be articulate in Party speak, even among the cadres.

'But there is no reason why we shouldn't protect *our* interests, wouldn't you say?'

'I understand, boss. We'll get on this.'

Hongbing's astute reading of his superiors was one of the reasons he was favoured by the powers that be from the Party. He excelled in deciphering the shades of meaning in words. He instantly understood that Lan expected any potential venture to be killed before it was able to see the light of the day. He fervently agreed that in the all-important national mission to originate a superchip, it was unwise for UFITC and UFI as well as UF-Clanta, to be distracted or, for that matter, for the state to spread its resources to another entity. UF-Clanta wasn't directly involved in the superchip project, but the JV had been instrumental in training Utopian engineers in the push for the most advanced semiconductor the nation was capable of producing. Equally so, he decided it wasn't the time to report on his meeting with his division heads a few days ago. No need to bother the great man at this point, especially when there was no considerable achievement.

Lan again offered his signature dry smile. He seemed pleased, and Hongbing seized the moment.

'Sir, there's just another small matter on which I need to consult with you,' he was careful with his choice of words. 'Our comrades in the JV are whispering that the Bureau of State Security has detained Cai Yiping of the superchip project, and this has proven to be unsettling for the staff.' He watched Lan, who didn't flinch. Guardedly, he continued, 'Can you advise me about the reason for this detention so that I know how to communicate with our staff? I'm sure you would agree that it is important to lessen their unease.'

Lan leaned forward for his packet of Utopia Lights and his gold-plated lighter. He lit up, took a long drag from his cigarette, and exhaled a long plume of smoke.

'I'm surprised by your scepticism of the Party.' Lan moved fast and hard. Before a dumbfounded Hongbing could respond, he fired a second round.

'We must have faith in our comrades at the SSB—they know what they are doing. Comrade Cai is an important member of our journey to realize the bigger cause, and it is crucial we never waver and doubt the Party. He was asked to assist with the investigation of a national security matter and that is all you need to know. I am confident that our comrades and the Party will do what's right. You should too.'

He flicked the dangling ash of his cigarette into the ashtray on the side table and took another drag before extinguishing it, by violently stubbing it out.

A slight panic seized Hongbing as he watched Lan. He was now desperate to rectify any misgivings the Party-Secretary had of him, especially of his loyalty.

'Please be assured that it's got nothing to do with my commitment to the Party, no, sir. And our team is equally committed and focused on doing what's best for Utopia.'

'If you say so,' his boss, looking hard and appraisingly at him, replied.

'You will continue to see it in my actions, sir.'

Hongbing was rattled, but he hoped he had straightened the record and he tried hard to appear unfazed. He suddenly felt torn between his friend and the Party. But he realized that there was no time to get emotional now or contemplate his mental dilemma as he glanced at his watch quickly. He was already ten minutes late for his next meeting with the director of the UFI, Yiping's boss. He politely left Lan's office, exiting with another slight bow and sprinted to the next building. He ran up two flights of steps, all the way to the second floor, past a series of doors to the end of the hallway and arrived at Yuan's corner office, panting. He smoothened his attire, used the back of his hand to wipe off the sweat on his forehead, and knocked on the door.

'Come in,' an annoyed voice grunted.

'Director Yuan, I'm terribly sorry I'm late. My last meeting overran.'

'Sit down, and let's get started,' commanded Yuan who was behind his desk. His face was still, but irritation was plain in his eyes.

Hongbing ran through the short list of mundane, regular update items, but he was racking his brain to come up with something to offset Yuan's displeasure for his tardiness.

His thirty-minute slot was almost over, and he could think of nothing. He needed to ask about Yiping.

'If there's nothing else,' Yuan said, drumming his fingers on the desk, 'you can—'

'Director, one more thing . . . it's outside our agenda today,' he blurted out in a last-ditch attempt, 'you know how our JV has been supporting the superchip development project. Well, we are concerned . . . I mean . . . our team is. . .' He felt beads of sweat forming on his forehead. The back of his shirt was drenched, and he was relieved it was covered by his outer jacket. Yuan looked pointedly at him, eyes piercing. Stammering, he said, 'Er . . . about why comrade Cai was taken.'

'It will not affect your or your team's work and performance. On the other hand, if you continue to push for information, it will certainly reflect on *your* performance.' With that, the meeting was truly over.

He walked out of Yuan's office, shaken. Two more meetings were scheduled, one with UFITC's senior finance manager and the second with the propaganda chief. He didn't think finance would have information on Yiping, but he tried his luck with the propaganda official, unfortunately, to no avail. What was discussed in the two meetings went by in a daze. At the end of the morning, Hongbing, who was always made to feel he was part of that elite inner circle, one of the chosen ones deemed for greater things, wasn't more informed than the previous night. Instead, he was slowly and rudely awakened to the possibility of facing a situation he had never anticipated.

* * *

UF-Clanta was UFITC's prized trophy and the model JV. The common man saw it as a cash cow, but it was, to Hongbing, the result of his blood and sweat. The Party held the semiconductor industry at an esteemed level like no other. After all, the semiconductor or chip was the computing power that would chart the country's future development.

He knew that having an edge in chip technology empowered a state to control—or disrupt—the world. For the Utopian leadership, which imported more chips than oil and energy, it was the key to freeing itself from the choke of its imperialist nemesis—the US— which had knitted allies like South Korea and Japan with its innovation infrastructure and ecosystem.

The main nodes of manufacturing in the value chain—design, fabrication, assembly, testing, and packaging—involved multiple countries. Every step of the process involved specialized knowledge that each company kept close to heart. Utopia occupied a small place in the complex system, and it was at the lower end of the food chain, or the downstream phase, reflecting its tech capabilities, which meant it helped mostly at the testing and packaging stages.

The South Koreans were at the top of their game and Clanta was one of the handful of semiconductor producers capable of carrying out all production stages. Hongbing knew that UF-Clanta—and Utopia—would benefit from acquiring its technologies.

The marriage with Clanta was a union of mutual benefits. The JV was managed by two co-heads, one from each side. The Utopians provided land and infrastructure including factory buildings while the South Koreans provided chip technology.

Like many, the early days of the marriage were pleasant. Both sides were eager and engaged. The Utopians were hungry for technical know-how and their foreign partners eager to please in order to entrench themselves deeper into the lucrative local market. Clanta hosted tens of thousands of UFITC officials at its Seoul headquarters and plants across the globe for workshops and training that involved technological transfers. For Clanta, it was also a channel to give relatively old technologies another lease of life, profiting a little through this. As Utopia flourished, it grew hungrier for more advanced chip fabrication technologies. Clanta wasn't always a willing party and didn't always accommodate these demands, but it was still deeply invested in Utopia. Over the years, UF-Clanta and Clanta East grew to become the South Korean tech giant's biggest overseas investment. So did Utopia's bargaining chip as its economy went from being the fifth to the second-largest in the world.

The differences between the partners also grew. UF-Clanta's 51–49 per cent equity partnership, with the foreigners taking the smaller stake, often left the South Koreans frustrated when important decision-making processes were stalled. In the capitalist world, time was money; in Utopia, politics trumped all.

At UF-Clanta, Hongbing soaked up all the foreign know-how that was made available and always went the extra mile to seek out more. South Korean tech experts from Clanta were posted to, or visited, the JV as part of the arrangement to transfer technologies. Hongbing made friends with all of them. He submitted regular reports to the UFITC, which were disseminated to all UF-affiliated entities, as well as kept a detailed personal journal of everything that went on in the JV. When his peers and other senior UF officials treated the Clanta-sponsored study trips as vacations, Hongbing diligently availed these learning opportunities to their full.

Hongbing rose up in the ranks, and gradually became a tough negotiator to his Korean counterparts. He would ask for numerous iterations of an expansion plan with very detailed specifications and breakdowns for each floor and each section. Each change or request would be packed with information and data that automatically infiltrated the entire UFITC organization, including the UFI.

The all-encompassing UF strategy formed the backbone to acquire technologies. Tactics were varied and, sometimes, even creatively and skilfully penetrated into every level of Utopian society, as well as on foreign soil—such as in universities—and were backed by the Party's deep pockets. Foreign scientists were wooed with millions of dollars in research funding either offshore or in Utopia. Utopians also sought out cash-strapped foreign tech companies to invest in. Often, money resolved a lot of the challenges.

Hongbing's teams were experts in deploying such schemes to build and win over assets. There were successes but also failures, like when a Utopian engineer with a US green card who had worked for fifteen years in an American aviation company was caught on his final day at the office stealing trade secrets. The engineer transferred hundreds of gigabytes of data to an email account which, routed through layers of accounts in between, was linked to a unit of the military.

His people were involved in planting intelligence as military officers, in foreign technology companies, or in political and business organizations. They also conducted cyber espionage. In the last two decades, his team had also worked the academic circle extensively. They wooed their own students and other academics by playing the nationalism and patriotism cards as well as courted foreign scholars to carry out their tasks, thoroughly exploiting the openness of a democracy—the very ideology they despised—to get what they wanted. The Party viewed such manoeuvres to be simply an 'expansive approach' while the outside world categorized them as 'espionage' and 'theft'. Such allegations angered Hongbing, his fury exacerbated when the South Korean government waded in to join the US, the European Union, and Japan, in condemning his country. *Outrageous! Clanta's been short-changing us over the years, transferring dated technology, we're just getting what is rightfully ours*, he rationalized.

The acquired technologies would fulfil the national strategy of 'military-civil fusion' with the grand objective of simultaneously empowering the military while also achieving Made in Utopia 2030. The entire society was mobilized: every business and individual was incentivized, co-opted, and compelled to participate. Non-participation was construed as unpatriotic.

* * *

As the relationship between Clanta and UFITC progressed over time, friction increased between the two. The biggest flashpoint came around the tenth year. Quietly, UFITC had established a parallel operation of three subsidiaries to produce identical chips that were made by the JV to sell to the domestic market. The South Koreans were incensed by what they saw as a backhand practice.

'What the hell, Hongbing!?' His Korean counterpart, Jay Kang, who at that time also ran strategy for Clanta at the JV, had stormed into Hongbing's office one morning.

'Whoa, good morning to you. What is what?'

'I'm talking about you secretly going behind our backs with parallel companies selling the same chips made from the technologies we imparted to you!'

'Jay, you need to calm down. Here, sit down. What's going on?'

Jay told him Clanta analysts in Seoul had stumbled upon an obscure research report about Utopia's semiconductor industry in which a few small paragraphs mentioned the prospects of a certain UFITC unit that was making chips and selling them to third- and fourth-tier cities in the country and in some African states.

Hongbing had heard through the grapevine of the unit but wasn't privy to its detailed business operations. Even though he spent most of his waking hours at the JV, which was located just outside the UFITC grounds, he stayed in touch with his HQ connections, knowing from early on in his career, the importance of creating and maintaining an internal network. At a personal level, he felt ambivalent about the UFITC chip offshoots, but legally, the SOE had breached no agreement terms, as Utopians had never promised exclusivity to any foreign business or investor. The JV was signed under the auspices of an offshore vehicle held by a UFITC-owned company. What's more, he was not about to get entangled in matters concerning his bosses. Still, Jay, who felt ambushed and embarrassed before his superiors and colleagues in Seoul, needed to be pacified.

'I'm sorry, Jay, I really have no information about this. But I guarantee you that our interests in the JV are the same. So, give me the day to find out what's really going on. I'll get back to you as soon as I know more.'

That evening, Hongbing called Jay on his cell phone after office hours to set up a breakfast meeting the next day.

The first meal of the day was arguably the most important, and Hongbing hoped Jay would draw the same parallel that Utopians had for their JV partner. As an offspring of the Utopian system, personal and trust-based relationships at all levels surpassed any agreement or documentation, and the ability to influence the course of a JV rested on that, even outside the company.

'I spent the afternoon at the UF headquarters yesterday. These days I'm not completely looped in on every detail of what's going on at the group level, but as you know, I came from the mothership, so I still have some contacts.

'Here's the thing. The group has invested in a few small start-ups making chips. They are really miniscule, it's just the state supporting graduates, young innovators.' Jay listened carefully without interrupting.

'It's coincidental that they are selling similar products. But, look, what's important is that they are restricted to small and inconsequential markets in some remote counties. These guys are not in the major league like us. It's nothing like our JV's exposure—top cities and exports to developed economies. Personally, I would say their quality is inferior to what we produce.'

At that moment, the waiter interrupted them with trays carrying their breakfast. Hongbing took a bite of his toast as Jay scooped up a mouthful of scrambled eggs. They munched in silence for a while.

Then, Jay asked thoughtfully, 'I know that Clanta cannot restrict your parent company from partnering with other firms, but these so-called start-ups are selling products that are so similar to what the JV makes that you can't blame us for being suspicious. Some Clanta folks back home feel like we are being screwed over, to the embarrassing point of technology being stolen by your side and then unilaterally profited from.'

'I know how this looks Jay. If I were you, I'd think likewise.'

'You know you don't exactly have a good track record, SOEs are not completely innocent,' Jay went on. Hongbing pursed his lips but didn't respond.

'Didn't your own court recently rule against another SOE, New Frontier, for setting up a subsidiary that mirrored the operation of its JV with the French? Frankly, I don't wish for this to happen to our JV.'

'No, it will definitely not come to this. You're overreacting, aren't you?' Hongbing said, with an anxious laugh, trying to lighten the mood. Jay looked back intently, with a look that essentially said, *are you kidding me?*

'All right, all right, I get your embarrassment with Clanta. Let's do this. You and I put together a plan to get approval to expand our geographical reach within Utopia. It's time to sell to the tier-three cities.'

On a personal level, Hongbing didn't want to fall out with Jay. They went back a long way. The South Korean had been assigned by Clanta to join the JV just three months before production was to commence at the first chip fabrication plant—when everyone at the JV was high-strung and the company felt like a pressure cooker. It wasn't the ideal time to arrive in a foreign land. Hongbing helped him settle in. Through Hongbing's real estate agent classmate, Jay found a nice apartment where he set up a home. Hongbing's wife, Sara, took Jay's wife, Min-joo, under her wing, helping her familiarize herself with their neighbourhood and the city as well as introducing other working professionals to her. The women stayed friends but weren't exactly close. The husbands, who were about the same age and big soccer fans, hit it off quickly. They set up a UF-Clanta football club and organized biweekly matches with teams in Unitas, the capital city. After Jay's son was born in Utopia and when the family needed extra help, Hongbing introduced a distant relative to work as a live-in nanny and helper in Jay's household. The two men's relationship deepened over time. Hongbing supported Jay at work and beyond, and, in the most organic way, planted his eyes and ears around his friend's office and his home. Jay's nanny for his son, the housekeeper, and his chauffeur met with him every quarter and also when needed to give update reports. Apart from the above-market salaries that their Korean employer paid these workers, Hongbing topped up with an allowance. In return, they showered him with gifts in the hope of getting more benefits and employment opportunities for their family members and relatives. There was always no shortage of such jobs, as the need for surveillance only grew. This model was replicated on all senior Korean executives and other foreign executives and officials in Utopia.

As for Jay, he saw Hongbing as an often-conflicted man with a good heart.

While Hongbing succeeded in pacifying Jay with the stop-gap measure, the work behind the scenes required more effort.

The Clanta analysts who stumbled across the start-ups felt indignant and decided to leak the information to an international news agency in Seoul. A reporter in Seoul dug further and discovered that two of the start-ups were headed by the offsprings of a few top Party leaders. The chips produced were selling well and the start-ups had ramped up their production. She wrote up a story and called Hongbing for a comment.

'Hi Mr Shan, I'm Kim Ye-jin from InfoStream News.'

'Er . . . How did you get my number? I don't think we've met.'

'I have my sources,' Ye-jin said. 'I won't take up too much of your time. I am writing a story about UFITC's start-ups.

'How do you feel about these start-ups competing with the JV with similar products? Why did UFITC play out Clanta?'

Momentary silence.

'Hello Mr Shan, are you there?'

'Yes,' he paused. 'I have no knowledge of what you're talking about. Please go through our public relations department. Don't call me again.'

With that, he hung up on the reporter. After that, he quickly called the agency's director of sales in North Asia, a jolly Hong Konger who had lived in Utopia for more than two decades. He conducted business with much flexibility and was always accommodating of his customers.

'Hongbing, what a pleasant surprise. I meant to call you over soon for lunch.'

'Hello, George, I will skip the pleasantries for now and get to business. This is urgent.'

'Okay, how can I help?' Anything to please one of the most influential customers in the agency's biggest market.

'Your Seoul bureau is going to run a story involving us, I need this to be shut down or . . . '

'I got it,' George cut him off. 'I'll circle back later today.'

True to his word, George called him back in two hours to relay the good news that there would be no story, without sharing the details on what and how it was achieved. But Hongbing could easily guess, as this wasn't the first incident nor would it be the last. George would have called the managing editor of North Asia and emphasized the political and financial significance of the Utopian market and UFITC to the company. It was the old wine in a new bottle tactic, and it always worked. Ye-jin's article was thus buried forever.

'That's great, George, thank you, I can always count on you.'

'Of course, anything for an old friend,' the salesman said with a boisterous laugh. 'Now, about lunch, are you free next Tuesday? There's a new French Michelin-starred restaurant in the eastern district. They have an exquisite wine list. I thought we could continue the discussion about the ten additional InfoStream data terminals UF-Clanta and UFITC are planning.'

George had been a long-time reliable ally, an accomplice in censorship via commercial pressure. He and Hongbing valued each other's friendship, and how much they mutually benefitted from the relationship.

Ye-jin's story might have been killed in the InfoStream newsroom because of the company's zealous sales team, but the information found its way to a local Korean publication.

Clanta, South Korea's leading tech giant has been played by its Utopian partner, which invested in three start-ups in the authoritarian state that produce semiconductors similar to those manufactured by its $20-billion chip JV, according to sources close to the JV's operations.

The start-ups are believed to have earned an estimated combined revenue of $1 to $2 billion in the past two years—not bad for start-ups—internal research reports at Clanta revealed. While the impact is measured to the JV, Clanta sources pointed out the greater damage was the scale of such 'backhanded practice involving technology theft'.

'We think this is the tip of the iceberg,' said a senior engineer at Clanta headquarters who was involved in the design of the JV plants.

A Clanta spokesman declined to comment. UFITC and the JV UF-Clanta didn't return phone calls or emails.

The story also revealed the founders of the start-ups and their allegiance to the top Party officials. This was to be understood in the context of UFITC and how the SOE was run and controlled by a government, which relied on the United Front's strategy—tapping a global network of assets and spies with persuasive and coercive tactics to expand Utopia's influence and get what it wanted.

The UFITC officials fumed silently but there was little they could do beyond their shores. The great Utopian firewall was effective in censoring all elements deemed inappropriate for the people's 'well-being' or that threatened their 'security', with the assistance of tech companies like UFITC. It was part of a national programme to build the database with records of every citizen and foreigner residing in the country that connected to the security agencies in phases. The national censorship and web surveillance system was also a precursor to the Social Credit System, which expanded surveillance to cover all aspects of life, a huge leap from the state watching what information a citizen could consume. Those who attempted to bypass the blocked websites or social media platforms through virtual private networks (VPNs) achieved limited success because the internet police were like ruthless mercenaries and quick to kill. Utopian media reported only triumphs without tribulations. The SOEs and selected private firms were model businesses that had transformed the global economy with their indigenous, game-changing technologies and products. The public would never know of any dodgy practices, the likes of which UFITC and UF-Clanta performed. Utopia's leaders had the most effective surveillance system and internet control, harnessing digitalization for authoritarianism. The snag, however, was these important technologies relied on and ran on chips that were foreign-made and imported. The irony was the further it progressed towards tech superpower status, the more it needed advanced chips.

UF-Clanta executives—on both the South Korean and Utopian sides, including Hongbing—seldom did media interviews. The South Koreans had no qualms with a stronger media presence but were asked by their partner to keep a low profile. The Utopians were scarred from an experience some years ago.

At the JV's eighth anniversary, the then Utopian co-head, who had also been a board member of UFITC, consented to a joint interview with his South Korean counterpart. The interview went along an agreed script until the reporter followed up on a response by the co-head, which Utopians saw as a hostile, offensive move that showed them down against their partner.

'Mr Dai, you just stressed that you'd be able to leapfrog two generations of nanometre technology, ahead of schedule,' the reporter had asked. 'How will you do that when the world's semiconductor leaders, including Clanta, are only realizing the next-generation node?'

Dai had been caught off guard. Bragging without accountability was second nature to many Utopian officials in a state where one only talked about the country's prowess. Dai was livid and humiliated, more so because the interview was conducted alongside the Korean partner.

He had stormed out of the interview room, leaving his Korean counterpart rather astonished.

Hongbing had later pressured the global news agency that did the interview to kill it or face commercial repercussions.

Thereafter, the interviews that the JV executives gave were confined to the domestic media and pro-Utopia outlets from other authoritarian states. In Utopia, there were only glowing stories of UF-Clanta, UFITC, and the achievements of the semiconductor industry. Clanta received some credit as a spillover mention now and then.

The start-up debacle was neither an isolated case nor the only alarm bell set off for the Koreans. They had suspected the Utopians of shifty undertakings or behaviours that veered from what had been contractually agreed. If these behaviours didn't have major consequences, the Koreans preferred to close their eyes, lest the consequences become dire. Over a beer, Hongbing's people sometimes hinted to Jay's team to be 'more accommodating'. And Clanta executives had witnessed the disastrous outcome suffered by a rival South Korean semiconductor manufacturer, Kotech, which had sued its Utopian JV partner in a South Korean court for stealing technology. Over the course of a three-year period, two JV employees—a Korean and a Utopian—had been sent to a Kotech R&D lab in Seoul for espionage, stealing trade secrets worth billions of dollars that were channelled to the Utopian SOE partner. The court in Seoul ruled in favour of Kotech and imprisoned the two staff members. Exposed and humiliated, the Utopians made sure Kotech paid for its folly. They rejected the JV's plan to expand production capacity, which essentially stifled sales and drove the business to a loss. A smear campaign against Kotech was launched, which not only ruined the reputation of the South Korean company but also of the JV's in Utopia and Utopian-allied markets. There were other roadblocks. Sourcing raw materials became difficult and supply deliveries weren't on time. The residence visas of senior Korean executives were renewed only on a short-term basis and approval for newcomers was denied. The costs piled up to a point where even sustaining a presence in the world's biggest consumer market made no commercial sense. Three years after their sweet legal victory, Kotech exited the Utopian market.

One JV less meant nothing to the Party because there were many more foreign investor suitors that would make up for the departures. Kotech's fall honed in the message. Clanta's management convinced itself to focus on the bigger picture: expanding its pie in the world's biggest consumer market, which aligned with one of UFITC's objectives. To keep a constant check also would be to question their partner's respect for the rule of law, if there was any at all. Rather than taking on the impossible, it was wiser and easier to follow the money, and make as much as one could.

At times, when Clanta kicked up a fuss, like Jay did with the start-ups, it was a veiled protest against the Utopians, who went overboard in taking advantage of their goodwill. These were also done in a measured manner.

Jay had known Hongbing since the early days of UF-Clanta. Both men rose in rank in their respective capacities and each's scope of responsibilities grew. Along the way, they had conversations about the difference in doing business—the international practices.

One of the sticking issues was how UFITC partnered with other foreign tech companies that competed directly with Clanta. Clanta's top leaders had protested but UFITC's president held his ground.

'We can't offend other companies,' he told Clanta's chairman. 'And all Clanta has to do is sell one computer and one mobile phone to half our population,' he shrewdly emphasized, highlighting the tired concept of how South Korea was only a thirtieth the size of the Utopian market. 'It's all about the fairness and the level playing field that your democratic societies promote,' he added, smiling.

It was never UFITC's concern of what and how existing partners would react to its ventures with others, and it was a reality that all foreign investors had to live with. On one hand, there were other structures to contemplate—like a wholly-owned subsidiary—but they weren't allowed in the lucrative high-tech industry, where national security was at stake. On the other hand, the Utopians desperately needed the foreign investors as their chip capability was at least a generation or two behind.

'Your leaders can't always use the potential of your market size as the carrot to take our IP,' Jay protested. 'Especially if Utopia wants to be considered a global player. Bullying and coercive tactics breach all international standards and practice.'

'Oh, like your country, Japan, and the West haven't gone out of line ever,' Hongbing shot back. 'Here's where you and all foreigners are wrong in assessing the world order. After centuries of the Western democracies leading the world order, why can't a non-Western country with an alternative model of governance take the lead?' Hongbing refuted. 'Where is your democratic spirit?'

If there was ever a question of what the biggest ability of a Utopian Collector was, it was the artful skill of manipulating the opposing party's own values as a counter to deflect criticisms. There were good lies and then there was the 'Utopian truth'. The education curriculum was subliminally embedded with the ills of democracy versus the greatness of the Party's ideology, intending for every child to be thoroughly steeped in patriotism, readying them to come to the nation's defence at any time. The great firewall blacked out most of what the Party deemed external vices. By the time the country opened its doors to foreigners and investments as well as allowed overseas travel, no amount of international influence could shake Hongbing's entrenched perspective of the world.

* * *

The world's most advanced chip maker possessed the one-nanometre (nm) technology. Utopia was only at ten nm by the time Hongbing took charge of the JV.

JVs were the easier route to obtain as much data and information as one could get from foreign firms. UF-Clanta began as a greenfield project, a mammoth advanced Integrated Device Manufacturer facility built from the drawing board. The first two fabs took three years to complete. Multiple versions of plans and blueprints changed hands, which meant intellectual property as well. They were necessary documents and files to get the project going, then mulled and debated over, and filed away in the cloud, state-owned. They sat next to files of Hongbing's weekly analyses and detailed reports of his Korean colleagues' movements.

The JV's scope and scale had expanded vastly, hence the amount of paperwork and reports to the higher-ups. As one of the several project managers transferred from UFITC to the new outfit when it was established, his main responsibility then was to review documents and blueprints for the plant and cross-check the details according to the agreement signed. His bosses were demanding, and the foreign partner was pressured to revise and submit countless revisions. As he scrutinized each revision, he meticulously picked up every bit of technological knowledge, however small, and pooled the data together into analytical reports that were filed away in the UFITC's server for the JV, which a handful of approved non-JV personnel could also access.

Hongbing built a highly efficient and state-of-the-art filing system that was steeped in complex security but easy to use at the same time. It was mostly automated, and could ship off reports easily and efficiently. The infrastructure eventually extended to the Link. And then it was connected to the national surveillance system where officials could cross reference any suspicious individuals to the multi-year archives for their detailed backgrounds. Few, like Party-Secretary Lan, had clearance and access at this level. Hongbing didn't, but he was the architect of the system.

For a nation that monitored its own people so closely, the surveillance of foreign visitors was, of course, without question. Each Collector who worked in a company where there's foreign interest was responsible for a few foreign co-workers and had to be sure of their subjects' status, especially if there were significant changes in behaviour and thoughts. It would be part of the performance assessment done by the Party.

Hongbing diligently reported every detail he could find on his Korean colleagues, Jay included. If the notion of spying ever crossed his mind, it was never dwelled upon, and he made sure it was fleeting and gone before his next breath. He was enamoured with the righteous dream. In fact, he took pride in cleverly blurring the line between the professional and the personal to excel in what the Party expected of him, all while honouring the friendship with the Korean colleagues he had befriended. He believed the state's surveillance of Jay and his countrymen at the JV was for their safety, just as it was for all Utopians.

As most of Hongbing's waking hours were spent at the office and the plant, his colleagues, Jay and a number of Korean co-workers became his extended family. Inevitably, the rift with his wife, Sara, and his daughter widened. Sara was irked by her husband's unquestioning commitment to the Utopian ambition. She had once believed in the Party like Hongbing. She had once worked for an SOE, promising a bright Utopian future, as devoted as any twenty-something-year-old could be. Then, her invalid second aunt, living in a remote mountainous county, suffered a stroke. The transport infrastructure in the mountains was poor, and hospitals only dispatched first aid and ambulances for a monetary price. Her aunt lived alone, as Sara's cousins had left the desolate county for the cities in search of better jobs and a better life. By the time her neighbours found her unconscious, some time had already passed. Her neighbours then had to spend another twenty minutes trying to raise the money to pay for the ambulance. By the time her aunt arrived at the hospital, doctors declared her brain was too far gone, and left her to die.

Sara had hired a local human rights lawyer to sue the hospital and the healthcare authorities in the local courts. Her lawyer was confident there was a case, as several neighbours had witnessed the ordeal and had also agreed to testify. Everything was in good order, she figured, as her lawyer filed the lawsuit. She believed that the judiciary would do what's right. When the court rejected the case, Sara was dumbfounded. An appeal to a higher court was also declined on the grounds of inadequate evidence and witnesses. Her lawyer found out that the local bureaucrats had gotten to the neighbours, silencing them with a mix of threats and payoffs. She even flew to the village to persuade the villagers to reconsider, but they were too afraid to defy their local chieftains.

She had sank into depression after that. Hongbing tried to talk to her.

'It's unfortunate that your second aunt died, we are all sad about it. But she was old and already suffering from other ailments.'

'Yes, she was old, but they had no right to end her life prematurely,' she had whimpered, cradling her head with her forearms.

'Look at it another way, at least she's no longer suffering.'

She had looked up and glared at him, with a face full of disbelief. 'That's not the point. As someone who's given to the Party all her life, contributed to this damn Utopia building, she is entitled to this basic right to decide when she goes! Doesn't the Party promise that everyone has equal rights!? What's wrong with you?'

'All I'm saying is, have some perspective. Can't you see how your doggedness in chasing this alleged corruption is stressing you out with no end? For all you know, you could be barking up the wrong tree! When was the last time you asked about your daughter's well-being?'

'In this country, you either need money or connections to those in power. Without them, we're nothing. You have to acknowledge that reality, and secure at least one of these before risking the loss of any more of your family members.'

Sara had broken down. Not that she thought he was right, but months of pent-up frustrations and dejection came to a breaking point and Hongbing's pep talk provided that release trigger. Her aunt, who had little, brought her up while her parents went to work in the city. She was indebted to her. Her tragic demise changed Sara's beliefs and her faith in the *people's* Party. *So much for equality!* Money and connections were the only reliable commodity that ran the national system. So, Sara quit her SOE job and took the real estate agent exam. At first glance, it seemed like she went for the money. The property market was booming and before three years were out, she had made her 'first bucket of gold', as Utopians would say, that is, the first million.

From then on, all that had mattered was making money. Naturally, her husband disagreed with her changed philosophy of life—the Party wouldn't condone it—but he didn't mind the wealth she was accumulating. It afforded a comfortable lifestyle, one where he could focus on the greater cause as she became the primary breadwinner of the family. After that, Sara began to see him in a different light too. Their relationship had been agreeable, but their common interests decreased. Their views and perspectives and, therefore, their values diverged, and she no longer knew how to communicate with him. One day, in desperation to blow off steam, she called Yiping because he knew Hongbing well. They had tea and Yiping was sympathetic as he was experiencing similar tensions with his wife. She found comfort in opening up to him.

* * *

Meanwhile, the Koreans kept track of their Utopian partners, albeit with a vastly different agenda. Like all foreigners eager to raise exposure in the local market, they were focused on building relationships and networks, connections that would enhance their investments. Every relationship formed was characterized by a calculation of benefit and loss. It was a culture that resonated, in fact, close to home. Jay also watched Hongbing like a hawk. He knew that over the years, his friend had transferred at least half of his assets to South Korea, acquired a property outside Seoul and established a shell company, actions that were common among Utopian elites. In Utopia, the biggest corporations were state-owned. There was little room for private firms or individuals to succeed or accumulate substantial wealth without the Party exerting some kind of control over them. Once, the biggest and most successful technology companies had been private and the owners became billionaires. The Party allowed for them enough time to advance and flourish, only to tighten their leash on them and assume their technological expertise to use it for greater control of the state.

I guess Hongbing has to protect himself against techno-totalitarianism too! Jay mused. He never mentioned this to anyone, nor used the information. Not yet.

Chapter 3

Shades of Grey

The death of Sara's second aunt prompted Hongbing to transfer some of his wealth offshore, a contradictory and counterintuitive action for a Party loyalist. Yet, in a way, it was an almost default reaction, a form of unconscious, subtle, and implicit denial against the grim realities hidden beneath the surface of the Party. But whatever conflicting emotions he might have experienced, he was just being pragmatic, he rationalized. *My devotion didn't waver, not one bit. No, I still love and believe in the Party,* he told himself. *The offshore assets are meant for my daughter—to give her an option,* he constantly persuaded himself. Senior Party officials had done this for decades, and he was only following their 'good' example. Frequent business travels to South Korea made it easy. When Sara began to strike gold from booming property sales, she also moved her wealth to Seoul, and even to other countries, unbeknownst to her husband. She never felt conflicted about this, not even for one moment. The Party had forsaken her aunt and her. She was reciprocating in kind.

Few people knew about Hongbing's fortunes overseas. Jay was aware, but they seldom talked about it. His personal assistant was privy to some information but not to the whole picture. A couple of his subordinates suspected their boss of having secretly moved his money out of the country, but they were not about to snitch on their superior, especially when the assumed consequences would be greater than the benefits.

Hongbing was on the rising path, in the Party hierarchy and his ambition to further rise up the ladder only intensified his willingness to do whatever it took. Sara had awoken to a side of her husband she was unfamiliar with—Hongbing's increasingly blind loyalty was becoming more sinister than she'd like to acknowledge. *Would my husband's thirst for climbing the ranks and serving the Party propel him to unthinkable actions?* His determination to achieve a goal, no matter what, unnerved her.

Her ambitious spouse was just the head of the Strategic Planning Division at that point, but the Party had indicated he would be on the fast track to the top job at the JV. Encouraged by the prospect, Hongbing slogged even harder. He disallowed himself from missing any opportunity to contribute to the cause. Besides slave-driving his underlings to collect more intelligence and increase their working hours, he also scoured acquisition targets to add to the UF-Clanta universe. Any notable chip-related start-ups and tech outfits in and around the capital city were gobbled up by the JV in a shopping spree that their Korean partner had little say over. Until a particular bid for a tiny AI chip maker in Silicon Valley backfired royally and worsened geopolitical tensions, which Utopians, in their arrogance, brushed off.

Niutel (homophonic short-form for new intelligence) was an obscure chip maker established in the Valley less than ten years ago by a pair of engineers whose last names were Huang and Fung. It began by making chips for the video gaming industry, before a successful pivot to focus on more advanced chips for AI and deep learning. Hongbing met the founder pair at an AI fair in Hong Kong.

His positive impression of Huang and Fung was predicated on the fact that the two men had kept their firm private and small over the years but had established a reputation within the industry for cutting-edge technology. The pair tried very hard to fly under the radar and never spoke to the media. Even in this highly connected world, the men and the firm had a minimal digital footprint.

Hongbing instructed his people to dig up as much information as they could; he wanted to buy the firm. Once he thought he had secured the vital information, he moved to woo Huang and Fung by inviting them to visit to exchange ideas. He flew them first-class to Utopia, brought them to see UF-Clanta's sparkling new plant and then inundated the duo with propaganda of the humongous size of the local market as well as a customized workshop with Yiping, where the two sides sparred on semiconductor technology so advanced and specific that even members of his own senior team could not make sense of it. At the end of the week-long visit, Huang and Fung flew back to the US, with both sides keeping in contact in the ensuing months. Hongbing thought he had successfully created a rapport with Huang and Fung. He felt confident Niutel would come under the UF-Clanta fold, even if a total buyout wasn't achieved, a majority stake was certain.

He made his move in the fourth month.

'Hello gentlemen, how have you been doing?' he cheerily waved at the large TV screen in a video call.

'We're fine,' Huang responded softly with a mere fraction of Hongbing's enthusiasm. Hongbing didn't notice.

'I must say that over the last few months, we've struck quite a bit of rapport. We are very impressed with what you've achieved at Niutel. We think you can scale greater heights if we work together closely as long-term partners. Utopia is already the world's second-largest economy, and I can't think of any top global tech brand that isn't interested in this market and collaborating with the UF group. The UF group is highly selective of who we work with.

'But because we are one people, speaking the same language, sharing a 5,000-year-old culture and history, I'm sure you'd agree we are the perfect partners to work together. It will be a win-win scenario. Particularly because of our bond, I didn't want to get our bankers and lawyers to start this conversation, like a typical global company run by Western countries would. Too cold.'

Fung winced at Hongbing's allusion to him and Huang being one of 'us' but kept quiet and let the Utopian continue. He stole a glance at his partner whose face had reddened a little. Befuddled, they looked at each other, wondering at which point in their interaction with Hongbing had they indicated their interest in merging.

'Hey, Hongbing, it was good to have spoken today. Frankly, what you've brought up is a total surprise to us. We don't recall having indicated, anywhere in our conversation during these past months, that we plan for Niutel to head this way.'

'Well, Fung, maybe you haven't thought of it,' Hongbing wasn't about to take 'no' for an answer, 'but didn't you and Cai talk about how you could come together to make a cutting-edge chip?'

'That was just a discussion, engineer to engineer,' Fung grimaced.

'Ooookay . . . Now that you know, there's no reason why you shouldn't think about the prospect. UF can only make Niutel better. In fact, you will have the entire UFITC behind you. Just think . . .'

'Ummm . . . Hongbing, we gotta go now,' Huang interjected, glancing at his watch. 'A client is waiting for us in the meeting room with an emergency matter. Thanks for the chat and the idea. Take care.'

The Niutel founders promptly shrugged off the proposition. They were more amused by Hongbing's proposal than repulsed. Hongbing, on the contrary, read the response as neutral. *Who wouldn't want to grab a slice of Utopian market, and work with UFITC?* he mused.

He figured that since he had extended the courtesy and raised the matter with Niutel, he'd pass it on to the bankers to follow up. The investment bank appointed for the deal was United Valley Global Finance, a JV between the financial arm of UFITC and a Silicon Valley-based institution. The JV bank was set up specifically to support the state-owned company's tech ambition nearly a decade ago. But years of constant bickering between the partners had tired the Americans who were looking for an exit opportunity. Most of all, the JV bank was not profitable enough to offset the unseen costs.

As financially enticing as a successful acquisition of Niutel could be in fees earned, the Utopia-based Silicon Valley bank representative had doubts about the deal. He had asked around his network in the Valley and he didn't think Niutel was the type of firm that would sell itself to the Utopians. His tech contacts told him that Niutel was at the top of their game, financially strong, and guarded its proprietary technology religiously. Being the seasoned banker that he was, he concluded that there was no reason for the founders to divest, nor the firm's backers, whom he also found out were not as straightforward as many would assume. He smelled trouble and questioned if the bank and his client should proceed. In fact, he told his headquarters to take this opportunity not just to walk away from the deal but also the JV set-up.

His boss, the president of the US bank, was in favour and called a board meeting to vote.

The board voted for them to exit, but the smoking gun was provided, interestingly, by one of the board members, who was acquainted with Niutel's main backer. The member's intel sealed the outcome.

When the representative raised the issue of a divorce with his partner, the Utopians were indignant. They felt snubbed and the displeasure was authentic. Yet, deep down, they were relieved and even glad. Utopia was rising in the world, and UFITC was more than capable of running its own investment bank engaged in the biggest global deals.

'The Silicon Valley bank will only weep in regret when we pull this off,' Hongbing bragged to the team from United Valley Global Finance, now minus the foreigners.

Unfortunately, his dream of a UF-Niutel outfit to produce the world's most powerful AI chip was crushed before it ever began. What the UF intel failed to uncover was behind the corporate facade of Niutel's main investor was an incredibly low-key tech billionaire who was a native of a democratic state, which the Party had a tense relationship with. The billionaire held Niutel through a myriad of structures and firms. Needless to say, the bankers only secured a fifteen-minute courtesy meeting with Niutel's founders before a written letter of decline.

News of the acquisition bid travelled through the grapevine and found its way to the American media, which also offered its two cents in on the 'Utopian scheme' against national security. Hongbing was livid when he read the report, which the global news wires picked up, and the story looped around the world. Utopian media countered with a special editorial package of stories to commemorate the seventy-fifth anniversary of the UFITC and its role in changing the lives of the people with the innovation of cutting-edge tech. The coverage gave Hongbing some comfort and allayed his fear of professional and personal repercussions that would set him back in his career path. He relentlessly worked his network and lobbied the senior UF officials and Party members, carefully reminding them of all his other successful acquisitions in the expansion programme and the triumphs of UF-Clanta.

Eventually, Lan called him to his office.

'We understand you only had our interests at heart in trying to buy Niutel. This matter is done and dusted. Niutel is a small fish in the big pond. In the time to come, we will be the big pond.'

'Thank you, sir. I will continue to do my utmost,' he promised Lan.

It was a defining meeting—Hongbing was on track to rise in the ranks. He was relieved, and felt so generous that he only reprimanded his team for the missing piece of intel about the elusive billionaire. The blow quickly went away with the wind, and he was more grateful to the Party than ever.

After the Niutel debacle, Hongbing shifted his focus back to the regular operations of UF-Clanta. Not getting Niutel was regrettable, but he had already taken over no fewer than five domestic chip companies that needed to be integrated into the UF group or UF-Clanta. In the past years, working with his Korean counterparts—and while squeezing more technology transfers from them—he doubled production output and, hence, sales. He was thrice named the best annual Collector among the supervising Collectors across Utopia, bringing in the largest amount of intelligence and, perhaps more significantly, information used to outwit the enemies.

Hongbing's world moved on nicely and he was promoted at work. He felt content and his job satisfaction was at its peak. The only missing piece was if he could join the rank of Utopia's Code of Honour, a title that recognized the individual's contribution to the people. The Party Hero status. A lifetime of Best Collector awards would not even get one close to a Code of Honour recipient.

The Code of Honour was a coveted national award given out to 'deserving' individuals at Utopia Party's milestone anniversaries, every decade. The Honour roll included the seven revolutionary heroes from when the Party seized power, the inventor of Utopia's semiconductor, the virologist who developed a vaccine to contain a virus that originated in Utopia but went on to kill a million people in the world, the entrepreneur who built and commercialized the country's first electric vehicle, and an engineer who developed an app that helped the Party consolidate its national surveillance system.

Only a handful of model workers had the privilege of receiving the Code of Honour. The hundredth was next, and this award would be most important to date, as it would mark the momentous centennial milestone for the establishment of the Party leadership.

* * *

A few weeks after Yiping's unexplained disappearance, Hongbing received a dinner invitation from Lan, at the restaurant where senior Party members hosted visiting foreign diplomats. Normally, he would be on cloud nine about such an invitation. But having irked the great man just last week with his question about Yiping's whereabouts, he brooded during the run-up to the dinner appointment, trying to guess Lan's agenda. A few possibilities emerged, most less than positive scenarios, although he could not be certain.

Lan was dissatisfied with UF-Clanta's performance, which would mean the quality and amount of intelligence for advanced technology that could be sucked from the Koreans had not met his expectations. Or he wanted to discuss Yiping's situation. *The latter*, he thought, *is highly unlikely*.

On Friday at 5.30 p.m., he left the office under a cloud of uncertainty. The restaurant was tucked away in a remote alley above a hill that overlooked the Party headquarters, inaccessible by public transport. Hongbing took the company car and had the chauffeur drive him there, one of the few occasions in a year where he utilized the perk. As the car wound up the narrow hilly road, he shut his eyes and slowed his breathing, to brace for what was to come. He was met at the restaurant by one of the senior waitresses and led to a private dining room.

'Chief Lan hasn't arrived, please take a seat. What would you like to drink?' the waitress asked.

'It's all right, as I'm early. I'll wait for Chief Lan,' he took off his jacket, hung it on the back of the chair, and sat down.

The private dining room was no larger than two hundred square feet, where a heavy mahogany table for four stood in the centre. One wall of screen windows looked into a garden inspired by Utopia's ancient dynasties. An old calligraphy painting featuring a Utopian proverb for eternal glory hung on another wall. At the corner below the painting was a waist-level high porcelain vase with silk flowers.

At 6.31 p.m., the wooden sliding door opened to reveal Lan standing behind the waitress.

Hongbing jumped from his seat and bowed slightly. He waited for Lan to remove his jacket and sit down before following suit.

'Hongbing, how are you?' Lan asked, picking up the rolled hot towel from the bamboo towel tray to wipe his hands.

'I'm very well, sir.' He was slightly embarrassed for not initiating the pleasantry.

The sliding door opened, and the waitress brought in a bottle of rice wine with rice wine cups. She poured them each a cup.

'Let's see, when was the last time we shared a meal together . . . must have been quite a while.'

'You are very busy, with the tremendous technological milestones you've achieved in the last decade. A toast to you, sir,' Hongbing picked up his cup.

'It's a team effort that we have come this far,' Lan said, his tone devoid of emotion.

'Not without your leadership,' he was extra careful with his words that evening. The last thing he wanted was to steal Lan's thunder.

'I always knew you'd see the big picture,' the older man responded with a half-smile, the skin of his cheeks hardly moved when he spoke.

'The two generations before me toiled extremely hard, sacrificing enormously. My generation has done our utmost to not let our forefathers down and I think we are doing all right. But, of course, more needs to be done and our road ahead is not getting easier, especially when our nemesis is bent on containing our rise as a global power.'

The waitress slid the door open again. This time, a second waitress followed, and they began to serve the food.

Once the servers left the room, Lan continued. 'So, as we work towards our common goal, we must tread carefully and not be distracted by smaller issues, be it domestic or petty manoeuvres from those who don't want us to succeed.

'Indeed, our friends and kin are important. That said, we must always focus on the overall picture and our rationale to serve.' He picked up his chopsticks and also gestured to Hongbing to tuck in.

Hongbing remained silent as he nibbled his food, replaying Lan's words carefully. If he read correctly, the Party Chief was telling him to put aside Yiping's case, which had been preying on his mind since he had met Tian Li.

Clearly, asking questions was not welcomed. He began to feel difficulty in swallowing his food. He choked and hurriedly drained his glass of water.

'How's the food?' Lan asked.

'It's excellent, thank you sir,' he murmured between small coughs before clearing his throat.

'Good, good.' Another half-smile.

'As I was saying . . . right, our common goal. The senior leaders have recognized your contribution for all these years. First at UFITC and then at UF-Clanta. The latter is not an easy assignment, where we have to manage an ally of our nemesis. You've done an outstanding job, and the recognition will come in due course.' Lan raised his wine cup for a toast.

'And never miss the forest for the trees—or one tree,' he warned.

* * *

Lan delivered on his word. Five days before the hundredth anniversary of the Party's foundation, Hongbing received an official letter from the secretariat that as a Code of Honour recipient, he was to attend a dress rehearsal for the award presentation. The Party Leader himself would be giving out the award, and for that, no mistake, no matter how small, would be tolerated.

Hongbing was ecstatic. To be a Code of Honouree—also known as a Party Hero—was his ultimate dream. The biggest state media published articles about the year's recipients of the award. Hongbing also appeared in the official social media post on OneAll, Utopia's all-in-one app that provided text messaging, voice calls, video conferencing, sharing of videos and location, as well as a mobile payment. OneAll, developed and operated by a UFITC sister company, dominated the domestic market due to a lack of competitors. Foreign apps were banned, and the few other domestic ones were limited to what they could offer. The information sector was always the most sensitive sector and OneAll made it easy for authorities to track and analyse people's online activities.

In the euphoria of learning about the award, he called Sara.

'I have been bestowed with the Code of Honour! The award ceremony is in five days and the family is invited to attend!'

'Well, congratulations,' his wife scorned. 'I hope you think all your devotion and loyalty to the Party is well worth it. I'll be travelling for work, so you can count me out. Enjoy your moment.' At home, Sara didn't bring the subject up at all.

* * *

The award ceremony on a Friday morning boasted of the usual pomp and fanfare as with all events graced by the Party Leader. It was at the cavernous auditorium called the Great Unification Hall of Glory, which was reserved for Utopia's most important ceremonies. The hundredth anniversary was the mother of all celebrations that would last a hundred days. Streamer flags hung on the external walls of the Great Unification Hall. Inside, it was decorated with scilla and chrysanthemum flowers, as well as red roses, a favourite of the incumbent Party Leader. The piped-in scent of the scilla flower was diffused throughout the building. Next to the auditorium was a special exhibition of the Party's achievements over the past century, with a special section towards the end singling out the current Party Leader's work.

Everyone at the ceremony that morning was all smiles. Hongbing came along, without any family or friends. His parents were too old to travel across the capital city from where they lived as retired state workers. The whereabouts of Yiping, who was like a brother, remained a mystery. He was just surrounded by his colleagues and co-workers, people whom he had transactional relationships with. *Is this the moment that I've been waiting for all my life?* he wondered. He had dreamed of what it would be like to be at his peak. Now that he had arrived, he only felt alone with no one to share the joy. He had also endured a stressful week so far, which was now topped with a three-hour ordeal where he had to put up a smiley front throughout. Jay congratulated him at the ceremony but they both knew it was just a greeting and nothing more. His distant relatives and former classmates whom he hadn't spoken with for years called. They simply wanted to connect so that they could brag on social media that they knew the Party Hero.

After the ceremony, everyone went back to work. His subordinates threw him a huge customary celebration party at a Japanese restaurant to be followed by karaoke. There was plenty of food and much more booze. The party drank till the early morning before everyone was wasted and went home, bracing for a weekend to be spent nursing a hangover.

Following his dinner meeting with Lan, Hongbing promised himself to discard his concerns about Yiping's detention and focus on the *big picture*. But as he was recovering from a nasty hangover on Saturday, his head throbbing so violently that he thought it would explode, desolation enveloped him in his empty house. He could not distinguish between the consequences of the previous night's drinking and the heightening internal struggle within him for abandoning Yiping in exchange for personal glory. His deepest conscience was waking up. He missed Yiping even more. Yiping understood him, and he understood Yiping.

As much as Hongbing had tried to persuade himself otherwise, the dinner with Lan had been, in essence, the Party telling him to make a choice. Although he chose the Party and glory over his conscience, in his heart, his inner voice was telling him something else and it was growing louder.

Also, what was strange was that in the days before the ceremony, the dynamics in the workplace had also shifted. As a Code of Honouree, you would think your status would be cemented as part of the inner circle of power, not only at his current level of the Party hierarchy but also as an indication of rising through the ranks. In reality, he began to be left out of the most important and confidential meetings—meetings that he had been a big part of before he received the award. The most telling was his exclusion from the quarterly meeting that he and Jay had with senior Party official Zhou Fanren, who oversaw Utopia's most important foreign JVs and held the same ranking as Lan.

Except for special Party-related occasions, Zhou never cancelled a session—which reviewed the operations and strategies of UF-Clanta—nor chaired a meeting where the Utopian representative was absent. Three days ahead of every meeting, his assistant would send an agenda to Hongbing and Jay to add any discussion items that they may have. When Hongbing didn't receive the agenda for the upcoming session, he had his assistant call Zhou's office.

'Sir, the meeting's been postponed,' his assistant reported back.

Hongbing looked up from his reading, raising one brow.

'It's odd, sir, because Mr Kang's assistant told me he was gathering data for his boss in preparation for the meeting.'

Hongbing quietly nodded towards the door for his assistant to be excused as perplexity gushed in. He was so sure he had cleared the air with Lan and the senior leaders. What's more, he was a Code of Honouree! *Surely, that represents everything!* Yet, it seemed not. *So, that Code of Honouree was their bribe to shut me up?*

He was certain the Tuesday meeting would go ahead. He forwarded a meeting invitation to Jay with a lame excuse to discuss the technological specifications of the new plant during that particular time slot. It was declined without explanation. After that, he tried to suss out information from the Korean with no success. It was unheard of that the Party senior would only meet with the foreign partner of the JV.

Days later, he was excluded from a special meeting among all UFITC senior officials who ran the group's core business units. UF-Clanta was beyond the core category, in the league of major businesses.

You could say that one exclusion was inconclusive, but to be excluded twice from strategic discussions within a week was no coincidence.

He attended his celebratory party with a heavy heart. He felt like he was being left in the dark; he had no perspective or context. *Wasn't I part of the inner circle?* Now, he was only so in name. It was a million times more troubling and unbearable than Sara giving him the cold shoulder. His decades of loyalty seemed to have been overlooked in one instant. He scanned his memory for any overlooked misstep and couldn't think of any. The recent biggest error made had been the failed attempt to buy Niutel but hadn't that been explained and forgiven? And more recently, his unwelcome questions about Yiping's whereabouts. However, the latter was just a question and nothing else. Unless his bosses saw it as more than a question. For the first time in his life, a seed of doubt for the Party emerged. *Does the Party always act for the good of the people?* He was no longer certain. His journey of awakening commenced as he was forced to search for answers. Unlocking the puzzle to Yiping's detention might provide the answer. He sighed. This weekend was proving to be longer and more unbearable than the previous ones.

Chapter 4

What Is Honour?

More often than not, Hongbing's weekends were as unbearable as jail time. This weekend, in particular, had been excruciatingly painful—the wheels were coming off. Yiping's arrest, coupled with that feeling of neglection, served as catalyst. Conflicted and as much as he thought he shouldn't be questioning the Party, he refused to deny himself the freedom to allow his feelings to flow. And the consequences were beginning to unfold and the stakes were stacking up.

He was tormented, perhaps not by why his friend was arrested, but by the Party's apparent questioning of his loyalty; initially through keeping him in the dark on Yiping's case, then by excluding him from critical work discussions. After all those years of loyal service and the numerous sacrifices he made, it was clear to him that the Party had failed to reciprocate his hard work. It was a betrayal. It proved that he was not part of the system. *But what more could I possibly do?* he asked himself repeatedly but could not find an answer. As these thoughts continued to emerge and swirl in his mind, Hongbing found himself trapped in a cage of resentment, and then . . . there was anger. *What have I done to deserve this treatment? What does being a Party Hero mean if my loyalty and devotion are in question?* The train of thought travelled through his mind until it struck him with fear. *Am I the next target?*

Ultimately, it was his own sense of security that completely tore him apart. The Party's thoughts and beliefs had been deeply embedded in him, but this was only because he was assured of his and his family's safety under the Party's guidance. All were meant to be safer and happier under the Party's supreme ruling. But the possibility of being unjustly arrested halted his loyalty—something he had never experienced before. His world was crumbling; he, who believed the Party to be his world. When the Party turned against him—a scenario he had never imagined possible—his world turned upside down. It was a painful feeling, impossible to swallow.

'You may think you're a bishop, but you are just one of many pawns on their chessboard,' the burglar's words from years ago came around to haunt him, whispering in his ears, piercing his heart.

To assuage his fretting, he walked towards the bookshelf to reach for the Party history book, his usual weekend literature, which he hoped would offer a much-needed perspective, perhaps dispel any early symptoms of the lèse-majesté'. A layer of dust that had collected on the book flew into his nostrils as he pulled it from the tightly arranged row on the shelf, sending him into a rough coughing fit. He flung it away in disgust as he tried to catch his breath again. He didn't lay eyes on the title for the rest of the weekend.

Monday arrived. Alas, it was no longer sacred. He dreaded going to work. Besides, he was a wreck, having lost sleep. Fatigued and disoriented, he sagged against the front door before reluctantly dragging himself out. He just didn't have the energy to face the world of Utopia. In his altered state of mind, leaving home would plunge him into the world of surveillance, strip him down naked, revealing his doubts and worries. It was almost impossible to fraud the Party's emotion-detection technology, and he knew it better than anyone. He contemplated calling in sick or taking a day off. But his paranoia that it'd raise suspicion compelled him to discard the idea. He could also picture the smug satisfaction of his subordinates in the office if he were not to turn up. *The idiots, always waiting shyly to see me fall.* He wouldn't put it past them to propagate some false rumours about him, a tactic that he often ordered his people to use against his political opponents.

Stepping outside, Hongbing was confronted with an army of surveillance cameras, on every street, every building, every floor. The Party reached into every nook and cranny of Utopian lives. It had once been a good thing to him. Not any more. As cameras scanned for any signs of contamination, he immediately mustered the little energy he had to convert his sullen expression to one of cheeriness. 'Another great day,' he said aloud, hoping to cast a spell on himself that would curb his face and body from giving away his real feelings.

Internally, a dispirited soul, he walked into the Link. He hugged his bag closer to his chest to reduce his sense of insecurity from the prying lenses. The piped-in odour of synthetic scilla reminded him of yet another means of the Party's pervasive reach, never leaving any human senses untouched. Hongbing came to believe the choice for the national flower—which was highly invasive and toxic with the propensity to spread out uncontrollably—was representative of the intention of those who ruled.

Awful, he thought while keeping a straight face and trying not to breathe in the scent for as much as he could. He lapsed into a slight wrinkling of his nose when holographic pictures of the Party's history were projected as he walked past the walls of the 'Great Hall of Glory'. For the first time, he questioned its authenticity. His favourite parts of tanks, ammunition, and Utopian people's bloody combat against evil imperialists no longer appealed to him. It had awoken him to the fact that it was simply designed to brainwash, to demand his obedience. The air around him turned still, its heaviness compressing him into the ground. But he was anything but sure-footed, his heart rate accelerating as he slowly lost control of his calm.

'Subject 4201. Collector at UF-Clanta. Access granted for Platform 8,' the Scanner said.

'Orange,' the death-dealer machine added as Hongbing walked towards the platform. He stopped short, petrified.

Orange? Around him, horror-stricken Collectors momentarily froze before swiftly distancing themselves from *the Orange*—a reflex to protect their ideological purity. Sweating, Hongbing speeded up to platform 8, also staying clear from those who had overheard his newly labelled status. He was utterly embarrassed for what he assumed was derogatory for his seniority. He chided himself for not driving instead. Human beings were creatures of habit. Strangely, though, irritation accompanied his fear. *Why am I not aware of what Orange stands for? How and why are they interpreting my data?* His unease grew with each passing moment, realizing he had never been completely privy to the inner workings of how the Party really operated. All that he was exposed to was information that merely scratched the surface; if he'd known better, he would have been informed about what happened to Yiping. He hadn't been matriculated into the inner circle, but he had foolishly believed otherwise. It pained him to admit the fact that he had barked up the wrong tree.

'Wake up, bureaucrat, you are not a real player here,' the mockery of the burglar continued to haunt him. Time had not weakened his angst against the petty criminal, but those words had hurt his pride then and were humiliating him further now. He put his hands over his ears and shook his head hard to shoo away the voice. 'You'll never really get it until the system hits you.'

'Next train arriving in the next twelve minutes,' his smartwatch vibrated with an alert.

'Hi, Hongbing,' Jane greeted him at the platform as she waltzed towards him. It was the first time she had appeared since her medical treatment. She looked *fully* recovered, even energetic. 'Congratulations on becoming a Party Hero!'

'Hi there,' Hongbing murmured without looking her in the eyes. 'You look good. Glad you're back.'

'Yes, I'm fine now, ready to work again for the *New Utopia.*'

'So you don't have all those questions any more? Found all the answers?'

'Oh cut it out, please. I was just silly, you know,' Jane shushed. 'This great authority of ours comes with great responsibility, and if you can't stand the heat, you just need to leave the kitchen, right?

'Think I was just too stressed and wasn't myself. All those silly questions I had were nonsense.'

Whatever *treatment* she had been administered, it had worked well. She was reborn. Hongbing sank deep into despair. Not for her, but for himself. Jane would have been one of the few that he thought he could confide in. Now, that possibility was eliminated. His perspiration increased and he felt the blood draining from his face.

'Are you okay?' Jane asked

He shook his head. She was startled by his response, and her face turned uncomfortable. She didn't press further, as she had learned to protect her interests. Hongbing ignored her intention and volunteered more information. He needed to vent.

'Jane, you know that machine turnstile gate . . .'

' . . .'

He went on, 'It assigned me orange just then.'

'Hah?' she whispered, genuinely frightened. 'I don't follow.'

'It assigned me orange, not green.'

The colour from Jane's face faded as her eyes gazed away. 'Don't worry, you'll be fine,' she choked, desperate to escape his hounding.

'You have any idea what these colours are supposed to mean?' He wouldn't give up.

'What are you talking about?' She continued to gaze away.

'I mean these colours. These *greens* and *oranges*. Have you ever stopped and thought about its meanings? Ever?'

'Don't know. They aren't important or relevant.'

'How can that be?' He was relentless, his emotions gradually running high. His impression of Jane tarnished and turned to disgust, conveniently forgetting his own unempathetic attitude towards her when she had been troubled.

'Stop,' Jane cut him short in a clear irritation. 'If the Party doesn't tell us, I'm sure there's a good reason there. Don't you trust the Party? We all have our roles here and they're all different.'

'Yeah, but the thing is, they're collecting data from us and we're completely in the dark about it. Even as a Party Hero, I'm left out of the loop,' he replied indignantly. 'Is that fair?'

'Hey, hold on a minute,' Jane retorted. 'You are a Party Hero, so act like one. Our job is to fulfil our designated roles. That's how we move a step closer to the New Utopia.'

'Jane, please don't give me that textbook answer.' Hongbing was clearly annoyed. She was prescribing the same medicine that he had dished out to her on this same platform weeks ago.

'It's like an orchestra,' Jane continued. 'We are the ones playing . . . say . . . the cello, and others are playing trumpets, violins, flutes, oboes and it is the Party Leader who conducts the music, not us. So, we don't need to learn how to play other instruments apart from the cello.'

'Cut it out, Jane, what I'm trying to say here is—'

'Trust the Party and stick with its guidance when waves roll over,' she cut him cold.

'Yiping got arrested, without any explanation. You still don't see a problem here?

Ding

The red train whizzed into the station, drowning out Hongbing's question. He was sure she'd heard him, judging by her stunned face. But she maintained an oblivious expression, which amplified his internal anger. He knew exactly what she was doing; she was mirroring his previous behaviour to stay ideologically clean. He silently cursed her although he knew that, in theory, her antipathy was completely expected by Utopian standards, as she was simply looking out for herself. *Coward. This could also happen to you. And when that happens, I won't bother to help.* He stopped talking and so did she. They rode the train quietly throughout the forty-minute ride.

'Let's head off for another great day ahead of us,' Jane remarked to him as the train arrived at their stop. 'Another great day . . . indeed,' he enthused with sarcasm, before quickly squeezing out his remaining energy to put up the most joyful face he could come up with as he faced more cameras at the UF-Clanta building.

After changing into the UniDress, he queued up for the Kilgate. Grinning, he tried to relax his rock-hard facial muscles, anxious to pass the Party's emotional assessment.

If I can censor my emotions and regulate my expressions, I might be able to outsmart the system . . . But is that even possible? What if they realize that my outward emotions differ from my true feelings? The thoughts in his head did little to calm his nerves. His feet grew heavier as he moved closer towards the gate. Worrying thoughts and questions continued swimming in his head, driving him mad.

Clink

His smart fabric was activated as he reached the Kilgate. In a last-ditch attempt, he clasped his trembling hands together tightly behind his back, lifted his chest, breathed deeply, and tried to recall his happiest memories.

The first display that day was an old footage of the Party Leader inspecting a construction site in a city devastated by a major earthquake. In the video, he blasted the local officials for not promptly implementing aid measures. He then announced his *three-stage development plan*, where the Party provided free houses as well as educational and cultural facilities, to those affected. People waved flowers in praise of his benevolence, with some even crying in joy. Hongbing sailed through this first assessment smoothly, concealing his emotions well, in part because he was still somewhat genuinely happy to see Utopian people benefitting from those Party measures. With some confidence returning, he tilted his head slightly upwards for the cameras.

The table was soon turned when the next footage was shown. It documented the life of an old sculptor, who produced the Party Leader Statue, and the Monument of the Party Foundation that commemorated Utopia's wars against the Western imperialists. A national treasure, he was naturally honoured as a Party Hero, showered with an elaborate event where a top Party official presented him a Hero Medal in recognition of his service to the Party. The sculptor was thereafter given a myriad of social privileges such as tuition fee exemption for his descendants, access to classified information as a member of the *inner circle* and officially labelled as a *political reliable*.

'The political reliables are provided with a sea of social benefits,' said the voiceover. 'For instance, three years ago, the political reliables were given prior notice on classified information regarding a treason incident that was being plotted in their village. Everyone in the village was punished except for the reliables who were given time to prove their innocence.'

Hongbing started to breathe unevenly.

The narrator carried on. 'Just a year ago, eight people were also prosecuted for stealing. Two of them were acquitted because they showed remorse, and their fathers were Party Heroes who had contributed to building our beloved Utopia. We reward those who serve us well with everything we have.'

A total lie! Access to classified information? I had no idea about Yiping's arrest, and when I asked about it, they treated me like I was causing trouble. Hongbing lost his cool. The flimsy mask he had worn to hide his emotions fell apart as a sense of disgust emerged from his tightened mouth and knitted eyebrows. As contempt threaded his mind, he could feel his face flushed with an adrenaline rush, which the

UniDress was almost certain to detect. He desperately attempted to control his breath, but his biometrics had already duly exposed his raw emotions.

An orange frowning face was displayed on Hongbing's UniDress and was also floating above him as a hologram.

'Warning. Subject 4201 suspected of *Diversity-Disorder*,' the silver-coated machine at the end of the tunnel announced.

A string of 'Oh-My-Gods!' rippled through the small crowd in the lift lobby, albeit in a hushed tone, some covering their mouths in shock. They reflexively pulled away from him as though he was some sort of contaminant.

He wanted to scream: *I didn't do anything*. But he held his tongue. No one would have cared. They were too terrified to handle the situation. The last time a Collector was labelled as having a Diversity Disorder—a condition caused by deviating from the Party's principle of uniformity—was more than five years ago, and the person had never made it back to the office.

'Technical glitch,' Hongbing exclaimed aloud, making one final attempt to smooth things over in desperation. 'Clearly, a mistake.'

'Who do you think you are?' yelled a familiar voice from behind. Jane's. 'Challenging the Party's technology is like challenging the Party's authority.'

'Seriously? Jane, I said I . . .'

'Stop seeding doubts in us,' she cut him off. She spoke loudly to accentuate her loyalty to those behind the cameras. 'Don't you dare compromise our value of uniformity,' she howled, a final blow to erase her personal ties with Subject 4201.

'Says someone who wasn't pleased with the Party just weeks ago?' he retorted. 'Seriously? You know I didn't do anything wrong.'

Jane and those around had hurried away towards the elevators. Almost out of nowhere, two armed men in black suits, double his size and with chained machine guns strapped to their shoulders, appeared. Hongbing's breath halted, fearful and shocked. Time was running out. He needed to prove his *iron-clad* loyalty.

'I'm a Party Hero and my loyalty remains unchanged.'

'Don't worry, 4201,' one of the two leaned forward and whispered as the tip of his chained machine gun brushed against his thigh. 'Everything will be fine if you cooperate.'

'I can prove my loyalty.'

'Of course,' the guard replied, one corner of his lips curled up. 'Come with us, 4201. We'll be escorting you to a mind-read session.'

* * *

Hongbing was led through a long, dark corridor, with the two bulky men, each on one side. They were three levels underground, in a damp and humid environment, surrounded by the musty smell of mould and mildew. He dragged his feet, dreading what was to come.

'Faster,' one of the escorts hissed and used the butt of his gun to push him forward. Not seeing it coming, Hongbing stumbled, his body succumbing to gravity's pull.

'ARGHH!' a sharp shriek suddenly pierced through the corridor. The deafening sound crushed his lungs, and he froze.

'What was that?' he asked the minders nervously.

The two just grinned at him.

'Where am I? Look at me, I'm a Party Hero, a Collector. You think I'd end here? Soon, I'll return to where I belong, and when that happens, you two will not be forgotten.'

'Passing the Hard Interview Zone here,' one of the escorts said flatly. Hongbing's quasi-threat seemed to have worked.

'A hard . . . what? What goes on there?'

'Rebuilding their happiness.'

'Is that where I'm being sent?'

'No. It's only for those who don't learn their lessons—the reds, not oranges.'

His body further stiffened in panic. Orange wasn't too far off from red. 'Can't they be closely monitored anyway? So why the need for torture?'

'It's not torturing, it's rebuilding happiness. If they can't retain the Party's ideology, they'll at least remember the . . . process of rebuilding their happiness. That way, they won't make the same mistake again. It's very effective, you know.'

'Ah, don't worry,' the other man interrupted. 'You ain't going there. Besides, we've never had a Party Hero there.'

'Where am I being sent to then?'

'The Soft Interview Zone.'

They turned a corner and arrived in front of a heavy door. It swung open to a dimly lit room. His minders gave him a nudge.

'Thank you,' a woman who appeared to be in her forties said as she walked towards them. Her voice was charming, yet her eyes remained cold and distant, a sharp contrast to the radiant smile she flashed at Hongbing.

It was a tiny, windowless room, which could only pack around four adults. A yellow light flooded the top of a steel table, and a pair of chairs was nailed to the floor in the middle of the room. A jukebox-like machine with blinking green and red lights stood against a wall. Across the other side was a mirrored partition. It was almost certain that a group of people on the other side were watching him through a one-way mirror.

'Please, take a seat,' the woman said, calmly. 'I'm Dr Chow from the Mind Division of the United Front's Fifth Bureau. I'll be the one running your mind-read session today.'

He had not heard of the division nor knew what a mind-read session entailed. He tried hard to conceal any sign of being perplexed, but Chow saw through him.

'Oh yes, we'll read your mind,' she added with a wink.

It was then that he saw tiny, protruded dots on the low ceiling and around the corners of the walls. They were so miniscule that he couldn't clearly tell whether they were high-definition internet protocol cameras or sensors. Pressure zone microphones were embedded in the table and near Chow was a grey, helmet-shaped device connected to a machine.

Once he saw the machine, the last hope of him outplaying Chow's interrogation and concealing his true emotions, completely vapourized. He bit his lower lip, sensing that he didn't have much longer before his emotions would be fully exposed.

'Dr Chow, please listen,' he begged, 'this must be a mistake. I'm a Party Hero and my loyalty never sways under any circumstances.'

'No need to sweat in advance,' she smiled but her eyes didn't, and cuffed his wrists to the table on top of the sensor pads.

'We'll just run a few non-invasive tests for your mental well-being. That's all.'

Where are my rights to decline all these tests?

'We're just trying to help you here,' Chow said, as if she could hear his thoughts. 'We're providing the best assistance we can as a nation state, especially when your mental health is under tremendous stress. This is to help you return to normalcy.' She then placed the grey helmet on his head, her brown eyes glowing.

'Clearly, you are not listening,' he cried out. 'I have served the Party for decades and my loyalty has never been compromised.'

She ignored him, and calmly made her way out of the room. 'What's this for?' Hongbing went on, yelling at her back, enraged by her indifference. His chin nudged up, infuriated.

'Oh, you mean the helmet?' she turned, giggling. 'It will track your brain waves, which will then be compiled with other biodata—your pulse, respiratory rate, body temperature, and muscle tensions— collected by your UniDress.

'We'll watch the electrical activity of your brain . . . from the other side of the room. You do not need to do anything but relax. Let the tech, and our chips, do the work.'

Following her exit, he sat, deflated and silent.

Test 1: Image Test

A hologram popped up from the table, indicating 'Functional Magnetic Resonance Imaging Mode Activated', with a simultaneous announcement from the helmet.

'Instructions,' continued the audio. 'An image will appear for twenty seconds. You are to look at the image and then to recreate it in your mind three times, trying each time to create an image identical to the one shown.'

A high-definition portrait of the Party Leader promptly appeared in hologram. His charismatic, sparkling eyes glowed as his charming smile belched out the smoke of deceit. The image disappeared precisely twenty seconds later.

'Now, reconstruct the image in your mind.'

Behind the mirrored wall, a group of UF bureaucrats were monitoring the reconstructed image being sketched in Hongbing's mind. They also observed the comprehensive data analysis displayed on a pair of large high-definition screens. Based on his neuronal activities from the functional-MRI scan, the Party's AI algorithm was translating Hongbing's brainwave signals into a photographic image.

Hongbing's recreated image was closely identical to the first attempt. The second try deviated slightly as his subconscious began to act out. By his third rendition, his intervening inner thoughts had taken over his mind. The shiny glow in the Party Leader's eyes turned into an evil gleam, making him appear villainous. Shadows under the cheekbones made him look like a starved werewolf prowling for his prey.

'Gosh!' the audience of two men and a woman behind the mirror gasped.

'The image test is completed. Thanks for your cooperation,' a holographic projection announced.

It then signalled, through a hologram and the monotonous voice, the commencement of the second test.

Test 2: Reaction Test

'A list of phrases will be read and shown to you. You are to just listen and read them to yourself,' the voice said.

Uniformity Is Diversity
Conformity Is Harmony
Prosperity Is Freedom

The familiar slogans emerged as a hologram and were also being read aloud at the same time by a mechanical voice. By this time, Hongbing could hardly muster any positive thoughts, and his brainwaves were reflective of this disturbance, exacerbated by the his certainty of the presence of bureaucrats monitoring the mind-read session.

'The subject under a state of confusion,' read the screens in the monitoring room.

Creak

Dr Chow returned to the Soft Interview Zone with a metal box in her hand, flashing her standard emotionless smile. Hongbing eyed her and the box with fatigued hostility. He said, 'I question the validity of all those machine assessments. Sure, they might pick up some changes in my emotions, but can they truly understand why?' Hongbing asked, sensing that he hadn't passed the tests.

'You have a point,' Chow replied apathetically with a sickening grin. 'That's precisely why we checked your brainwaves—to read what you think.'

'Nonsense! How can a machine possibly fully comprehend the complexity of human minds? And what if it's wrong? How can you be so sure that it's 100 per cent accurate?'

'We're aware that there are sceptics questioning the accuracy. But like any scientific method, there's a margin of error that is considered acceptable. Thus, we treat the assessment results as factual.'

'But people can't be prosecuted when there is a possibility of error. If you're using these tests to prosecute someone, shouldn't they be completely accurate? How does that align with our judicial system's promise of absolute fairness and equal rights? Is this the treatment a Party Hero deserves?'

Chow ignored his rant. 'Were there any recent grievances that you had with the Party?' she asked, as she walked around the table to his side. She then removed the lid from the metal box. From the corner of his eye, he saw a couple of syringes and two small vials in it. Before he could find his tongue in his state of shock, she said with an evil chuckle, 'Oh it's not lethal, please don't panic. We respect our Party Heroes wholeheartedly. It's just a truth serum. Think of it as a booster against the attack on your virtues.'

The truth serum was commonly used by Utopia during enhanced interrogation to acquire information from unwilling subjects, especially in criminal cases. Code-named TRUTH-911 and a Utopian creation, the soluble, colourless drug would cause the subject to lose control once it was injected into the body. Similar drugs were also administered in democratic countries. The difference was that the use of such a drug to induce an involuntary state of mind was regarded as a form of torture in those states. But, in Utopia, that mattered little. It dismissed the possibility that the subjects' testimony under the influence of the drug could be a fabricated reconstruction from their unconsciousness.

'Sharp scratch now,' Chow whispered perversely in Hongbing's ears. As the needle penetrated his skin, he felt a sudden onset of drowsiness. Chow's face blended into the yellow light, her voice trailing off, 'Let's begin—is there anything about the Party that you were displeased with recently?'

He came back to consciousness at the sharp prick of the second vial Chow injected him with.

'The Party thanks you for your cooperation,' were her parting words as she showed him to the door, where his two minders were waiting to escort him out.

* * *

'Where's my coffee?' Hongbing yelled at his assistant through his office door. 'Get me my coffee within ten seconds or you're fired.'

Back on *his* turf, he allowed his pent-up anger to explode. His staff and colleagues were stunned to see him whoosh back to the office the next day, energized, but in a negative manner. News of his disgraceful orange rating and mind-read session had made its rounds within his office; the bureaucrats had already placed him on their radar. Jane was most shocked. She gave out a little yelp when she saw him in the common corridor. He gloated at her dismayed face, his eyes staring at her as if to say, *challenging the Party's assessment is challenging its authority*. Historically, oranges didn't return to their lives in the short term. *Let them think it's the Party Hero's social and bureaucratic privilege*, he thought. Deep down, he knew that the repercussions would be far-reaching, and it would never be the same again. More importantly, he could never view Utopia and the Party like he had before. The doubt they had cast upon his lifelong loyalty was something he simply couldn't take. Something he just couldn't forgive.

'I said I need my coffee,' Hongbing screamed again. His manner was far more abusive and aggressive than usual. It was his way of reminding the subordinates of his undiminished influence, which he felt slipping away.

'Here it is, sir,' a subordinate said, running into his office with Hongbing's mug, 'your assistant has stepped away to the bathroom.'

'Why wasn't it here earlier? You people think I wouldn't come back?' he roared.

'You've been derelict in your duty, and therefore, are suspended from work the rest of this month.'

The poor staff was shell-shocked and froze.

'Get out of my office. OUT!' He then stormed out of the room and called out to the floor.

'I want my assets in my office.'

'Yes, sir,' a staff member replied loudly.

Summoning his people was only an excuse. He was neither in the mood to work nor felt the need to. *How could the Party treat me this way?* He was conscious that these were blasphemous thoughts detectable by the numerous cameras throughout the building—but these were thoughts he simply couldn't contain. A random meeting with his underlings would distract him and offer temporary respite from the undesirable line of thought he was certain would aggravate his standing and risks within the system. Summoning his people would also reinstate his authority, particularly after his assistant had failed to ready his coffee, which was perhaps the most infuriating issue he was struggling to stomach and let go of. *The minions must be reminded of their place in the food chain.* Whatever the assets reported, he was ready to give them a hard time.

Unfortunately, he soon learned things wouldn't go as intended. Fifteen minutes passed, and no one showed up. His rage was rebuilding inside him.

'Get me my assets here right now,' he yelled into the phone to his assistant as loud as he could to cover his emerging fear.

'Er . . . we have a problem, sir,' his assistant said meekly. Paused. Then she continued, 'It would be impossible, physically, to have the meeting today.'

'Nonsense! Tell them to drop whatever they're doing and come to my office immediately or they'll spend the rest of their careers as cleaners.'

'They were called to another meeting just ten minutes ago.'

'What the hell are you talking about? I'm their immediate boss. Tell them to walk out of whatever meeting right this minute.'

'I can't—it was a Controller who requested their attendance, sir.'

Hongbing sank into his chair behind his desk, humiliated.

'When was the meeting called again?'

'Ten minutes ago, shortly after you called for one.'

He blinked his rage-filled eyes, his mind momentarily blank. He looked at the recording room next to his office, which he didn't have access to. He had to remember that he was being monitored in his office. Slamming the receiver down, he stood up and steered himself to refocus on his next move. He concluded that if he couldn't hold a meeting with his subordinates, he'd force one with others.

Kicking open his office door, he instructed his assistant, now visibly shaken by her enraged boss, to arrange for an immediate meeting with the Clanta executives.

'What should I say is the agenda for the—'

'Actually, just tell them I'll be there now.' He ran four floors down by foot to level eight where the top Clanta officials were. *All are equal in the New Utopia,* a catchphrase cropped up from a screen on the landing between the eighth and ninth floors, which made him want to shatter it to pieces.

Nursing his broken pride, he put his nose higher in the air and marched into the foreigners' office. The few senior executives present were puzzled by his sudden appearance, not to mention the request for an ad hoc meeting, even though his assistant had called ahead. One of them—Choe, who had opposed the latest deal with Utopia—wore his displeasure of Hongbing's unplanned visit on his face. The Korean had no tolerance for his wilful behaviour.

'Hello, all. How's it going?' Hongbing said brightly, ignoring the cool reception. 'How can we help you?' asked Kim—the woman in the spy video who favoured standing with the Utopians against the *imperialists.* Hongbing knew her very well, as they were partners beyond the JV. That said, the relationship was strictly transactional. Through her connections, he had relocated some of his wealth to Seoul. He was also careful to spread his risks by tapping into other channels. Like the Party psyche of divide and rule, never let any one party grasp the whole picture. Hongbing was created from the system, and these were some concepts that had embedded themselves in his psyche and wouldn't be erased easily.

In return, he showered her with whatever bureaucratic benefits he could offer; he watched her back within Utopia. After what he'd just been through, he began to realize that a transactional relationship was far more reliable and realistic than the 'blood bonding' the Party had brainwashed its citizens into. Here was a foreign imperialist, who, with money and benefits, had tied them together in a relationship where he always knew what he was getting into. *Now that's real transparency.*

'I just wanted to check whether everything's going all right with you all,' he said in his most snobbish tone. If his own people were defiant, he was going to exert his superiority over the foreigners.

'Okay,' Kim replied politely with a baffled smile. 'Thanks for asking, we're well. Actually, we were just wondering—'

'Everything's fine,' Choe hissed, cutting her short. His abrupt interruption took his Korean colleagues in the room by surprise. Hongbing, too, was taken aback by the discourtesy extended to him. He didn't realize that Choe had no patience or time for him. The Korean executive took an instant dislike to him from the moment they had met and had since suspected Hongbing of selling Clanta short and stealing their technology. 'Mr Shan, we'd appreciate it if you would at least notify us of such a meeting . . . at least an hour before you turn up to our office.'

Hongbing's ego was already bruised but Choe dealt it another blow. To be humiliated by foreign partners was unprecedented. They had only strived to flatter and flood him and other senior Utopian officials with requests—on both business and personal fronts—lobbying for concessions in Utopia. They would be knocking at his door on the twelfth floor.

'Oh, am I interrupting an important meeting here?' Hongbing asked lamely, hoping to find himself a gracious exit path as well.

'No, I just think what we need here is mutual respect,' Choe
torpedoed him, looking straight into Hongbing's eyes. 'All are equal in
Utopia, right? We would like to stick with the principle.'·

Hongbing opened his mouth, but no words came out. Choe cannily
used Utopian values to his advantage. He couldn't argue against the
Party's slogan, especially in his current state. But he also sensed that
there might be a deeper ploy at play—engineered by the Utopian
bureaucracy—which gave Choe the leverage to behave derisively.

'We were actually about to start our internal meeting. Do you mind?'
Choe gave him a final glare.

With an awkward smile, Hongbing quickly said goodbye and quietly
left. He was overwhelmed with mortification and vowed to make Choe
pay for humiliating him openly. *Just you wait . . . when I find dirt on you.*

'Mr Shan,' Kim called from behind, her heels clicking rapidly
as she caught up with him. She looked slightly embarrassed as she
pushed her glasses onto her nose and gently tapped his shoulder in a
friendly gesture.

'Yes, madam,' he nodded to her. He grappled with a confluence of
emotions: comfort and a sense of relief that he still mattered, as well as
a renewed feeling of superiority as a Utopian official. 'How can I help
you?' He felt as though he had regained some dignity.

'Just giving you some background here,' she whispered. 'We've been
told by your Controller this morning to communicate directly with him
for the next few weeks.'

'What?' His last remaining shred of pride was wrecked. Then,
again, came anger. 'Why?'

'We don't know, as if we could ask any questions here,' she muttered.
'Look, I've been investing in you for years and I don't have any other
channels other than you. Make sure you clean up whatever mess you
have ASAP.'

'When did they contact you, what time?'

'About ten minutes before you invaded our office. And also, that
just completely exposed your desperation, you know that, right? Please
think before you act. You need to be a bit more strategic.'

With that, she turned around and walked back to her office, the
clicking of her high heels fading. Hongbing watched her back for a

moment. He turned her warning in his head. She was right. He needed a strategy, a plan—and to not let emotions get the better of him. All around him, they were watching. The future was bleak, but he was not going to give up.

* * *

Hongbing threw his brown leather bag on the sofa as he shut the front door behind him. It was only 7 p.m. but he was already home. It was a remarkable first time. He would no longer voluntarily work until 10 p.m. to contribute to the Party's journey of building the New Utopia. He found his motivation rapidly waning. His Controllers, without spelling it out, had stripped him of his authority. His assets never responded to his calling, the gossip about him buzzed behind his back, and foreign partners humiliated and deserted him. Above all, his life—the living hell he was experiencing now—was topped by a sense of paranoia about the increased monitoring of his movements in the office. The clock ticked slowly at work. Being out of the Party's favour meant nothing was in order. The scilla scent stank, and the legion of cameras that he once felt protected him from harm, turned repulsive overnight. *Why hasn't anyone complained? They won't know until the system hits them directly. Fools!* He cursed, forgetting he had been one himself.

His house was ice-cold. The temperature had dropped, as had the level of family warmth. Sara was away again on one of her numerous business trips. He tried to keep a tab on her whereabouts but was indifferent to her life. The lukewarm interest was mutual, and she likely wasn't aware of his Party fallout. He remotely remembered that she was due to be home this evening. *She must be picking up our daughter after work,* he rationalized his daughter's absence, and didn't think it was a big deal.

'I'm home,' he muttered to himself. He made his way to the kitchen and pulled out some finger food from the fridge. He was glad to be alone, to have time to think, to *strategize*. The flat was eerily quiet, but he didn't want to turn on the TV, it was best to avoid more Party propaganda. His thoughts must surpass the realm of propaganda. The question was—what exactly could he possibly do against the Party? He racked his brain, but fatigue consumed him. He dropped himself into the nearest sofa and stretched out his tired body. Before he knew it, he'd fallen into a deep sleep.

* * *

He woke up in a panic. He had a nasty dream where Sara and his daughter were pursued and taken. It was dark around him except for the dim kitchen light he had left on earlier. The digital clock on the wall showed that it was 12.15 a.m.

Sara wasn't back. Neither was his daughter. Given his state of mind, he envisioned the worst, sure that something must have gone wrong. He reached for his mobile phone on the dining table and called her. It went directly to her voicemail. He tried again and again to no avail over the next half an hour. Then he remembered the home security cameras that were installed after the house was burglarized and his graduation ring stolen. Perhaps the home surveillance system had caught something.

He wasn't disappointed. The timestamp was 4.20 p.m. Sara and his daughter, carrying a hand luggage, were walking past the sofa, when they simultaneously turned their heads back to the front door. Sara turned around and moved to open the door where two dark-suited men stood. Hongbing let out a small gasp—the pair were the same men who accompanied him to the Soft Interview Zone for his mind-read session with Dr Chow. One of them flashed his ID.

'Who are you and what do you want?' Sara asked, shielding her daughter behind her.

'We are from the Party,' the quiet minder told her. 'You need to come with us for an interview.'

'What interview? I'm just a private citizen.'

'There's no cause for panic. We just want to ask you a few questions.' She stepped back, reluctant to go with them.

'Questions about what?'

'Your lover, and what you both are plotting,' the minder told her as he glanced up to look into the camera. 'You better come with us.'

A lover? How strange of the minders to address me this way. It was clear that the Party was suspicious of him.

'What do you mean?' She rebutted. 'My husband and I hardly talk.'

'Oh, we know that,' the other man said. 'We weren't referring to Mr Shan, and you know that. We were referring to your *lover*, not your husband.'

Hongbing stopped breathing.

'I have no idea what you are talking about,' she raised her voice, telling her daughter to go to her room. 'Get out of my house, now.'

'He's just a family friend,' Sara said feebly, voice trembling.

'It will be just a few questions,' the other minder told her calmly. He took out something from the inner pocket of his jacket and showed it to her. Hongbing froze the screen and zoomed in.

'Don't make this harder than it needs to be.'

Sara lowered her head. Then she asked, so softly that it was almost audible in the footage. 'What's Yiping charged with?'

'We're not at liberty to say. But we do know that he'll be in deeper trouble if you don't come with us now. So, shall we?'

She nodded in silence and left the flat, still carrying her hand luggage. The minders also took their daughter.

The shock paralyzed Hongbing. Then, overcome with rage, he leaped forward and with both hands swept everything, including the monitor, off the desk.

The three things that he had lived for—the Party, his job, and his family—had all let him down. He felt caged by his anger, furious that everything he had believed in was one big lie. Writhing in despair, he didn't turn up to work the next day.

* * *

Bang! Bang! Bang!

Hongbing woke to the sound of door-banging. He was lying on the sofa in his study where he had languished for two days—only getting up to feed his growling stomach and go to the bathroom when needed. Unshowered and unshaven, he was a wreck. There was no word about the whereabouts of Sara and his daughter nor had anyone from the UF universe hounded him. In his temporary peace, he managed to catch some sleep, even if it wasn't fully restorative and could hardly make up for the traumatic stress he had encountered.

'Mr Shan, we have a message for you,' came the voice of an enthusiastic young man.

'It's from the Party.'

Bah, he sneered, covering his eyes and ears with a pillow to muffle out the noise. But whoever was at the door remained persistent. It was clear he wouldn't leave until he fulfilled his duty. Grunting, Hongbing lifted his heavy legs and walked to the door.

'What is it?' he asked gruffly.

'Good afternoon,' smiled a suited young man with a cropped haircut. 'I need you to come with me immediately.'

Hongbing's pulse quickened as the temporary peace of the past two days dissipated. As long as he lived in Utopia, he would never be able to live a quiet life. He was forever marked.

'Why?' Hongbing snapped.

'Shall we talk inside?' the man responded gently, stepping forward to pressure him back into the flat.

'No need,' Hongbing assertively pushed back with full strength. Curious neighbours and passers-by were beginning to gather outside his patio. He lived on the ground floor of a vast estate, with a small mall nearby, so there was quite a crowd. Any conflict between a Party Hero and a bureaucrat made good entertainment in Unitas, the model zero-crime capital city.

Hongbing's pushback wasn't in the young man's playbook. 'Well, we'd like to kindly invite you to our Happiness Rebuild Session. Please cooperate.'

'A Happiness Rebuild Session?'

'Yes. Treat it like an interview. You do not need to prepare anything. Just come with me.'

A Happiness Rebuild Session? Alarm bells went off in his mind. Flashes of his mind-read session and the screaming from the Hard Interview Zone resurfaced. He was released the first time, but he wasn't sure he would be as lucky the second time.

'Shall we?' pressed the young man. Impatience brewing, he grabbed Hongbing's arm.

Hongbing realized that he needed to react strategically without giving away his desperation, as advised by Kim. He glanced to where about two dozen people had crowded around his patio. It sparked an idea. *The people and their perception of the Party propaganda.* What the Party's afraid of the most. He rolled his dice.

'How could you defy the Party's principles?' Hongbing shouted at the top of his voice. 'It is the Party's dearest principle to honour and respect Party Heroes who have contributed endlessly to the society, which makes Utopia, Utopia.'

The crowd grew. Some were recording the spectacle on their phones.

'Taking a Party Hero against his will violates the Party's principles. Moreover, I've already informed you of my illness. I demand your name and rank, young man. I intend to report your actions to higher authorities.'

The young messenger's face flushed, and he opened his mouth, 'Sir, I am only—'

But Hongbing was having none of that. He continued, 'Party Heroes warrant social privileges, and that's why people strive to become one.

'What's the point of devoting all the time and effort to serve the people and stake your loyalty to attain Party Hero status if something as fundamental as being taken against your will can't be ensured? Are you implying that what the Party has been advertising is a lie? That would be a criminal act.

'Go through your Party principles again,' Hongbing added.

The onlookers looked puzzled and more gathered around, and he knew his rant slash monologue had succeeded in sowing seeds of doubt. But he was also aware that this tactic would only work for the time being, partly due to the inexperience of the young official. The face of this young messenger was a picture of shock; his eyes widened and his mouth opened, but he was unable to retort. If he forcibly took Hongbing, without a legitimate claim to answering the questioning audience, he would seriously compromise the integrity of the Party's social management system. He couldn't afford to shoulder that burden and would rather accept whatever punishment to be issued for failing the assignment.

'Now, back off,' Hongbing gave the young man a gentle push and banged the door shut.

Inside, with his back against the wall by the entrance, his knees gave out and he slumped onto the floor with a weak smile. Relief, and a sense of small jubilation, filled him, even though anxiety and fear lingered on. *I don't have a lot of time before they come back for me.*

I need to run . . . to Seoul . . . where my money is, he decided.

Realistically, it was the best option because he already had his business visa to South Korea and the bulk of his money and assets were in Seoul. Seoul, however, would be a stepping stone. He would then make his way to another country that hadn't signed an extradition treaty with Utopia.

With his mind made up, he ran a bath, relaxed in the hot tub for a long while, shaved, and put on some clean clothes. Feeling refreshed and energized, he made his way to the safe tucked away behind the clothesline in his wardrobe, and took out his passport, all the cash, the jewellery, and the watch collections. He packed as many valuables as he had in the flat into a backpack, along with essential clothing items into a carry-on trolley suitcase. He would have to avoid the bank—ATMs and credit cards—anything that would leave a digital or paper trail. He then went into the kitchen, found the smallest knife, and shoved it into his coat pocket.

His concern for his own survival was so profound that at this point, he found himself unable to worry much about Sara and his daughter. *Sara will take care of her,* he told himself. At the door, he turned back and scanned the spacious flat. The coldness of the space reflected his own sense of emptiness, which had been brought about by vanity and gullibility, as he had blindly embraced the Party's ambitions. By backtracking and questioning the Party, he had lit the fire, and the flame was now out of control, maliciously burning everything he had built. And he knew that when you can't fight the fire, the next best thing you can do is run from it. *Do I have a chance against the Party's surveillance?* He didn't know, but he simply couldn't stay put and hand over his fate to the Party. *How is this Utopia when it is the Party that dictates the fate of each individual? Utopia for whom?* He could go on and on this philosophical track, but what good would that do? *Stop!* He scolded himself. He looked at the clock on the wall. It was close to midnight.

With one last glance at home, he put on his cap and shut the door behind him.

It's time . . . and I will survive.

Part II

Echoes of the Mirror Hall

Chapter 5

The Fugitive

Bright lights, big city. The fugitive's shrinking frame was amplified against the illuminated propaganda hoardings in Unitas, the capital city. The infrared technology of the surveillance cameras trailed him, like a shadow he couldn't shake off. Hongbing ducked his head, attempting to conceal himself as much as possible. A Party Hero who had to keep his head buried was a painful notion to accept. But survival took precedence.

His plan was to leave for the airport from the neighbouring Wose, a third-tier city seventy kilometres away from the capital. From there, he'd purchase a one-way ticket to South Korea. Strange as it was, he was confident that the authorities were yet to ban his foreign departure. The administrative adjustments within the system tended to be slow and inefficient, especially in the third- and lower-tier cities, thanks to factional bickering among bureaucrats. He didn't think anyone would have pre-empted and bothered to obstruct his departure unless ordered by the Controllers. The working level was not about to take on additional responsibility that could change the status quo. Now, that's how the Party *really* worked. What's more, he was yet to be formally charged. Utopia's practice had been to brag about its capabilities before they were perfected, and the propaganda-first approach was adopted at every level of the government for the indoctrination of all citizens. Information also travelled slower in the smaller cities and rural areas, as the most advanced core technologies were prioritized for the capital and tier-one cities. He could probably gain some advantage from his Party Hero status in these backward towns, he hoped. On the other hand, the major cities had installed the latest technologies that put the Social Credit System

in operation. This meant all public transportation—including taxis—
required a face scan, which was verified by the United Front Social Credit
Data to assess whether the subject was clear in using the service. Taking
a sleeper bus or any mode of public transport to Wose was out of the
question. A remote option was to rent a car to drive to Wose. The Social
Credit System, while comprehensively laid out across the public sector
in the capital city, was still at the early stage of incorporating private
businesses, which car rental firms usually fell under. Car rental shops
were naturally required to check their customer's social credit, but it was
a one-way screening process. Only delayed data would be fed to the
national system after twenty-four to forty-eight hours had lapsed. He
would be out of the country for good when shit hit the fan, Hongbing
thought as he arrived at the front of a twenty-four-hour rental shop.

'Rent your car today with your social credit', read the neon sign
hanging on the glass door.

'Greetings, sir. How may I help you?' A youth with bright eyes came
to the counter, as the customer pushed through the glass door. The staff's
enthusiasm only saddened Hongbing. Here was another brainwashed
victim, he sighed under his breath. 'Hello,' he responded lethargically.
'I need a car, just anything that you have available now.'

'We can sort that out for you right away, sir. Do you have a
preference for a particular type?'

'Any type,' he was short with the staff, voice raised slightly. 'Anything
that's ready to hit the road now.'

The young man drew a momentary blank. He appeared lost at the
free range given by his customer. Like the average Utopian, he was
unaccustomed to recommending, what more, to making decisions.

'A cheap one,' he said, with his voice tone tinged with urgency. He
had no time to waste.

'Oh, of course,' the staff said. 'Oi, Muchen, pass me the pamphlet
please,' he called to his colleague, who was dozing off in a glassed office
behind the service counter. Per Utopian regulations, all shops must be
operated by at least two people at any one time, which the rental shop
observed strictly.

The pamphlet showed the terms for lease of three types of vehicles available for rent:

Class 1 (Luxury Sedans): Social Credit Score of over 95
Class 2 (SUVs): Social Credit Score of over 90
Class 3 (Economic Vehicles): Social Credit Score of over 85

Hongbing jolted, internally. He realized that he had never been conscious of his own Social Credit Scores. As a Party bureaucrat and a Party Hero, he had never had to be conscious of his score to do anything. He realized that he was enjoying all the privileges as a member of the ruling class of Utopia. Hongbing glanced at the young man in a subtle flurry, then fixed his eyes back on the pamphlet.

'Class 1. Thank you,' he pointed at the pamphlet, without giving it much thought. He figured that with his position in the hierarchy of the Party, he didn't need to worry too much about his Credit Score. As part of the ruling elite, and a Party Hero, his face and Party ID were sufficient to tap whatever services he wanted to access. Now that he was leaving for good, he intended to make the best of whatever he was entitled to. The very least he could get back from a system that had grossly abused his devotion and unfairly punished him when he had done no wrong.

'Right away, sir. Your ID please.'

The youth took his ID card and scanned it in a machine placed behind his monitor. 'Won't be long,' he assured his customer.

Beep

The staff frowned, and Hongbing's heart quickened. He looked away, as the beeping carried on.

'I'm sorry, sir,' the youth finally said, blinking nervously. 'I think we have a problem.'

'What's the matter?'

'It says your social credit account has been suspended.'

'Suspended?' He put on a surprised look, biting his lower lips. 'What's that supposed to mean?'

'Sorry, sir,' said the employee, who now looked helpless, 'I've never seen this before.'

Hongbing went quiet for a moment as he tried to calm himself. He stared at the young employee who was probably half his age. This was bad. The Wose airport was seventy kilometres away—too far to walk. He was at a standstill, and the clock was ticking.

Amid the struggle to come up with an alternative, the youth said, hesitantly, 'Er . . . Sir . . . May I . . . ? Are you . . . Mr Shan Hongbing, the Party Hero?'

Hongbing's breath stalled. Instinctively, he grabbed the knife in his right pocket.

'You are! Right?! Oh my . . . I am so honoured to meet you!' the employee continued. 'May I take a photo with you?'

'No. No photos,' he told the youth curtly, even though he read the latter's behaviour to be more harmless fanship than a calculated move to rat him out. Just to be on the safe side.

'This must be some silly mistake,' said his young admirer. 'Machines are machines, after all. Humans are still superior! I mean I don't need to have some data to recognize you.'

His colleague, Muchen, sitting at the back, on the other hand, observed them in silence, looking rather indifferent.

Seizing the opportunity, Hongbing said, 'Could you do me a favour, young man?'

'Of course, anything you need!'

'I need to get to the Wose airport, urgently. Could you drive me there?'

'It's been my dream to become a Party Hero like yourself, so—'

'You're not answering my question.'

'Oh . . . you mean you want me to drive you there? But why would you need someone like me to do that?'

'Don't ask. It's a Party matter. Listen, this could be your chance to serve the Utopian people.'

'Er . . . actually,' the staff murmured, rubbing his chin. 'The Wose airport is quite far from here. The return journey would take more than two hours. It would cost me my job here.'

'You in or not?' Hongbing pressured, unconsciously slipping into the manner that he adopted with his subordinates at work.

The young man looked stunned and worried. *I can't offend the Party Hero.*

At the same time, Hongbing also realized that he wasn't exactly in a position to demand anything. A soft strategy that took advantage of the staff's naivety was a better bet.

'Sorry, young man,' he offered an apologetic smile. 'I'm under tremendous pressure, racing against time . . . because of this mission I must complete. You do understand, right? How about to the Central Station then? Do you think you can take me there?'

'Central Station? Oh, that I can do! It'll probably take an hour to return. That, I can take the risk!'

'Great! I'd pay you in cash. Let's move then. No time to waste,' he instructed.

The young man went into the office, took some keys from the hanging panel and came around the counter, leading the way out to where the rented cars were parked. The other guy, Muchen, looked slightly puzzled by his colleague's unusual behaviour, but he maintained a somewhat indifferent demeanour that was difficult to read. Rushing out, the young man pushed a button on his car key and a sharp crimson-coloured—the official hue of the Party—car beeped.

'What a conspicuous colour,' Hongbing remarked.

'Yes, all our vehicles come in the Party colour. Our boss applied and paid the United Front Group for copyright to use the colour,' the young man said proudly. 'Please, get in.'

The Utopian road system in the first-tier cities was unquestionably world-class. In Unitas, regardless of where you were located, the Central Station was within reach in thirty minutes. The Party had a vision that connecting railways with highways would accompany a myriad of economic benefits, and it was spot on. An average of 50,000 kilometres of highway were built and put into use every year. The roads, of course, were installed with hundreds of thousands of surveillance cameras, at least one at every three kilometres. The Party preferred its people to use ground transport rather than air, where monitoring the commute was easier. To steer them in that direction, it had to make the ground facilities more convenient and accessible.

'Er . . . sir,' the staff said, after they had been on the road for ten minutes. 'It has been my dream to become a Party Hero, like yourself. Can you share your experience . . . on how you became one?'

'Why would you want to be one?'

'Why?' the staff laughed. 'It's the Party Hero! Who wouldn't want that title? With all those social privileges and the elevated status!'

'So you want to become one to get social privileges, a way to somehow whitewash your social status?'

'Oh no sir, please don't get me wrong,' the staff immediately defended. 'Loyalty is a given, of course. You see, I'm not an elite like you. I mean . . . I didn't go to the University of Unity and am not a bureaucrat . . . it would be really hard for me to prove my loyalty to the Party because I don't have any channels to reach the above.

'There are so many things that I can contribute to the Party. I want to be a part of the history of making this country the most powerful state on earth.'

'And why would you want to make Utopia the hegemon?'

No answer. After an awkward minute or two of silence, he asked Hongbing between chuckles, 'Is this some kind of a test?'

Hongbing didn't respond.

'Well, for the people's glory, of course!' he continued. 'We're all better off when our country becomes the hegemon!'

'How exactly are we benefitting?' Hongbing's dark eyes narrowed.

'If the country gets stronger, the Party will redistribute its resources to us and that way, we'll all better off!' he reasoned. 'And I aspire to become a Party Hero, as I want to be a player to realize that. I don't want to always be on the receiving end.'

'Do you really think you can be a player in this system?' Hongbing laughed, bitterly. 'You can never be a player. Neither can I.'

The staff stole a very quick glance at him as he needed to keep his eyes on the road; he was perplexed by Hongbing's admonition. *Why so negative?*

By then, their car had arrived at the drop-off point at the Central Station. Hongbing got out of the car, thanking the young man.

Keen to end on a better note, the staff said, 'You know, I know your questions were really a test. My loyalty to the Party is unwavering, and so is my will to serve for the glory of our people. My name is Jin. You know where to find me.' Smiling brightly, he waved and drove off.

Hongbing watched the red car sped off until it disappeared from his sight. The exchange with Jin reminded him how alone he was in this fight.

* * *

It was 4 a.m. Hongbing stood at the entrance of the Central Station gathering his focus. He was about to leave the comfort of the darkness of the night that had briefly shielded him from the Party's surveillance. The shade of his cap was now his only shield against the multiple prying eyes scattered throughout the station. He pulled his cap as low as he could and huddled towards the entrance. He had only Lady Luck to count on and he hoped she could help him evade the cameras, or at least delay detection.

Swing

The automatic door swung open, pulling him into the marvellous station. In the wee hours, the station was quiet and even tranquil. In the emptiness, minus the bustle of people, the station presented as quite the next-level facility and a remarkable piece of architecture. It was meant to represent the economic prosperity of the capital city, which had been nothing but vast swathes of farmland four decades ago. The glass ceilings and walls—including the massive smart glass panels fitted throughout—showed the weather of different regions in Utopia, the world's currency exchange rates, and the times of arriving and departing trains. A five-star hotel with a casino and a shopping centre were linked to the station, to entice travellers to spend. The internationality of the hardware however was adorned by a Utopian peculiarity. Every arriving traveller would be greeted by a propagandistic hologram. The one appearing before Hongbing now emphasized the seamless connection of the Central Station to different cities, both domestic and overseas, making Utopia central to the world.

Unitas, the Central City
Utopia, the Central State

While there wasn't any official acknowledgement, it was an open secret among the bureaucrats, including Hongbing, that the Party's One Ring Initiative (ORI)—the grand economic plan to link the railways and all infrastructure of 150 countries to knock out the current hegemony of the US—had not achieved its intended success. It was a reality that Hongbing had to grudgingly accept.

A staggering one trillion dollars—and counting—had been invested in these primarily cash-strapped, infrastructure-lagging countries. Hongbing had closely monitored the Party's pouring of its resources into promoting the ORI in international forums, intrigued by the endless financial injections from its state-run banks. Meanwhile, its think tanks announced their 'neutral' academic projections on how the ORI would boost at least 5 per cent of the developing world's GDP once the railway connection was complete.

Like with all things, Hongbing could vividly remember how the ORI started off positively. Developing economies were happy to see funds flowing into their drying coffers. But over time, they began to resent Utopia's resoluteness to ultimately absorb them into the its orbit of economic and political influence. The investments left many states with unsustainable debt. In some extreme cases, the amount Utopia provided for funding their railways was equivalent to half their GDP. Failure to meet debt payments gave Utopia the right to use these countries infrastructure facilities, such as ports. The Party then used these facilities as strategic footholds to counter American influence.

And that's when things had started to go haywire, Hongbing recalled. The resistance began to take shape in various forms. Local communities in the partner countries accused Utopian investors of a range of violations, from human rights abuses to environmental harm. As the people of the developing nations were exposed to some of the side effects of the ORI, the resistance grew, putting pressure on their governments to opt out of the project.

Hongbing was even aware of the specific allegations. For instance, Utopia had built a few multipurpose dams in developing states, integrating transportation infrastructure with the dams, aimed ultimately, at enabling railways that would connect those states to Utopia. However, the construction of the dams lacked environmental assessment and displaced thousands of people living both upstream and downstream of the dams. As the protest against the displacement of the people grew bigger, Utopia spent more money on lobbying and bribing officials who could suppress the resistance by force, focusing their energy on maintaining the initiative in the states, rather than compensating the locals. But it didn't work. Angry citizens in some states started to use force to hinder the projects. They attacked and bombed some of the construction sites, and sometimes, even targeted technicians and labourers from Utopia.

And yet, the propaganda machine in the station right now was doubling down on the ORI's promotion, because the Party would never admit to its misstep. Hongbing felt sick, wrinkling his nose.

He got to the ticket counter. He was taking a two-pronged risk; even if the surveillance cameras missed him, a face ID scan was required for the use of any public transport, and this could be the breaking point. But what choice did he have?

'A ticket to Wose,' he told the ticketing officer behind the acrylic window. He lowered his voice to a baritone in case the station's ticket sales database cross-checked, in real time, his biodata from where it was uploaded on the Social Credit System.

'What time?' the ticket officer asked, without looking up.

'The next train.'

'That would be in twenty minutes. Okay?'

'Yes.'

'First-class or economy?'

'Economy.'

'ID please.'

Hongbing hesitated. He had already hit a wall at the car rental. Would he encounter another rejection? The repercussions would most certainly be bigger at a state outfit. *The United Nations says in its Universal Declaration of Human Rights that everyone lawfully within the territory of a state shall have the right to liberty of movement. Everyone shall be free to leave any country, including his own.* He stopped short and willed himself from the unnecessary reference to international charters that Utopia essentially ignored. He pulled his cap lower, dropping his chin to the chest.

'ID please,' the ticket officer asked a second time, impatiently. When none was pushed through the slit above the countertop, she finally looked up. She could only see his face from the nose down.

'You got some problem there?' she asked, suspiciously.

'No. Here you go,' he slipped the card through.

Fixing her eyes on Hongbing, she took the card and placed it on the scanner.

Beep

Hongbing's body froze. His gut told him that something was amiss, and this time, he wasn't going to wriggle out of it as easily. His breath became heavy. Behind the counter, the ticketing officer did not budge, but her eyes glanced from her screen to Hongbing a few times.

'You're giving me the creeps,' he told her, laughing nervously. 'Is there a problem?'

'N-o, no,' she stammered.

'Then, please pick up your speed.'

'Of course.'

But she didn't budge, her hand with his ID was still on the scanner, while her other one lowered beneath the countertop. She then proceeded to type on the keyboard.

'Don't think you need to type anything to issue a ticket. Didn't you say the train's leaving in twenty minutes? Oh, it's fifteen now.'

As he drummed his fingers impatiently on the counter to pressure her, he saw to his horror in the reflected ticket window, two security guards pounding towards him from the back. She had called for security. *This couldn't be the end!* Once caught, he would be transported to the *Hard Interview Zone.* The guards were closing in. They were carrying batons, not guns, which meant that they were from outsourced security companies and not the officially trained United Front Police. He still stood a chance of getting away unscathed. But it had to be now or never.

'Damn!' he bellowed and banged his palm against the glass of the ticketing window before him as hard as he could, venting his anger at the ticket sales officer and her actions. He then pushed his trolley bag with all his might towards his advancing captors, who were now a few metres away, and dashed off towards an exit sign that was at the end of the futuristic hall.

'Stop there!' yelled one of the security guards as he tried to hurdle over the spinning trolley bag. Hongbing tried to shut out all sounds as he sprinted towards the glowing exit sign, he had fixed his eyes on. There was no time to think.

Another pair of shadowy figures was emerging from a distance near the targeted exit sign. These two carried guns.

'This can't be true,' he said, slowing down for a moment and looked back. Together, the two pairs were sandwiching him. He aborted his target exit, turned sideways into a connecting passageway and bolted. At the end of the alley was an escalator.

Kablam!

He thought his face had been crushed. It was a gunshot. *Did I just get shot?* His mind went into a daze, but his feet kept running. Distracted by his thoughts, he had also unwittingly slowed down his pace a bit. By the time he reached the escalator, he was alarmed that the guards with guns were merely a few metres away. As he raced up the steps of the escalator, he felt a powerful tug from the back, his body tilting backwards and on the verge of losing his balance. One of the guards had grabbed his backpack and was trying to stop him from fleeing. Hongbing jolted. He pulled his body forward several times, but gravity was working against him. That's when he decided on a make-or-break moment. In the blink of an eye, he pushed himself backwards and hard towards the guard, letting the weight of his body fall onto the latter. Unprepared, the guard lost his balance and, pulling Hongbing along, both men tumbled down the moving escalator. In the process, Hongbing hit his head on the corner of a step. A rush of warmth struck him, and he suddenly felt lightheaded. Bright red, lukewarm blood slowly streamed down along his neck. He scrambled to his feet, one foot stepping on the shoulder of the guard who was groaning in pain from the fall. Regaining his balance, he gave his opponent a hard kick in the groin, leapt over the agonizing body and dashed up the escalator, taking two steps at a time.

Upstairs, he followed directions from a smart glass sign board suspended from the ceiling, indicating 'To Arcade Shopping'. At the end of the hallway was a flashing neon sign with the name 'Arcade'. He picked up his pace.

Squeak!

The neon sign blurred before his eyes as a concrete wall slowly descended from the ceiling.

'Red Alert,' a mechanical voice blasted from the public announcement system, which echoed through the hallway.

'All passengers to remain in the station,' the voice added as the station's interior lighting turned red.

There was no time to lose, the wall was already halfway down, and he was still about a hundred metres away. He ran as fast as he could. The two pairs of guards were hot on his heels, just a few metres behind. He prayed for a miracle.

The wall was already four-fifths down by the time he reached the entrance. The hand of one of the chasers grazed his back again, sending a chill down his spine but also unleashing an unexplainable spurt of power. He threw himself on the marble floor, letting his body skid through the dark, narrow gap between the shutting wall and the ground. Just as he rolled into the other side, the heavy wall came down.

Bam!

AHHHHH!

Muffled and agonized screams of pain penetrated through the wall as he lay on the floor catching his breath. Less than arm's length away, three crushed fingers stuck out beneath the dropped wall in a bloody pool. He turned away quickly from the grisly scene, which made him want to throw up. As nauseated as he felt, he still wasn't out of danger. Just as he was pulling himself up, gunshots were fired.

Bang! Bang! Bang!

He immediately dropped to the ground to dodge the shots. Fortunately, the concrete wall was too thick for the bullets to puncture. Nonetheless, his breath quickened and turned shallow as he tried to get up a second time. The gash on his head continued to bleed but he couldn't care less.

All that dominated his mind was how to escape from the building in the fastest way possible. Soon, the wall would roll back, and the chasers would resume their pursuit. Only in the dark outdoors could he take a breather. *But what next?* He dithered and shook his head vigorously in exasperation.

The power room! *If I can cut off the power supply here, I may be able to buy more time.* With no time to lose, he went into the shopping centre in search of a directory to locate the power room. There was hardly a soul in the shopping centre at this hour. He did not see any staff either. *They probably fled the scene when the wall came down,* he thought. He ran past the cosmetic counters and towards an unmanned information desk. Behind the counter was a touchscreen directory. With shaky hands, he desperately typed in his enquiry. Basement two, the result showed, with an accompanying map that had directions via emergency staircases. He then placed his hand on the screen and, using his palm, he tried to rub off his bloodied fingerprints.

Scanning for emergency exits, he quickly spotted a green exit sign. *Creak.*

As he opened the door, he heard, from a distance, the concrete wall rolling back up.

Thud.

He quietly shut the door behind him and started to race down to basement two. The further down he went, the darker it got. Strangely, no sensor lights were installed on the staircase, which was illegal. The shopping centre's management had likely bribed the authorities to get away with it. He snorted.

Creak.

The door of the emergency staircase opened up to a dimly lit car park. It was bright enough for Hongbing to see where he was going. But it also meant that the surveillance cameras were back in business, able to pick up his tracks. Ducking his head, he moved rapidly through the car park to the power room that was located next to a cargo lift. He turned the doorknob, but it was locked.

'Attention, all security personnel. Subject in basement two. Repeat, subject in basement two,' a hysterical voice bellowed through the PA system. Hongbing looked around frantically for an object to smash the door lock. A fire extinguisher by a pillar caught his eye.

'Stop right there!' a security guard yelled from the emergency exit as the extinguisher came down hard and knocked off the doorknob. There were now more than six guards charging towards him. Kicking the door open, he dashed in, hanging on to the fire extinguisher as he scanned the room for the main power source box. As luck would have it, he spotted a large grey metal box above a cracked and partially torn black leather sofa. *This better be it.* He didn't have a second to lose. Inside the box was a tangle of wires and tons of switches. Heavy footsteps of his hunters were within earshot. 'Arghhh!' He bashed the power box with the fire extinguisher. His face was red and the veins in his neck protruded. *Please help me.*

Bang!

And the heavens above answered his pleas.

Kaboom!

The thundering noise not only numbed their ears, but the sudden blackout threw them into a frenzied chaos as they lost their bearings and sight of the target.

One of them shouted, 'Everyone, stay close!'

Hongbing crouched down behind the sofa. In the pitch darkness, he sensed that the six men were hovering near the door. There was only one exit for the room and his pursuers only had to block it off by staying put and his chance of escape would diminish drastically. He held his breath and started thinking. As he leaned his forehead against the back of the sofa to focus, blood from his wound smeared against the leather surface. The scent of his own blood gave him an idea. He put his right hand in the pocket and took out the knife, grabbing it as firmly as possible. *What now?* He had no chance in a hand-to-hand fight. Six against one was a clear no-win. As the shuffling footsteps grew louder, he instinctively grabbed the tip of the knife and flung it like a dagger as hard as he could.

Whoosh!

'Arrgh!' One of the men screamed at the top of his voice.

Boom!

'Aaarrrrggghhh!'.

One of them started shooting in the air randomly. Moments later, one of the men turned on the torch on his mobile phone, which only partially exposed the bloody commotion among the guards. Hongbing's knife had slashed the face of one of them and the man was bleeding profusely. One guard had also been mistakenly shot in the leg by his colleague, which triggered a fistfight among the six. Hongbing shrewdly waited for the brawl to build up. *This is my one and only chance.* And when the screaming and shouting climaxed, Hongbing snaked his way past the fighting men towards the door. He tumbled as one of the guards grabbed his legs. But he managed to kick the hands away, picked himself up and stepped on them several times, brutally breaking the fingers, before he headed towards the entrance and escaped.

He was going to head back from where he came but stopped short when he heard rapid footsteps descending behind the emergency staircase door. An image of the lift next to the power room flitted through his mind. He crawled cautiously, staying clear of the cameras, to where he thought the lift was. When he reached a wall, he started tapping the concrete and slid sideways until he heard the sound of steel. His fingers deftly found the crack of the lift door and using all his might, he opened it by force.

Hongbing could only see a little in the lift shaft. Green and yellow lights from small power boxes installed on the walls of the shaft in the tunnel enabled him to see dangling wires and some toeholds above him. Being able to see what was above meant that the lift was below him, and he could only climb upwards. Without thinking further, he jumped and grabbed one of the dangling wires. He hooked his foot onto the wires and swung himself towards a wall. His face was wet with a mixture of sweat and blood. Panting, he began climbing upwards. His arms and legs were shaking, unable to move at times. Ignoring his pounding heartbeat, he slowly ascended, one step at a time. Although there were only three floors below him, a slip of his sweaty hands could still be fatal. He shuddered at the thought. After he had climbed three stories, he couldn't breathe any more. His legs felt paralyzed. The weight of his backpack and coat was weighing him down as well. Wanting to rest, he stretched out one of his legs onto a rusty power box with flashing green and red lights next to him and gently leaned his weight against the leg to check if the box's bearing capacity was stable enough for him to stand on it. The steel box remained unyielding, neither moving nor warping under the partial weight of his body. Still firmly grabbing the toehold above him with his hands, he placed both feet on the box and let gravity take hold of them. The numbness subsided as his body relaxed, allowing him to breathe better, and he saw heaven in hell. His paranoia permitted him to rest a good two minutes. And then, came the dreaded squeak.

Before he could move his legs back to the toeholds, the screws that nailed the box to the wall loosened all at once. Dislodged, the box plummeted into the darkness down under.

The sudden loss of footing caused his body to tumble, legs swaying and dangling mid-air and the forces of gravity threatening to pull him down. He clung for his dear life with both hands grabbing onto the toehold firmly and then rapidly pushed his body close to the wall while his feet desperately searched for more toeholds to step on. When his body was stabilized, a series of loud clunks reverberated through the shaft as the power box shattered into pieces at the bottom of the dark pit.

He panted. All this sound would surely give away his location.

Sure enough, he heard a voice shouting, 'Found him!'

'Come over this way!' the same voice continued, followed by loud bangs on the lift door.

He tried to stay calm as he glanced up and down several times. He felt some optimism as his chasers were a few floors behind. Breathing deeply, he steadily continued the upward climb. Except for the remote pants of his chasers who had stopped shouting after him to focus on climbing, the shaft was quiet.

Hongbing finally reached the top of the shaft, which was oddly fitted with a square lucarne. Without much thought, he bashed it open with one elbow and shoved his body through. Cold, fresh air slapped his face and then the rest of his body as he stood on the rooftop of the building. He saw several pieces of abandoned furniture placed near a few outdoor air conditioning ventilation fans. He picked the biggest and heaviest items—a broken bookshelf and a sofa—and pulled them to the lucarne. Closing the lucarne, he desperately pushed the bookshelf on top of it, then tilted the sofa diagonally to lend weight to the bookshelf. It would buy him at least a second, he thought.

Clomp, clomp, clomp!

The sound of footsteps came from the emergency staircase across from the lucarne.

Bam! Bam! Bam!

Whoever had come up the emergency stairs was now trying to barge open the lucarne. The heavy banging coupled with loud swearing was like the worst deluge that he could no longer cope with; his knees buckled and he fell backwards. He half crawled and half walked to the edge of the rooftop. He peered over the ledge. A tangle of unsightly wires extended from a cable management box anchored towards the ground. They dangled down to the second floor, above a massive advertisement poster board. Realizing it was his only means of escape, he didn't hesitate. He grabbed the wires, vaulted over the ledge and let the wires slide him down against the exterior wall. This happened just as he heard the sound of his pursuers forcefully breaking the emergency door open. By the time he landed on the advertisement board, he could see several heads bobbing over the ledge, looking down. It would be risky for them to follow in his footsteps because the big bunch of wires he used, which were stretched by the weight of his descending body, had snapped just a few inches before he reached the advertisement board. The remaining few wires were thin and hanging loosely.

What now? He was still at a height at which he was not confident of jumping to safety. Falling would no doubt break his head open. He looked up—one of the guards had jumped onto two flimsy wires and was sliding down gingerly, hanging on for his life. As he shifted his focus back to himself, he scrutinized the structure of the advertisement board, looking for any materials he could use to cover his last mile to the ground. The board consisted of a rectangular steel frame, supporting canvas banners that were secured to it at the edges with ropes. Hongbing assessed the situation and decided that if he could untie just some pieces of rope, and then hold on tightly to the fabric as he jumped, he might manage a safe landing. After untying the first rope, he shifted his position, gripping one corner of the banner with one hand. Once he had the second rope untied, he extended his arms, holding the edges of the canvas as far apart as he could. Taking a deep breath and at the count of three, he jumped, praying that the banner would provide him the buffer to slow down the speed of his free fall as gravity took charge. When he saw the ground floor to be at a reachable distance, he bent his knees, released the banner and let his body fall.

Crash!

An alarm pierced through the silence of the city as Hongbing's body crashed into a car, shattering the windshield.

'Arrghh,' Hongbing winced in pain, as he lay on the hood. He thought that his body must have shattered into pieces. Opening his eyes, he saw one of the guards perched on top of the advertisement board. But he could not move further. There wasn't another banner. He dragged his sore body off the top of the car. He could hardly stand up, but he didn't have a choice. Waddling, he disappeared into the night's darkness. Behind him was the fallen banner that had saved his life: the image of the Party logo was emblazoned across it.

* * *

Hongbing walked briskly for a good twenty minutes before nearing an old bridge. Behind the bridge, the sky was gently turning into subdued hues of orange. To him, it was the ugliest sunrise ever. The sun would bring light to the authorities and pitch darkness to him, exposing his every move to those who wanted to put him away. He took shelter under the bridge, at a blind spot of the surveillance cameras. He yearned to close his eyes and rest his sore body to lessen the tremendous stress that he was carrying, but he was terrified of slowing down. Utopia's surveillance system wasn't *perfect*, as he just proved, but it should never be underestimated. He surveyed his surroundings and saw a tunnel near the river, which looked like a sewage facility. It would stink like hell, but it would be the best camera-free shelter available. Still somewhat reluctant, he lifted and made his way to the tunnel. He ducked his head and squirrelled into the cylindrical hole.

Although he had been enduring the stench of his own sweat and blood for the past hours, it had done little to prepare him for what lay ahead. The thick and fetid odour of rotten foods and human excreta shocked all his senses. He avoided looking down, aware that through the soles of his shoes, he was walking on slimy and sticky matter. He trudged through the tunnel for about twenty minutes and came to a connecting shaft with a small, rusty ladder that dropped from above. The ladder led to another tunnel, one that was approximately the same size as the sewer tunnel but without the dampness and the stink. *I can lie down here.* Unable to walk any further, his body collapsed onto the ground. Then, he stared through the darkness. His head was bleeding less, but now it was his hands. The skin was torn from gripping the toeholds, wires, and then the banner during his dramatic escape from the station complex. He could almost see his blood glow in the dark, brutally illuminating the grim reality he was facing.

He gulped down his tears. Just days ago, he had been one of the most popular men in Utopia. Everyone had looked up to him, wanted to take a photo with him, and wanted to *be* him. Yet, here he was, a bleeding fugitive, seeking temporary refuge in a sewer. It was painful to accept that he had lived in vain for most of his life—it had taken him decades to become who he was, but just days before its complete demolition. *Death would be less painful,* he thought wretchedly. He was lost. Seeing only what he wanted to see, he had worked all his life towards one ideal—to make Utopia great, for the people's glory. But with the goal's demise, he was now suffering an existential crisis. Perhaps he would have been better off if he had died in the shopping centre. His emotions hovered between self-pity and anger.

Hongbing then started wrestling with a flood of conflicting emotions. *What are my legal rights? None. Since when could the Party do this? Always.* The reality of his situation was slowly downing him, and it completely contradicted his long-standing loyalty. *The people must take responsibility for all this,* he blamed. No one spoke out against the Party's dictatorship, and no one spoke out when the Party implemented measures to solidify its control. When the Party Leader prosecuted and imprisoned his political rivals, the people kept their heads down for fear of suffering repercussions that would affect their lives. Moreover, the Party indoctrinated the people with the concept that the struggle for power was common in all nations and economic prosperity took top priority. And so, this rationale was used to build the Party's principles around defying political diversity, outlawing independent journalism, civil societies, and unions. It was easier to close one eye so that there would always be food on the table.

So entrenched were the values of obedience and compliance in Utopian culture and society that when the Social Credit System had begun its run in the test bed cities, no one questioned its violation of a citizen's rights or its abuse by those in power to advance political agendas. Confused, Hongbing had always believed uniformity was only beneficial. But protesting—if ever—would have been pointless anyway. The Social Credit System would name and shame naysayers, making their lives a living hell.

It's all their fault! After a tumultuous mix of emotions churned within Hongbing, it was anger that ultimately took hold, consuming everything else. *If someone had spoken out to put an end to this totalitarianism or at least put a brake on it, I wouldn't have been in this stinky mess. Cowards!*

'Common prosperity for all, and all are equal in Utopia', was the propaganda lynchpin, but Hongbing now realized that it was full of contradictions. Those in the Party's inner circle had no desire to share any power and prosperity with the people. Similarly, the rich did not intend to redistribute their wealth and give some to the less fortunate. So, the privileged stuck together and made sure the system continued to operate for their benefit.

Carrying anger, particularly under such demanding conditions, was an exhausting emotion. However, for Hongbing, this period of reflection proved to be a vital detoxifying exercise. It helped him release some of the mental stress and gather the strength he needed to pull himself together and move forward. Sitting in the middle of his sewer refuge, he became able to think, with clarity, about alternative options to leave Unitas and Utopia. He would wait for sundown, when, in darkness, he would be freer to move and take his next step. As he planned, his eyelids grew heavy, his upper body glided slowly to the ground and he eased into a deep slumber, in the safety of a sewer.

* * *

Squeak, squeak, squeak.

The sound of grey rats scurrying by Hongbing's ears woke him up. The tunnel remained pitch dark. Disoriented, Hongbing was clueless about both the time and how long he had been asleep.

He grunted, holding his head with both hands after shooing the rats off. He had the worst headache, stemming from both his injury and the mental strain. Physically, his body felt weak and uncooperative, resisting his will to move. Squeezing his eyeballs as hard as he could before releasing them wide open, he psyched himself up to focus.

Laboriously, he dragged his body towards a dimly flickering light at the far end of the tunnel. Squinting, he managed to read the time on his analogue watch—it was 1 o'clock. He valued analogue watches for their untraceability, but the downside was evident now; he couldn't tell if it was one in the morning or afternoon.

Putting his cap and backpack back on, he started to mobilize again, walking towards the entrance. He had to get to Wose. Considering the risk posed by the sea of cameras installed along the roads, Hongbing was well aware that travelling on foot was far too dangerous. He hoped to find an opportunity to hitch a ride instead.

Upon reaching the entrance of the tunnel, Hongbing was relieved to find that it was nighttime. Finding solace and comfort in the darkness, he rushed into a thicket of bushes and small trees. No sirens, no gunmen, no police cars. He was relieved that the Party was yet to pin down his location. Navigating through the thick underbrush, Hongbing made his way to a nearby highway. Ever cautious, he slowed down at the edge of the field, stopping a few metres behind the curb that separated it from the road. Before him was a highway, brightly lit, with lamp posts at ten-metre intervals—a troubling sign. *Damn!*

He quickly turned around and headed back towards a smaller road— it was more of a sandy trail—which he had encountered earlier among the bushes. He knew the city thoroughly and small roads with fewer cameras were a safer bet. Ahead, in the direction of the highway, a giant electronic display board was broadcasting Party news. Hongbing shifted the brim of his cap to the side, directing his attention to the screen to see if the authorities were publicly denouncing him. But the news items focused on the Party Leader's efforts to enhance the quality of life for citizens, the alleged malevolent actions of the US and its allies in attempting to isolate Utopia, and the latest domestic technology incorporated into Utopia's newly constructed aircraft carrier. He was puzzled, albeit relieved, by the authorities' decision to stay silent, especially after previous night's episode at the Central Station. Surely, declaring him a wanted man would be the quickest way to hunt him down, given the thousands of Utopians who were eager to be in the Party's good standing.

On second thoughts, however, it was about face, upholding the Party's dignity. How would it look if the recently minted Party Hero was turning his back against its ruling? The Party's reputation could be tarnished even among the most loyal and obedient Utopians, revealing the cracks in its social control. The Party Heroes represented the apex of its control—devoted subjects of Utopia, treated like pets and nourished with social privileges in return for their complete submission to the system, ultimately designed to steer public behaviour. To its foreign adversaries, the idea of mistakenly selecting a traitor as a national hero would be seen as a ludicrous display of poor judgment. So, *they want to get me, but under the radar? Hah!* He snarled, as he thought of the ticketing woman who had turned him in at the station last night. Knowing the system, he figured that her circumstances wouldn't be any better. She might have believed she was doing the right thing, but the authorities would have likely taken her into custody to prevent any word of the Party Hero's rebellion from spreading. Dried branches brushed against his coat and fallen leaves rustled under Hongbing's feet as picked up his pace. Tree roots sprawled above the ground like a tangle of snakes, ready to trip him if he wasn't careful. Hongbing started running and was soon on a winding two-lane road that led to the city of Wose. The road was an unfavoured alternative to the highway, a much longer route to take. It was dark as hell and there were hardly any cars on the road. He stood by the edge and waited for the next vehicle to drive by.

Hitchhiking was a nerve-wracking endeavour, particularly for a middle-aged Party bureaucrat who had never had such an experience before. It meant he needed to swallow his pride completely and beg for a favour. He swallowed whatever was remaining of his pride. Waving his arms in the air, he yelled, 'To Wose'. And he repeated it several times for practise. But except for the small wild animals that scampered past, the road remained empty. Frustrated, he sat down to take a breather, preparing for a long wait. Suddenly, a distant gleam of headlights entered his line of sight. He bolted up and edged out to the road. 'To *Wose*,' Hongbing waved and yelled at the top of his voice, over and over, driven by a mix of desperation and elation. It was a truck.

Vrooom!

The truck zoomed past him, mere inches away, almost grazing his outstretched limbs. 'What the—' He managed to swerve away in the nick of time. He couldn't die like this after all that he had been through.

He might have hit a lucky streak that night, though. In just less than a minute, he saw another set of headlights glaring into his eyes. In a flash, Hongbing threw himself on the road as a human roadblock. He wasn't going to let the vehicle get away without stopping.

Screech! A red sedan came to an abrupt halt.

'To Wose?' he shouted at the dazed driver trying to come to terms with what had happened.

Done! Hongbing ecstatically jumped up from the ground and ran around to the passenger seat.

'Thank you! Thank you! Thank you so much!' He attempted to open the door, but it was locked. The car's passenger window then slid down, revealing a young man in the driver's seat, gazing at him. 'Thank you!' he gushed out once more. 'Unlock the door, please.'

'Get lost!' the driver shouted at him. 'If you're looking to end it all, find a building. Don't drag others into your mess!'

'No, no, no. I just need a lift to Wose. That's all,' Hongbing pleaded.

'As if I'd help someone like you,' the driver retorted, his face turning red with anger. 'Move, now!'

The young driver then accelerated sharply, the car nearly rolling over Hongbing's right foot, leaving him standing there, shocked.

'Bwahahahaha!' A peal of crafty laughter snapped him out of his shocked humiliation. Out of nowhere, a homeless woman had appeared. Wearing a long, tattered, and dirty tunic over a thick sweater, her head of unkempt and straw-like grey hair was bobbing up and down. She was clearly enjoying the show. She looked like she had been out on the street for a while without proper nutrition and healthcare. Her twisted fingers and deformed hands were clearly a case of severe rheumatoid arthritis. She presented a pitiable image, yet her strange and stern gaze somewhat intimidated him.

'That's the best circus I've seen in years!' she said, walking towards him.

'None of your business,' he retorted with contempt and retreated to maintain a safe distance.

'What brings you here?'

'What do you want?'

'Well . . . You don't look like you're broke . . . but here you are, in the middle of nowhere, at this ungodly hour, hitchhiking? So, what's your story?'

He was irritated and decided he wasn't going to give her the satisfaction of an answer. Instead, he countered, 'What are my chances here? Do you often see people successfully hitchhiking around here?'

'Bwahahaha!' She broke into an enormous belly laugh again.

'Some answers would be appreciated,' Hongbing said tartly, frowning.

'Take a guess,' she teased between sniggered laughter. 'Of course not! Not after that social credit thingamajig!

'There are penalties for drivers who ferry strangers from the roads! The Party's way of locking in fugitives . . . like you!'

'I'm not a fugitive,' he protested. 'But how can the Party keep tabs?'

'Of course it can't!' she tsk-tsked him. 'Not with the technology they have right now. But the scheme is working, and you've experienced it first-hand. All they needed was to make drivers *believe* the Party had the capability. After that, control becomes easy.'

'Shouldn't technology be there to . . . to liberate people?' he mumbled under his breath, but she heard him.

She stopped laughing and looked intently at him. 'Listen, you naive man. That applies only when the government is accountable.

'When a cow drinks water it becomes milk, but when a snake does, it turns into venom.'

Hongbing's head was throbbing with pain.

'It's none of my business, but if you want to flee from this city, you better find another way,' the woman said, before she turned around and quickly disappeared into the dark bushes.

* * *

Hongbing collapsed a few metres in front of a shop, out of breath. He was drenched with perspiration, so hot and wet that the cold, late autumn weather had little effect cooling him down. He also stank. Panting, he tried to calm himself down and normalize the pace of his breath.

Rent your car today with your social credit.

He had run for hours to get back to the car rental store, opting for a longer road to avoid the camera-lined highway. He had returned to seek out Jin. Hongbing opened his backpack and retrieved a shirt from inside. He understood the importance of appearing presentable to receive assistance in Utopia. His current state, as the woman had pointed out, was not conducive to garnering help. Knowing that Jin still believed him to be a Party Hero, he needed to at least look clean and not like a fugitive, as he intended to seek Jin's help. Both plans B and C—to take the train and hitchhike' to Wose—not only failed miserably but he also had to put up with the humiliation of being jeered at by a marginalized, homeless person. The only remaining option he had was Jin driving him to Wose. That was the only way out. What's more, flying to Seoul was no longer his plan. Buying a ticket was not possible, he now realized. His new plan was to be smuggled out there from a port in Wose.

Jin was his best shot. He ducked, bent his upper body, and surged forward towards the shop. He crouched in front of the waist-high wall and popped his head up an inch to look through the glass window. Inside, there were only Jin and the sleepy Muchen.

Thank God.

He stayed put for a few minutes to make sure that no one else was in the shop, before he stood up.

Ding.

The chime went off as he marched into the shop.

'Oh . . . my . . .' an astonished Jin stammered. A Party Hero who had
looked perfectly well a day ago now had a blood-stained, bruised, and
purplish face. His hair was dishevelled, his clothing was smeared with
dried sludge and his shoes were caked with mud. Hours of running had
left his legs wobbly, and he felt like a walking zombie. Hongbing's new
shirt did little to conceal the rest of his dishevelled state.

'Mr Shan . . . is that . . . you?' asked Jin after finding his voice.
'What happened? Are you all right?' The stench from his idol was so
overpowering that it woke Muchen who looked momentarily at Hongbing
in silence, then blinked a few times before returning to slumberland.

'I need your help with my mission,' Hongbing told Jin in a
directive tone.

'A mission?'

'Yes. You in or not?'

'Err . . . what's it about?'

'I can't go into details.'

Silence. 'Look, I need your help,' he softened the tone of his voice
to indicate a request. 'This is your opportunity to serve the Party and
contribute to the glory of our people. You could be a part of Utopia's
history,' Hongbing urged.

Jin remained quiet, but his eyes were already glowing, lured once
more by the same sugar-coated bait from the Party Hero.

Hongbing leaned forward against the counter and whispered, 'I'll
formally recruit you into the Party after all of this is sorted.' Hongbing
observed Jin, visibly overwhelmed, yet responding with an affirmative
nod. 'What do you want me to do?' Jin asked.

'Shall we talk about it outside?' Hongbing suggested, his voice
tinged with paranoia, concerned that Muchen might be feigning sleep
and eavesdropping on their conversation. 'For national security, of
course. Your cooperation is needed for the Party's wellbeing,' he added,
as he pulled Jin out of the shop.

Once outside, Hongbing grasped the shoulders of the excited young
man and stared intently into his eyes. 'Okay, you need to focus. Your
mission is to drive me to the Eastport Harbour in Wose. Can I trust you
with that?'

'Can do that of course . . . but when?'

'Now.'

'I can't leave now. I'm on my shift and I can't —'

'Young man, listen to me very carefully,' Hongbing said, unable to keep his voice from rising. 'This is your chance, perhaps your once-in-a-lifetime chance, to truly serve the people. But know that you're free to decline. There are many others eager for this kind of loyal service, like your colleague back in the shop,' he added, nodding his chin in the direction of the shop. As he walked past Jin, their shoulders brushed slightly.

'Wait!' Jin called out. 'Okay, I'll do it. Just give me a moment, I just need to ask my colleague to cover for me.'

* * *

When Hongbing saw the horizon of the sea, it was almost the break of dawn. A brilliant light-orange hue was emerging and slowly pushing away the darkness, as the first rays of the sun shone on the sea, like crystals sparkling on the waters.

'Thank you for your service, Jin,' Hongbing said gratefully as Jin drove his car onto the road leading to Eastport Harbour. Feeling refreshed by the turn of events, Hongbing had Jin stop at a quiet rest area so he could use the bathroom. He splashed water on his face and cleaned himself up with soap and a face towel that Jin had bought for him from the convenience store. He had also napped in the car.

'It's been my honour, sir,' Jin said as Hongbing woke up.

'This must stay strictly between us. Can I trust you on this?'

'Of course. For the people's glory.'

'Yes, that. Now, you'll be contacted by one of my men after I sort out all this mess. Until then, you can't disclose any of this to anyone. Understood? If someone approaches you and asks about me, that person is a foreign agent. Don't trust anyone.'

'Copy that.'

'Good. You saved many lives today. We will meet again soon.'

'Thank you.'

Hongbing got out of the car to walk the short distance to the harbour.

Hongbing picked up speed. He knew exactly where he was heading. The winding road leading to a small seafood shop was all too familiar— it was the channel he had used to relocate his wealth to South Korea over the last decade. All transactions of Party bureaucrats were tightly monitored and controlled. But that didn't stop them from parking their assets abroad. He relied on the old-school way of smuggling his cash abroad via a boat. Primitive and sloppy it may seem on the surface, but it worked and hadn't failed him yet. Through his Clanta mole, Kim, he had been able to connect with a Korean politician Yeon Soo-jin. A veteran politician aiming for Korea's top office, Soo-jin was constantly building up her war chest, and nothing was cleaner than cash. She used her authority to press the South Korean maritime police and cleared the way for Hongbing's agent vessel to reach hers in the open sea that divided the two countries. The cash was then transferred to the Korean vessel, which was then picked up by another agent from Seoul. The agent then exchanged the cash in a black market at Namdaemun in Seoul.

One-third of the money had then been allocated to Soo-jin. Hongbing detested her insatiable greed but using her was a sure bet. The remainder of the money would always be safely delivered to his Korean bank account. Soo-jin guaranteed that. She was very clean in that transactional way. But this time, the situation was different and Hongbing didn't have the luxury of time to contact Soo-jin or Kim, which would have been a risky move anyway. In the past, on the Utopian side, he had always relied on backchannel intermediaries to communicate with the agent, a strategy used to stay under the radar. However, now there wasn't time to follow the same tried-and-tested route. Moreover, involving more people only increased the risks for him. Resolved, he decided to deal with the agent directly, a meeting that was just a few minutes away.

Squeak!

Hongbing pushed open the shabby door of a sloppy seafood shop.

'Afraid we're not open yet,' grunted a grubby man who bore the rugged appearance of a fisherman. One hand holding onto his bottle, he waved his other arm to shoo him away, without once looking at him.

The man, clad in his fishing bibs, was seated in the middle of the shop, positioned behind a seafood display fridge. He was absorbed in watching a morning news entertainment show on the television. His eyes were glazed as though he hadn't got any sleep and had just returned from sea. The tiny shop smelled of cigarettes and alcohol. The fridge displayed some small fish, like gazami crabs and sardines. There was no way he could make a living with these.

The marine ecosystem of the East Utopia Sea had suffered devastating damage over the years. Two decades ago, larger fish like seabass, yellow croaker, and groupers, constituted approximately 70 per cent of the sea population. However, in recent years, their numbers had dwindled to less than 40 per cent, overtaken by smaller fish species. Rural Utopians, who had been bypassed by the nation's economic growth, began to venture deeper and farther from the shores, indiscriminately catching even the small fry. The United Front Maritime Research Centre was well aware of the deteriorating situation, but the Party's political decisions overruled any environmental concerns. In their view, if allowing such practices meant keeping the marginalized rural population content and maintaining social stability then the environmental cost was deemed a necessary sacrifice. This was a reality that Hongbing, like many others, was acutely aware of, yet felt powerless to change within the current political framework.

'Hello. I'm speaking to you,' Hongbing said, standing next to the TV and knocking on the edge of the set.

'Did you not hear me?' The fisherman tilted his head up. 'Not open yet. Out!'

'I've been one of your paymasters over the past decade. Remember all that cash you've been shipping out to Seoul? That was all my money. Does that ring a bell?'

'The hell . . .' the fisherman murmured and turned back to the screen.

'I want you to take me to Seoul, *now*,' Hongbing raised his voice while his hands pointed towards his chest affirmatively.

'No idea what you're talking about.'

'I can contact my source in Seoul to clear the way,' Hongbing went on. 'This time, we're going all the way into Korean waters, and you will drop me off there. You got that?'

'You got the wrong guy, mister.'

'No, I haven't. My last order was two months ago, on 19 September. Think that's pretty precise, no? I'll pay you 300,000 PD for the trip. Are you in or not?'

There was an ominous pause. Out of options, Hongbing could only continue to press him.

'You're aware of how much I've stashed away in Korea, so you understand I'm not trying to deceive you,' Hongbing said. Seeing the fisherman's unmoved expression, he continued in desperation, 'Okay, I'll offer you 400,000 PD. Deal or no deal?'

'I still am not sure what on earth you're talking about.'

'Oh cut that crap,' Hongbing banged his fist on the counter next to the TV. The fisherman jolted.

'Okay . . . let's say, hypothetically, I am the person you're looking for. How can I be sure that you're really my client?'

'I just gave you the exact date of the latest transaction. Wasn't that precise enough?'

The fisherman went silent. Just blinking his eyes in silence and looking at Hongbing in a daze.

'I want 500,000 PD and paid upfront.'

'What?' Hongbing lost his cool for a moment before recomposing himself. He had zero bargaining power. 'Okay. 500,000 PD it is. But you'll get that once we reach Korea.'

'No. Money first.'

'I don't have that kind of money on me right now. You'll get the cash once we get—'

'No deal then. OUT!'

'Then I'll just report you to the police for smuggling,' Hongbing threatened. 'You know I got evidence.'

The fisherman burst into a fit of cackles. 'Ha! Says someone who wants to be smuggled,' the fisherman snarled. 'You got my offer, and that offer is final. The ball's in your court.'

He had been checkmated, even if refused to admit it. The drunken fisherman was no doubt smarter than Jin.

'Fine,' he conceded grudgingly. 'Won't be long.'

Coming down on his hunkers, he opened his backpack and rummaged for cash. He knew that he had nowhere near 500,000 PD. Most of the cash he had was in the trolley luggage bag that he had flung at the security guards in Central Station.

After rummaging through his backpack in total silence for a while, Hongbing finally spoke up. 'I only have 12,000 PD with me now. But I promise you when I get to—'

'No deal.' The fisherman was merciless.

'Please, I need to leave now.'

'Not my problem.'

Hongbing felt his blood start to boil, his gaze fixed intently on a sabre mounted on the wall, just a few inches from the fridge, beyond the fisherman's shoulders. He was momentarily lost in his thoughts, absorbed by the sight of the weapon, until the fisherman's voice snapped him back to the present.

'You go and get your cash from an ATM or use the OneAll credit transfer using my phone,' the fisherman suggested.

Now, that was the worst possible alternative one could ever come up with, Hongbing thought. Using an ATM for withdrawals or conducting a transaction via OneAll would automatically alert the central system, effectively revealing his exact location. Hongbing was also certain that the authorities had already disabled his bank accounts. Transactions made through OneAll were under close surveillance too. Individuals marked with a 'tainted ideology' were almost instantly suspended from using these services.

'You know I can't do that.'

'Beg, borrow, steal. It's not my concern. If you don't have the money, get out or I'll seriously report you.'

Hongbing paused, as gravity pulled him heavily down south. With a deep breath, he approached the fisherman as he requested to use his phone. Hongbing sat there and just stared at the phone for a while, before he hesitantly dialled a number etched deep into his memory. The line buzzed, and then, a familiar voice answered.

'Bao Keqiang speaking.'

Chapter 6

Betrayal

'Old Bao, I'm glad I got you.'

'Hongbing? To what do I owe this pleasure, a call from a mighty Party Hero?' Bao, a friend and local tycoon based in Wose, teased.

Sigh. The Party Hero in question exhaled softly. 'I need to call in a favour.'

'No problem, any time! You know I owe my life to you. What do you need?'

'I need half a million PD . . . in cash. And within an hour.'

There was silence at the other end.

'Hello? Bao?'

'Yes, I'm here. That's a lot of money, in such a short space of time . . . May I ask what the money is for? Are you in some kind of trouble? I heard some rumours from my channels—'

'Hey Bao, how long have we known each other? Have you forgotten how I've stuck my neck out for you?' Hongbing countered. Then, catching his breath, he quietened down, 'I can't divulge the reason as it's a state secret. It's urgent and I wouldn't have troubled you if it wasn't.'

'Don't misunderstand, I will definitely help. Just thinking about how to gather enough cash at such short notice. Let me figure out how. I'll ring you back on this number in ten minutes.

'Okay, I will wait for your call. Thank you.'

Hongbing returned the handset to the fisherman. 'You heard me, I'd know how to get the money in ten minutes. You better be prepared to take me to Seoul,' he told the smuggler snidely.

The fisherman took a drag of his cigarette and slowly blew out a cloud of smoke. 'Chill man,' he glanced sideways at his tense-looking potential passenger with a smirk, 'my vessel is ever ready. Let's see if you get your money.'

Before the ten minutes were up, the mobile phone rang. Not recognizing the display number, the fisherman handed it over to Hongbing. 'Probably your money buddy.'

'Hello. Old Bao? So glad you called, thank you. Did you get the money?' Hongbing asked beseechingly.

'That's wonderful, thank you very much. Rejuvenation Lane in twenty minutes?' Hongbing looked at the fisherman who gave a nod. 'Yes, I think I can meet you there.'

He handed the phone back to the fisherman, who turned on the navigation app and typed in the meeting point.

'Here,' he showed the screen to Hongbing, 'Rejuvenation Lane is about four blocks from here. There's a Rejuvenation Department Store at the intersection, where it meets with the main road, Unification Boulevard, so you can't miss it. Rejuvenation is a dead-end street and the shophouse where your buddy will meet you is right at the end.'

'Okay. I will be back within the hour,' Hongbing muttered without looking at the fisherman. His eyes remained fixed on the screen as he tried to memorize as many details of the map as possible, until the screen was removed from his sight.

'Whatever you say, whenever you can pay up.' His potential accomplice only grinned.

Hongbing began to walk towards the city centre, moving away from the shoreline. He accelerated his pace to a quick jog. He wanted to be at the meeting venue ahead of time to suss out the environment before Bao arrived. He couldn't help being paranoid or overcautious, given his current circumstances. Beads of reddish-brown sweat trickled down the sides of his face, and his back and armpits were soaked in spite of the late autumn chill. He felt his head wound sustained from the escalator fall, begin bleeding anew, the slight flow of blood now mixed with perspiration. Fortunately, the cut wasn't too deep. He pulled out a piece of dirty tissue from his coat pocket to dab away the bloodied sweat. He had worn his overcoat throughout his escape but was now removing the heavy garment. He even felt sweat dampening the woollen jumper he wore over his long-sleeve shirt. With the coat draped on one arm, he picked up speed. He had quickly covered more than two blocks on the main thoroughfare when an enormous granite building came into sight, lit by the dimming streetlights and the glow from the half-moon. *That must be the Rejuvenation Department Store.* His heart was pounding. He was so close to the turning point that could change his life forever.

The quick jog turned to a brisk walk, which he then slowed down to a normal pace as he tried to catch his breath and calm his nerves. At the department store, he turned the corner gingerly and entered Rejuvenation Lane. It was a small street of less than 200 metres, lined on both sides by sad-looking, dilapidated shophouses and warehouses, barely lit by the two drooping streetlamps that would sway and plunge to the ground with a sudden gust of wind. Treading towards the warehouse meeting venue at the end of the street, he constantly turned around to see if Bao was arriving. As he reached the stretch in the middle, the sound of a car engine purred behind him before the vehicle glided to a stop. He squinted into the glare of the car's headlights. The driver remained in the car as the rear passenger door on the right side opened. A heavy man got out of the car, tugging the handles of a black duffel bag, and then giving it a final pull with a jolt. The bag fell onto the ground with a loud thud. It was Bao. He gave Hongbing a wave. The front passenger door opened, and a stockier man stepped out from the passenger seat and stood by the side of the hood. He had cold eyes. Together with the driver who remained behind the wheel, he was an unfamiliar face.

Hongbing had met Bao a few years after he was transferred to UF-Clanta from the UFITC mothership. Bao had established a trading company based in Wose, and having built a rather successful distribution network across the country, the business was at the point of shifting its focus to distributing chips, in a way heeding the national call to elevate technological prowess. A UFITC colleague introduced Bao to him when he was seeking a distributor for the JV's products.

He had remembered Bao to be leaner and less rotund then. He was dressed in understated khaki pants, a shirt, and a navy blazer, with a nondescript Casio watch on his wrist.

'I'm Bao Keqiang, owner . . . also janitor of Epic Trading Group,' he had said with a grin during their first meeting. Hongbing was struck by this seemingly down-to-earth businessman with a sense of humour. Over the next few weeks of the procurement process, Bao showed that he was honest and modest, and his company offered a very competitive price. Epic won the distribution rights and its alliance with the United Front Group opened many more doors to opportunities and accumulated more wealth for its owner.

The privately-owned conglomerate then expanded to become Utopia's biggest privately owned semiconductor testing and packaging company. It went on to successfully expand into the ORI markets. Bao had a humble start as an importer of low-end electronic devices from developed economies before the pivot to semiconductors. What many who had business dealings with him didn't know was how he also utilized distribution networks to smuggle imported cars and petroleum in the earlier years of his business. In order to lubricate his shadier operations, Bao bought over an extensive network of Utopia officials and Party members—from SOE executives to customs officers. Oddly, Hongbing was never on that payroll, and he purposely stayed focused only on the semiconductor aspect of business. The professional relationship between the two men extended into a friendship, one centred on exchanges and transactions for mutual benefits but without the involvement of money changing hands. Like when Bao's nephew wanted a job at one of the UFITC labs or when Hongbing needed a channel to move his assets abroad. On this small street tonight, it was in play again.

'Hu here and Long, in the car, are my two new bodyguards,' Bao assured Hongbing, whose face had tightened at the sight of the two unfamiliar faces. Bao was shocked at Hongbing's appearance—his eyes were red, his hair was clammy, and he smelled. Bao was about to open his mouth to ask when Hongbing beat him to it.

'What happened to Zhang and Lin?'

'Zhang retired, and Lin's mother was ill, so he went back to his home town to take over the family's grocery store,' Bao explained. 'Don't worry, it's cool.'

'All right,' he uttered. What choice did he have? 'Did you bring the money?'

Bao pointed his chin to the duffel bag in front of him. As Hongbing edged towards Bao, a gust of wind blew from his back. It also blew Hu's jacket open, which revealed a shiny metallic emblem badge clipped to his belt. It was made visible by the car's headlight, as he walked around the front of the hood towards Bao.

Unbelievable! Hongbing froze. It was the State Security Bureau badge. *Think, quick! Will I be able to circumvent Bao and his bodyguards, to grab the bag of money?* On one hand, Hu was now just an arm's length from Bao, where his burly figure shielded Bao and the bag from sight. On the other hand, if he forwent the money, slid sideways, and made a 100-metre dash out of the dead-end street, he might escape from the fix that he was in as long as the driver didn't get out of the car fast enough. His legs began to wobble, and they felt like they didn't belong to him. He tried to forget about them. Holding his breath, Hongbing darted off like an arrow, his eyes focusing straight ahead, and he ran as fast as his legs could take him. With the speed at which he was running, he could hear the sound of the wind blowing by his ears, draining out Hu's frantic but muffled screams to his partner to stop Hongbing. 'Quick, don't let him get away!' he heard someone say, among the sound of heavy footsteps. He dared not turn back to look.

As Hongbing turned the corner out of Rejuvenation Lane, he pulled up the screenshot of the local map from his memory. He had walked from the south, so a left turn in the northern direction would lead him towards the border to an adjacent town. Making the turn onto the main road, he glimpsed from the corner of his eye, Hu and Long trying to close in on him. While there was still a significant gap between them, there was no time to lose. Even for his love of the Party, at least until recently, Hongbing had no romantic illusions about the SSB. Out of all the Utopian uniformed divisions, the SSB was the most secretive and only a small group of Party officials knew what was really going on within the organization. SSB officers underwent harsh training to battle the toughest enemies and were trained to take down the most ruthless opponents. What was scary, even to Party loyalists, was that the division's operations were covert and did not need to be accounted for. Hongbing had no doubt that Yiping had been taken by the SSB.

He continued to run as fast as he could, reaching a winding road that seemed to lead to nowhere. He took it anyway because staying on the main road made him visible. He bet that, in the shadows still refusing to yield to the rising sunlight, he might just find a hiding spot to shake off his assailants. Physically, there was no way he could outrun the SSB officers. He followed the curving path that led to a fishbone-patterned area of narrow alleys lined with old, squalid houses, as dilapidated as the structures on Rejuvenation Lane. The sun was yet to fully rise and fortunately light was still scarce, emanating from the old streetlamps still glowing. For the first time, he came face to face with the reality of how ordinary people outside the big cities lived. There was always sufficient power to light up the streets of the major cities, to the indulgent extent of firing up glowing neon advertising signs in commercial districts. The roads were perfectly paved and wide, while buildings and houses were periodically repainted. In contrast, the shops and houses he ran past already looked ruinous in the dark, he shuddered to imagine how they would appear during the day. But ironically, it was this underdevelopment that offered Hongbing a chance of survival.

The first few drops of rain began to fall on his head and shoulders, bringing him back to his current predicament. The wind had picked up too—it was sharp and biting. The rain was also becoming more intense and drummed on the zinc and clay-tiled roofs of houses he ran past, drowning out any other noises there might be. He could only hear the sound of his own breathing and his heartbeat, which was pounding like a jackhammer in his chest. He turned into one of the numerous alleys—at the end of it stood a one-storey shophouse with a narrow zinc roof and a cluster of tall garbage bins tucked under. He slid behind the bins to hide, curling himself into a tight ball, and ducked his head as low as possible. The fetid stench of food waste and other garbage knocked into him, like a powerful punch to his stomach. After the prolonged hideout in the sewer tunnels not too long ago, he thought it would have been a while before he would be subject to such intense olfactory torture again or have his nostrils desensitized. But no. As revolting as it was, he willed himself not to throw up, as it would have drawn attention to his hideout. He gritted his teeth, clutched his backpack as tightly as he could, and tried to not breathe in the humid and nauseating smell that was being soaked up by his jumper, the overcoat hanging on his arm, and his skin. He threw his long overcoat over his head and face. The thick fabric only blunted the stench a little, and now he felt suffocated. Sweat and tears trickled down his face, and he wiped them off with the back of his hand.

How did a Party Hero fall into such a state?

Confusion and fear had gripped him since he ran, which was now compounded by growing anger. But there was no time to wallow in self-pity or anger. Unnecessary fury would cloud his judgement and cause him to make the wrong decisions. He needed to stay clear-headed despite his fatigue. His only objective was to be able to stay safe and get out of Wose as soon as possible. The rain pattered rhythmically on the zinc awning, which was not wide enough to cover his shivering body. But the pitter-patter of the rain had a calming effect, and his anxiety eased, and exhausted from the physical and mental stress he had endured, he dozed off.

* * *

Hongbing wasn't sure how long he hid among the garbage cans. He had also numbed his senses to block off the foul odour and, in the process, fallen asleep. Peering between the garbage bins, he blinked his eyes and awakened his senses. A glimmer from the streetlights shone at the start of the alley, which was deserted. He uncurled his limbs and stood up. The rain had turned into a light drizzle, but the biting chill was enough to make his body shiver. He hurriedly put on his damp and heavy overcoat. Hongbing thought he smelled of rotten eggs. He dug into to his backpack to check for cash. Luckily, the 12,000 PD was still in place. He hoped that this remaining cash would be enough to navigate the troubles on the next leg of his journey.

He slowly walked out of the alley and retraced his steps back to the main road, constantly scanning left, right, and over his shoulders just to make sure he wasn't being followed. His pulse began to quicken, and he took a couple of deep breaths to slow it down. The one good thing about being in a backward part of Utopia was there were fewer surveillance cameras, as local authorities had fewer resources to acquire the technologies needed. Many of the governments were either in debt, having heeded the call to invest in infrastructure or they were simply corrupt and squandered away public funds.

He walked about fifteen minutes before he arrived at the junction that connected with the main road, Unification Boulevard. Not a soul was in sight. The air was crisp as the skies cleared and the rain was gone. He finally felt like he could breathe with some relief. Although his head was throbbing horrendously, his mind was racing with a rush of complicated and conflicting emotions that he grappled to comprehend. There was so much to take in, but he hadn't had the time nor the energy to process any of it. Bao's betrayal, and his being wanted by the SSB, it was all like a bad dream. *I must be the first Party Hero fugitive*, he thought wryly. *Nothing makes sense. Or has anything ever really made sense?* He had thought it did or rather that everything the Party did was rational. *Have I been too blind to be discerning?* It was too exhausting to dig into his deepest emotions and values at the moment. Time was certainly not on his side. Soul searching could wait. He desperately needed an alternative plan, one that could offer him some reprieve from this surreal predicament. He needed help, but who could he turn to?

In his sleep, after he had dozed off amid the garbage, he dreamed of meeting his mentor from university. The former professor Li Wei had since retired and returned to his hometown. As fate would have it, his hometown was Fengshou, a town located some 100 kilometres from Wose. Awake and slightly inspired by his dream, Hongbing weighed the risks of seeking out the professor. He wasn't brimming with confidence about people he knew, as the sting of Bao's betrayal had barely passed. But he needed help, and an objective perspective to move forward. He hadn't seen the professor in a long while, although he remembered the scholar to be a man of integrity and honesty. On the contrary, Bao was a businessman whose goal was to make money. *I'll have to take the chance*, he decided.

Hongbing had not been to Fengshou, an agrarian town with five surrounding rural villages, but he knew about its significance. In its heyday, Fengshou had been one of the biggest rice growers in Utopia, with a population of about 200,000—which had now reduced to 10,000. The name Fengshou or 'bounty harvest' was a nod to the past, reminiscent of the better days, when it had been even hailed as a model city by the Party. But the opening up of Utopia's economy, coupled with cheaper rice imports from other nations had gradually killed the local industry. Young people began to leave for work in the bigger cities, leaving behind the elderly and the children. There was still a tiny farming community whose production output of rice, vegetables, poultry, and meat barely fed its own people. Fengshou's residents mostly relied on money that family members remitted back. The town's current diminished status of a place neglected by the Party made it the ideal next stop for someone on the run.

Unable to use the public transport system and given the risk of hiring a car at this point—not to mention his paranoia about trusting an unknown driver—Hongbing decided to walk those 100 kilometres to Fengshou. While it was twice the distance of a full marathon, he hoped that as he made his way deeper into the rural area, he might be able to get a ride from a passing farming vehicle. He would trust farmers more than the cunning urban driver. The money he had on him was more than enough to cover his passage to Fengshou, which he calculated would take a day. By the time the full sun was above his head, Hongbing had covered the rest of the Unification Boulevard and stepped onto the adjoining Wose No.1 Road that cut through Wose's rural outskirts, where it would connect to the seventy-five-kilometre Wose–Fengshou highway. Hongbing hoped he would be able to hitch a ride there, as pedestrians were barred from walking along the sides of Utopian highways. Fatigue and anxiety weighed on him. Neither had he eaten nor had a drop of water.

On Wose No.1 Road, a few breakfast shops were opening, and the smell of steaming buns and hot broth filtered out of the small eateries onto the sidewalk. Hongbing's stomach growled loudly in response. He pressed his palms against his stomach to hide the embarrassing sounds from the pedestrians hustling by. A few cast him nasty looks, and one even pinched her nose, but the rest were indifferent and went on their way. Embarrassed, he ducked his head. He saw a public toilet and entered it. At the wash basin, he pulled out a face towel from his backpack and wet it under the cold, running water before using it to wipe his face, neck, and arms. As he brushed his teeth with the toothbrush and toothpaste he had packed with him, he saw that the wound on his head had dried up once again. Looking at himself, even he was appalled by the face in the mirror. He ran his fingers through his hair, and then tried to wipe his overcoat with the damp towel in the hope of brushing off some of the stench. Feeling cleaner and more tidied up, he made his way back onto the street. He stopped by the nearest shop and sat down at one of the small tables. The eatery was a mere rectangular box, no larger than ten square metres, minded by a petite, middle-aged woman, whose face was etched with lines around her eyes and mouth. There was just room for three small tables and a long stainless steel standing counter with a noodle boiler and soup warmer next to each other near the shop's entrance. At one end of the counter was a three-tier steamer that was puffing out hot steam, creating a layer of mist in the environment that diffused the mild sunlight pouring in.

'Order at the counter. It's self-service here and I only take cash,' the woman called from the counter to Hongbing, who promptly got up.

'A dough fritter and soya milk.'

'30 PD.'

He handed her a 100 PD note. When she gave him his change, he saw that her hands were calloused from the daily grind of cooking and washing.

Hongbing was relieved that he wasn't recognized, thanks to all the bruises and his dishevelled looks despite washing up—in fact, he was even subconsciously pulling away from his own reverence of a Party Hero. In his present state, the inconveniences of a city less wired up were becoming more tolerable to him. He would have previously been scornful and irritated at such backwardness. Conventional practices like paying with cash, however, were working well for him. He took the food and drink back to the table and sat down. Soya milk and plain dough fritters had never tasted so good. Perhaps, it was because he was starving. He couldn't recall when was the last time he had dough fritters.

He thoroughly enjoyed the simple taste and the warmth of the soya milk in his stomach. Another customer walked up to the entrance to give his takeout order.

There was serenity in Wose. Surveillance was relatively light. Not every shop, or even alley, had an installed surveillance camera. Big Brother wasn't always watching. The residents of the city got on with their daily lives. They probably weren't caught up in any of the Party politics as those in Unitas would be, being close to the centre of power. On the surface, it almost appeared like a chicken and egg issue: Does the lack of surveillance allow for disengagement from the Party politics, or does their disengagement from politics contribute to the city's freedom? But at a deeper level, even those in Unitas, in fact, refrained from voicing their opinions on political matters too. The answer, then, became crystal clear. Ultimately, it was the people's will to fight against power that determined their freedom. Without it, change was merely a matter of time Without the will to fight, Wose was also destined to become 'Unitas-ized'.

Anyhow, Hongbing was glad that he didn't have to watch his back for now. He ordered and paid for another glass of soya milk and a bowl of piping hot noodles with meat dumplings. As he slurped his noodles with his chopsticks, he recalled in his mind the state of decay the buildings and houses he saw earlier in the morning while on the run were in. The shop that he was in was neat and clean but structurally, it wasn't in the best shape. Worn-out electric wires connected to basic light bulbs ran across the interior, just below the low ceiling. Hairline cracks and paint were peeling from the walls. It reminded him of his maternal grandparents' cottage in a township near the capital city three decades ago. Whether Utopia could produce the smallest cutting-edge semiconductor was probably irrelevant to the local people.

What is glory when ordinary people struggle to make ends meet?

Hongbing was amazed at how his perspective had swung from one end to the other. Personally, he was still grappling with the changes mentally, and the strain of being on the run. What was most daunting was he could not ascertain when and how this ordeal would end. For now, he realized it was fruitless to think too far ahead. Instead, he'd cross that bridge when he came to it. Looking up at the wall clock with its rusty steel frame, he was reminded that he needed to keep moving. The hot beverage and noodles, coupled with the glow of the sun, warmed his cold body. Even his damp clothes were drier and lighter. His spirits lifted. He was looking forward to seeing his mentor. The last time he saw Professor Li Wei had been five years ago at the latter's retirement dinner party in the capital city. *Those were happier days.* At the end of the evening of good food and wine, a slightly tipsy Li had pulled him aside.

'Hongbing, you have done very well, and you've made me very proud!'

'Professor, I think you had a drink too many. Let me take you home.'

'No, I'm not drunk! Listen to me, my good student. Serving your people is a respectable principle to uphold. But you must be wary of the wolves around and never be sucked in to lose your sense of self!'

'You are drunk, hush now,' Hongbing had hissed at his mentor. He was, then, rising through the UFITC ranks and paranoid about any comment or act that could tarnish his reputation. He dragged the older man towards the restaurant's entrance as he picked up both his and Li's belongings. He caught the eye of another former student and made an apologetic gesture for his early exit, pointing at the professor who had passed out.

Recalling the incident, his face blushed with remorse and shame. To exonerate himself from Li's little outburst, he had avoided contacting the latter in the last five years, except for the customary Lunar New Year greeting, which he purposely kept formal and cold. But in his present darkest hour, he now understood his mentor's wise words and the value of one's integrity. His eyes turned wet again. He found himself breaking down frequently in this vulnerable state. His dream of reuniting with Li had surely been a sign of the opportunity to return to the right path. Li was the sounding board he so desperately needed at the moment. Oddly, just the thought of seeing his old professor gave him a long-forsaken sense of calmness. He had only been on the run for no more than a few days, yet it felt more like a year.

* * *

The number of buildings diminished as he progressed along Wose No. 1 Road. The road also narrowed from a double carriageway in both directions to a single carriageway in each direction. Its condition also deteriorated as it cut deeper into the outskirts of Wose—turning gradually from a paved road to an uneven, unpaved one. Both sides of the road were lined with more trees and foliage, adding a layer of cool air to counter the sun.

After Hongbing covered about twenty-five kilometres, he fervently prayed for a vehicle headed to Fengshou to drive by and pick him up. Regardless of how strong his will remained, his flesh had turned weak, and his heels had blisters. He dragged his feet for another thirty minutes, before collapsing under a towering, ancient ginkgo tree. He leaned against the wooden, scaly trunk as the bumps of the bark pressed against his pressure points, giving his tired back some relief. He looked up above him and marvelled at the beauty of the tree. It was ironic, he thought, that he needed a setback as serious as this to appreciate mother nature. As he relaxed, his body began to shiver, his teeth chattered, and a cold sweat began dripping down the sides of his head, neck, and body. His head suddenly felt like it was burning, and he felt woozy. A truck drove past at that moment, but he was too weak to stand up to stop the driver. A second van followed and again, he couldn't find the strength to wave for the driver's attention. His eyelids became heavier, and he was soon half asleep. He barely heard a third vehicle pulling up by the side of the road a few metres ahead of him. The elderly driver and his female passenger got out of the battered pickup truck and walked towards him. Both were in their late sixties, dark-skinned as a result of long hours under the sun in the fields.

'Mister, are you all right?' the farmer asked, shaking his right shoulder gently. 'His coat is damp, and his face is so red,' he said to his companion.

The woman bent over and held her palm over Hongbing's forehead.

'Oh my goodness, he's running a temperature,' she exclaimed. 'Mister, what happened to you? Where are you heading?'

'Professor Li Wei, Fengshou, Professor, Fengshou . . .' Hongbing murmured.

'We live near Fengshou. We'll give you a ride,' the man replied. 'Can you stand up?'

He then turned to his companion, 'Quick, help me, support him on the left side.' She grabbed Hongbing's left arm to let it rest on her shoulder while her companion propped Hongbing up on the right side. Together, they walked back to the back of the truck slowly. They leaned his body against the truck and slid him up the truck bed. The man pillowed his head with a bag of potatoes. The woman retrieved a large, folded piece of old jute blanket tucked away among the bags of fertilizers and several shiny farming tools on one side of the truck bed. She shook it out and covered his body with it.

The couple then climbed into the cab of the truck and drove off towards Fengshou.

Chapter 7

Seeking Allies

A stream of warm sunshine woke Hongbing up. He rubbed his eyes gently and blinked at the afternoon sun's rays pouring through the window. It was indeed the first proper sleep he'd had in days, and it had reenergized him, both physically and mentally. The feeling of relief that entered him had done wonders—it somewhat eliminated the intense fear and perturbation that had consumed him for the last few days.

He was in the elderly couple's home—a three-room cottage overlooking the farmland that they had leased from the Party. He had been half awake by the time the pickup truck pulled up the dirt pathway leading to the one-storey house, having slept throughout most of the drive. He vaguely remembered being helped to the smaller bedroom to lie down on a daybed.

'You look less pale than when we picked you up,' the woman said as she entered the room feeling his forehead.

'Looks like the temperature has gone down a little. Think you need to go back to sleep.'

'Ai-hua is right. We know you need to get to Fengshou,' Qian said. 'But not in your current state. You can go to there when you get better. We are just a twenty-minute drive from Fengshou. We'll wake you up for dinner.'

Despite the hospitality, Hongbing, alerted to his situation, still remained somewhat wary. Gazing at the house's door, he pictured the Party guards bursting in to arrest him. So, when the tempting suggestion to sleep arose, his reluctance was palpable, struggling against slumber to stay vigilant, to stay alive. Yet, the elderly couple's comforting hospitality—their warmth and kindness—proved irresistible, gently lulling him back into sleep. Exhausted beyond measure, Hongbing soon succumbed, drifting into a deep, unknowing slumber.

* * *

He was awoken by the fragrance of fried garlic from the kitchen. He opened his eyes in a daze as he recalled where he was. The sun had set, and the house was dark except for the light from the kitchen. He got up, folded the blanket, and piled it on top of the pillow on one end of the daybed. He walked out of the bedroom, past the round dining table, which was set for three people, towards the kitchen.

'How do you feel?' Ai-hua turned around from the stove briefly.

'Much better. Thank you.'

'That's great,' she said as she returned to her cooking. 'Dinner's almost ready. Just frying the last dish of vegetables.'

'How can I help?'

'You can bring those out to the table,' she nodded sideways to a plate of stir-fried chicken with green pepper and black bean paste, and a bowl of tomato egg drop soup next to the stove. 'Can you also let Qian know we're eating soon? He's in the backyard.'

Tears brimmed in Hongbing's eyes as he sat down at the dining table. He could not remember when the last time was that he'd tasted a home-cooked meal with his family. But here was a couple in their autumn years, complete strangers, who'd taken him, a fugitive, in.

'Enjoy your meal,' Qian said, as he returned from the backyard. He picked up a piece of chicken and green pepper with his chopsticks and laid it on top of Hongbing's bowl of steamed rice. 'Try my wife's cooking. It's not too bad,' he chuckled.

'Hope you don't mind, the countryside, it's only plain tea and simple food,' added Ai-hua.

'Please don't say that, it's delicious.' He put down his bowl and chopsticks, looking from her to her husband.

'I can't thank you enough. You guys saved me from the pit,' his head dropped in shame.

'Come, let's eat first. Fill our stomachs and we can chat more after dinner,' his host interjected, and shifted the conversation to the couple's harvest this autumn and the joy of living in the countryside.

As Ai-hua finished up with the dishes, Qian fetched from the cupboard a bottle of rice wine. He brought in three small cups and poured the rice wine.

Hongbing took a small sip. 'This is delicious, it's nothing like what I've tasted,' he told his host.

'Glad you like it. We fermented this ourselves. Being in the countryside, you learn to become as self-sufficient as you can.'

'From the sound of it, you don't look like the you're from Party-controlled capital.'

'Nor are you, no? Haha.'

'Yes . . . you're right. Actually—'

'Both of us are actually from Warc. To be more precise, we were born in this region but we each left with our respective families for the city when we were primary school kids.'

'For Warc?'

Qian nodded. 'Yes, you heard me right. Now the Social Credit test bed city. So, we returned here few years ago.' He glanced at his wife who had joined them with a plate of sliced apples.

'Qian and I had enough of city life,' Ai-hua sat down across from Hongbing. Then, contemplating a little before going on. 'You looked like you've gone through a lot yourself . . .'

Hongbing smiled weakly.

'We worked at Warc Television for nearly three decades. We were the head and deputy producers of *Crime-Zero City*,' she said. Hongbing gasped. 'Yep, that show,' she grinned, sarcastically, and took a sip of the rice wine.

'At first, like all good Utopian citizens, we were honoured to do our bit. But to cut a long story short, we realized that it was not what we envisaged. We felt duped.'

Qian had taken over the storytelling. The problem for Ai-hua and him came when the authorities began to exploit the popularity of the show to take out their political foes. The number of low scorers were not just the figure that the audience saw from the show. In fact, the proportion of low scorers among the 300,000 Warc residents was insanely high, Qian said.

'Actually, the extra number of low scorers that the audience don't know about is the group between the top and low scorers, your regular guys,' he refilled his cup with rice wine. 'Unfortunately, some of these regular Joes pissed off the local bureaucrats for reasons no one knows, and as such, the bureaucrats found a way to take action against them that wouldn't reflect badly on them. So, the bureaucrats exploited the show's hype and slipped some names into the blacklist of low scorers. And you know what happened with low scorers, right?'

Qian drained his wine cup.

'Worse still, the climate also bred a culture of reporting on others to score brownie points. People ratted out their co-workers, their classmates and so on, accusing them of ideological incorrectness or disloyalty to the Party. Whether the allegations were true or not was another matter altogether. Such behaviours clearly show people's integrity withering away. This sent chills down our spines, as we felt like we were reliving the horrors of the Cultural Revolution decades ago when everything went amok.'

'We found out after the fact,' Qian said. 'But from our perspective as responsible producers, we immediately wrote a detailed report, proposing to end the show to prevent further social havoc that may ensue. It was submitted to the Warc Broadcast Commissioner.

'We then waited for the Commissioner's office to call us in for a meeting or some form of discussion, as would have been the usual practice.'

'Did you hear back?' Hongbing asked.

Qian shook his head. 'Next thing we knew, we received notice that we would be transferred to the archives department, cataloguing audio and video resources,' he leaned forward and picked up a slice of apple.

'We read the writings on the wall, so to speak,' added Ai-hua. 'Those above obviously didn't like to hear what we had to say and told us so in the most explicit manner. And as we were nearing retirement age, we decided to bring that forward. So, we left the city and came to this no-man's-land-like place.'

Her husband nodded. 'What we saw was a Cultural Revolution 2.0. Having gone through a version one in our teens, we didn't have the stomach, at our ripe age, to experience another round.'

'Anyway, after we returned and lived in the countryside, we realized that while overall conditions have improved, the gap with the major cities has widened.' Qian sighed. 'As we don't have families in the rural areas any more, we haven't returned to our home towns for a long while. Utopia is Utopia only in the big cities.'

'What about you? What's your story?' Ai-hua asked.

Hongbing glanced from her to Qian, and began to share his story, from the time when Yiping was taken.

* * *

The conversation with Qian and Ai-hua the previous night made him feel that he was no longer a lone voice in the wilderness. He was enlightened and felt encouraged knowing that there were others who felt the same way, who could all work together towards a common goal. He stretched and turned his body on the soft sheets and sucked in a long deep breath of clean air. The sound of birds chirping in the distance brought a smile to his face, as well as *hope*.

He scanned the bedroom. The room was probably a study, filled with memories of the old couple. The morning sun illuminated the tall bookshelf on one wall, and little dust particles were dancing in its rays before the photo frames and books that lined its shelves. The pictures told the personal history of the couple and of Utopia. Two, in particular, caught his eyes. They were of Qian and Ai-hua as teenagers. Qian was photographed with a few other teens, their pants rolled up to their shins and legs kicking in the water by a riverbank. They looked like regular kids enjoying a day out but the red scarf around each of their necks and their worn clothing told volumes about the tumultuous period that they had lived in. In the second photo, a serious-looking Ai-hua with a short bob cut just below her ears—as sported by girls during the Cultural Revolution—was pictured with nine other girls in what seemed like a class photo. A few of the girls had badges with the image of the then Utopian leader pinned on their drab military-like jackets.

Hongbing could see that Ai-hua's smile was forced. The background of their photos showed the real history of Utopia from the time it had been suffering from extreme poverty decades ago, and how people had lived through the Party's oppression. The couple's existence reminded Hongbing, who marvelled at the couple's strength, that it was no small feat to stay resilient and not allow the powerful forces of state coercion to destroy their values. For the first time in days, Hongbing felt invigorated, able to take on whatever fight came his way.

The aroma of coffee brought him back to reality. He made his way to the living area. Qian and Ai-hua were at the dining table, having their coffee.

'Good morning,' he greeted them with a smile.

'Good morning, Hongbing. Slept all right?' Ai-hua asked. 'Some breakfast? We're having ours.'

On the table were plates of sunny-side-up eggs, toasts, lychee jam, and a slab of butter. Ai-hua placed a side plate in front of him, as Qian scurried to the kitchen.

'Help yourself,' Ai-hua said as she savoured her buttered toast with a sip of coffee.

Hongbing grabbed a piece of toast, spread some butter and jam on it, and shoved it into his mouth.

'Oh, this is good,' he told his hosts. 'Best toast ever.'

Ai-hua grinned, 'Home-made lychee jam. Fruits from our tree in the backyard.'

Qian returned from the kitchen with a mug of coffee. 'You like it? Ai-hua, we should put your toast and jam in the Store,' he said loudly pointing to a drawer in the kitchen.

'The Store? What is it now, a safe house?' Hongbing laughed.

'Oh, it's just where we keep our valuables. We don't trust the Party, so we don't use banks here.'

'Thank you.' He ate quietly, enjoying the old couple's small talk. It was an unfamiliar experience. He couldn't recall experiencing such simple pleasures with his wife or his family.

'Thank you so much for your kind hospitality,' Hongbing finally broke his silence. He had had two slices of toast, an egg, and a cup of coffee. 'I hope I'll be able to repay it one day.'

'Oh, think nothing of it,' Qian said.

'It's quiet here, even boring, so we are delighted to meet a new friend,' Ai-hua added.

'You guys gave me inspiration about what to do next.'

'Oh no, that's heavy,' Qian chuckled, and the wrinkles around the corners of his eyes deepened. 'We can't be accountable for whatever you're going to do next.'

'He's kidding! Please relax!' Ai-hua also laughed.

'Seriously, I was just wondering . . . wasn't it lonely to distance yourself from the rest of Utopia to protect your values?'

'Definitely. Lonely as hell.'

'How did you survive?'

'Well . . . what else could we do? End our lives ourselves? Not us.' Qian laughed again.

'Are there any like-minded people?'

'There must be, I assume, but we can't be sure. We never talk politics outside this house. It's not like people would openly talk about it anyway. You know Utopians.'

'You've not tried?'

'No.'

'What if we can make a difference?'

'How?'

'I don't know . . . I feel like something needs to be done to fix how the Party runs things in this country.'

'Oh, Hongbing,' Ai-hua stepped into the conversation, 'we been thinking about this for a long time too, it's impossible to find like-minded people in this country.'

'But we met! Which proves it can be done.'

Hongbing spoke with a flow. His words were not planned in advance, but perhaps it was that these thoughts had been brewing unconsciously within him since this morning. The idea that there might be others who shared the same beliefs triggered a realization; if they joined forces, their voices could be amplified. Also, he understood that it wouldn't be fair or feasible to abandon his country—after all, it was his homeland. Fuelled by confidence and a feeling he hadn't experienced before, he continued to speak with greater conviction, empowered by this renewed internal inspiration. 'Yeah, but do you think it is possible, in this country, to form a political movement?' Hongbing asked.

'Now, that requires a bunch of people. A bunch of *brave* people. You'll probably get arrested while you recruit those people,' Ai-hua said.

'Well . . . I think the key here is to build momentum so more people can engage.'

'How?'

'We can start by building a network of like-minded people. And let them know that we're here.'

'Like how exactly? That's not concrete enough,' Qian interrupted.

'Oh, Qian, it's wonderful that he has the passion,' Ai-hua told her husband.

Then, looking Hongbing in the eye, she said, 'We don't mean to be a wet blanket. Maybe if we were as brave as you are now earlier in our lives, things could have been different. We're apologetic to you and your generation. But don't make the same mistake we did. Don't be apologetic to Utopia's next generation.'

Hongbing was touched by the couple's words. They empowered him with a renewed sense of purpose. Perhaps there was a way. He just needed to find it. Professor Li Wei could surely help him figure it out. He needed to act, for the people. Despite all that had happened to him in the last few days, he still loved his people. The greater cause wasn't flawed, he realized, rather the problem lay in how the Party structured, ran, and controlled government mechanisms using the cause as its propaganda tool. Those who saw through the real issues and weren't happy with the Party's ruling would have concealed their thoughts, for fear of facing repercussions. But the wider Utopian population simply wasn't aware of the issues at hand—including deprived basic rights—because it was constantly fed with the propaganda and only allowed limited access to the outside world. What was sorely lacking was a forum to raise awareness about the system. Even if there was a platform to gain knowledge, would it be able to put an end to the Party's power to abuse and control?

For decades, he had lived for, and done everything to seek, the Party's approval. Now, he was coming to terms with the fact that he would always be a target of the Party's wrath. *The Party has essentially brought this on itself,* Hongbing thought. They were the ones who eliminated his options to flee abroad, cornering him into taking this path. He was surprised by his own readiness, which could partly have been spurred by the desire to survive, as he couldn't leave the country.

He went back to the bedroom and changed back into his pants and shirt. Ai-hua had made him change into Qian's sweatshirt and pants when they had arrived yesterday and had thrown his soiled clothes into the washer-drier. She had also washed his sweater and sunned his overcoat. He picked up his backpack and headed out to the door, where Qian and Ai-hua were waiting. Hongbing had declined Qian's offer to drive him to Fengshou. Qian gave him quick directions to Fengshou by foot. 'I believe it's not too far from here, so you should get there after lunch.'

Ai-hua held his hands in hers. 'Take care of yourself. Here, take these!' She gave him a plastic bag. It was filled with hot baked potatoes.

'Thank you both, you saved me in my darkest moment. I will never forget.'

'Let us know how it goes,' Qian squeezed his shoulder. 'Make a difference. We're vouching for you.'

Hongbing walked along the gravel driveway, taking a moment to wave goodbye to the couple. He kept walking, waving until he reached the spot where the driveway curved sharply to the right and the couple disappeared from sight. Then, he followed a dirt path that led to the road and headed towards Fengshou, where he would hopefully meet Li Wei and seek his mentor's counsel once more during this trying time.

* * *

Hongbing arrived at Fengshou at around two o'clock. As he scarfed up the last potato from Ai-hua, his eyes were fixed on the horizon checking the presence of surveillance cameras. He constantly looked over his shoulder to make sure that no one was trailing him. When some people walked past him, he ducked his head as low as he could to hide his face. He must remain under the radar. While he felt the tremendous weight on his shoulders, his feet were light. He saw hope. He had called Li from the Qian residence, using the landline and asked to see him.

'What a nice surprise,' his mentor said. 'Certainly, you must come. I haven't seen you for a long time. My address is . . .'

Very soon, he would be able to tap into his mentor's wisdom to help in his fight, to make up for his lack of experience. How to safely communicate, how to recruit like-minded people, the best ways to mobilize resources—were some of the questions that he needed immediate answers to.

Hongbing walked towards a small, detached house in a Fengshou suburb. The afternoon sun was blazing through the boughs of several ginkgo trees that towered over the red-tiled roof of the one-storey house. Their golden yellow leaves had all but fallen and blanketed the sandy ground in gold. But they would stand strong till spring arrived, like a beacon of courage in defiance of the winter's bitter cold that was to come.

Li was sitting on a little patio outside the house, wrapped in a thick sweater, having a cup of tea, and reading a book. The rustling of leaves from his visitor's footsteps caught his attention, and he looked up. Hongbing was walking up the pebbled pathway, his hand raised to shade his eyes from the sunlight. 'Professor Li,' he waved, smiling sheepishly.

Li removed his reading glasses and stared hard at the advancing, but dishevelled man. He couldn't immediately make out who his visitor was.

'It's me, Hongbing.'

'Oh, of course! What a nice surprise for you to visit,' Li said, before he gave Hongbing a bear hug. 'Silly me, I don't think I've seen you in such a getup. I'm clearly getting old, haha.'

'It was time for me . . . for some change.'

'Oh, I like that. Come on in.'

He followed his mentor into the living room. Three walls of heavy wooden bookshelves surrounded an old brown sofa. They were overflowing with books, which spilled into numerous stacks on the floor, a coffee table, and an armchair by the sofa. The books were mainly of history and philosophy genres. One title stood out—*The*

Free Mind. The dog-eared copy was yellow with age. *How like Li to keep a copy*, Hongbing grinned. He had never read it, a title that the Party's United Front Ideology Protection Unit had banned a decade ago in a decree to wipe off its existence throughout the country, whether it was in the public libraries or in homes. The confiscated copies were thrown into furnaces. He spotted a few more 'politically incorrect' publications. The old him would have frowned at Li's act of betrayal, perhaps even severed ties completely. Now, he was relieved he had only kept a distance and not gone to the point of no return.

'Please take a seat,' Li gestured towards the sofa as he removed a stack of four books from the armchair and placed it by his feet as he sat down.

'What brings you here? How many years has it been? Five, six?' Li wondered aloud. 'And you look . . . unusual I have to say. Still, it's wonderful to see you.'

Hongbing fell silent as guilt consumed him. He blinked away a tear, ashamed of how he had treated his mentor.

Li sensed his discomfort and allowed the silence to sink in. Then he said, 'The past is the past. It's no use looking back.'

In a lighter tone, he asked, 'Tell me, what is going on here?'

Hongbing started to fill him in—from Yiping's detention up to the dramatic turn of events that had occurred in the last few days. As Hongbing related his story, he only saw disbelief on Li's face. Even for someone who knew the Party well, the tactics employed by the Party still shocked, and at the same time, overwhelmed him.

'I feel your pain,' Li spoke finally after listening to Hongbing's tale for an hour.

'My world turned upside down. What I can't stand the most is that everything I worked for till today was in fact restricting the basic rights of people.'

'It's not your fault.'

'I've been feeding all the high-tech materials of Clanta to the United Front. And they have been using this to control the minds and behaviours of people, including me!'

'Listen Hongbing, get a grip, it's not your fault. You didn't have much of a choice; you are part of the system.'

'How could this be? Technology should enhance people's lives but it's doing the exact opposite in this country.'

'I'm also worried about the impact on our freedom,' Li agreed.

'It's a tool to control and monitor people here. Nothing more than that.'

'Look, everything has two sides. Just like there's day and night, there's good and bad.'

'I get that, but it feels like we're only seeing the bad side here. Our first-tier cities are already so entangled with that technology, and it feels like I'm already on the wrong side of history.'

'No, you're not hearing me. Everything has two sides.'

'What do you mean?'

'Tech itself is value-free. Neutral. The problem lies in the intention of those who are using it.'

He looked quizzically at Li.

'Meaning —yes, it can be used as an oppressive tool, but it can also be used as a means for resistance.'

The brilliance of the logic made Hongbing sit up. The out-the-box idea was simple and straightforward, with a twist that could potentially change the game altogether. It woke Hongbing out of his recent preoccupation—and paranoia—that technology existed solely for the Party's manipulation.

'Like how?' He pressed, excitedly. 'How exactly can it be used as a tool for . . . resistance?'

'Well, for a start, it can be a vessel to amplify alternative voices. By using foreign social media platforms, you can spread the information you want, aimed at mobilizing people.'

'The Party would no doubt track the IP. And it would cut down Utopian people's access to all the "illegal material" on the internet. They would have cut off access to those platforms in the first place.'

'Of course. And they'll track and monitor you too. But there are ways to skirt around them and exploit technology to your advantage.'

'How?'

'There are a few options out there. You may access those platforms via encrypted messaging apps using blockchain technology or via VPNs to encrypt your internet connection. You may also use your own secure browsers.'

'I see. So, I can use this tech to penetrate the great firewall of the Party . . . and provide a space to exchange alternative views?'

'You got it. Consider it as an independent media, if you like, to hold those in power accountable to serve the interests of people, not themselves.'

'What should I say on those platforms?'

'I can't give you an answer for that. Think about it yourself. Something that could enable different people to engage and build bridges of understanding among themselves. You could also organize an offline meeting and decide on a possible plan of action when you meet them in person.'

'The Party would never allow that.'

'Of course it won't. They will be hostile towards such meetings. But the good thing about third- and fourth-tier cities is that the Party is yet to heavily invest its resources in surveillance. This means it can be done here. You can describe the meeting as a local charity or a study group gathering on the internet so it doesn't pop up on their radar.'

'Then what?'

'You'd then coordinate peaceful actions to counterbalance state power!'

Hongbing had always looked up to his mentor as a successful scholar for as long as they were acquainted. But to discover the activist in Li was a surprise he didn't expect. *Was this his secret life? How would he have judged me over the past decades?* Endless questions swirled in Hongbing's mind, yet he decided it was wiser not to voice them. All that mattered was Li gave him inspiration, which crystallized his thoughts into planned action. It gave him courage and a new goal in life. This time, it was a righteous one; to contribute to building Utopia, and for the people. It was then that realization struck Hongbing that Li might have some idea about the whereabouts of individuals like Yiping, and consequently, about Sara and his daughter. Given Li's apparent knowledge of how to resist the Party, he might also know of ways to bring his friend and family back.

'Sorry, I don't have any answers for that,' Li said when asked these questions.

'Any ideas at least on how the Party would treat them?' Hongbing prodded, as the harrowing scream he had heard in the Hard Interview

Zone corridor continued to haunt him. He hoped for any response from Li, anything that could contradict the fears growing within him.

'Well . . . I'm not entirely sure about the accuracy of this, but my latest intel suggests that the Party has established a test bed detention centre equipped with their newest technology. It's apparently designed to collect data on those the Party considers rebels and their families,' Li began, his voice tinged with uncertainty. 'I've heard that the people there are given a degree of freedom within the facility. The idea, as far as I understand, is to collect behavioural data on individuals acting freely, as the Party ultimately wants to study when and how rebellious behaviour manifests itself.'

Relieved, Hongbing was grateful to hear anything other than fearful references to the Hard Interview Zone. Still, his concern lingered.

'What happens to people inside that facility?' he asked.

'Beats me . . . I can't even confirm if that intel is credible. But . . .' Li trailed off.

'But what?' Hongbing pressed.

'I've heard that there's a chance for them to return as loyal servants of the Party,' Li replied.

This notion visibly disgusted Hongbing. Frowning seriously, he said, 'This is the problem with people here. They just lack the strength to fight. Once you understand your values, you should be ready to risk your life to defend them. It's attitudes like that which have shaped Utopia into what it is now.'

'Well, again, all of this is unverified. So, there's no need to get angry prematurely,' Li responded with a warm smile. 'Perhaps your focus should be on getting your family back first?'

'How?' Hongbing's tone was urgent.

'By starting your fight,' Li got up from his armchair, and walked towards the bookshelf. He gently pulled out a map between a couple of tightly arranged books on the right-hand corner of the bookshelf.

'Can you help me out here,' he said as he put on his reading glasses, and opened up the folded map, inviting Hongbing to come closer. 'This is a map of Tenfeng, have you heard of it?'

Hongbing shook his head. The map showed a comprehensive illustration of the town's roads and houses, providing a clear overview of the layout and distribution of houses and other facilities. Li pointed to a block of houses where there was a red dot marked on top of one.

'Go and find John. He'll help you . . . on how tech can be used for the greater cause. I'll write a letter for you before you take off, so that he knows you're one of us.'

* * *

Hongbing walked for about a few kilometres, passed farms and fields, and crossed streams, until he finally arrived at the neighbouring town of Tenfeng. He sped up when he reached the outskirts of the tiny town. He was hopeful that he could once more be part of something bigger than himself, to take on whatever challenges confronted him. He had, after all, gone through a few harrowing, life-and-death moments in the past few days and had survived.

The house circled in red on the map wasn't hard to find. The exterior was in a similar hue to that of Li's house, he noticed. But it was a bigger house. When he reached the gate, a man was strolling in the garden lined with intricately trimmed pine trees on one side, and brightly blooming autumn flowers—black dahlia and red poppy—on the other. It was a picturesque garden, a true escape from the rest of Utopia.

'Hello!' Hongbing called out brightly, walking towards the man. He looked stern, even unwelcoming, with a hint of suspicion in his eyes.

'It's Shan Hongbing here, a friend of Professor Li Wei,' he said, showing him the map he was holding, which had Li's writing with instructions and directions to John's house.

'Think you have the wrong house,' the man said, as he turned to walk towards his house.

'John!' Hongbing called out. The man stopped in his steps.

'Please, take this,' Hongbing said as he ran up to John who was about to step into the house, shoving him Li's letter. John took the letter and disappeared into his house, leaving a helpless Hongbing in the garden. Nerves crept in as he waited. He paced up and down the narrow driveway that separated the garden into two sides.

After a while, the door slowly opened, and John's voice came through. 'Come on in.'

A musty smell rose from the weathered wooden floor, adding to the mysterious aura of the space. The house was shrouded in cobwebs, and a thick layer of dust blanketed the worn, old furniture. The living room was filled with objects and both the window frames and the windows themselves showed signs of the space being neglected for a quite long time. Between the still air and the silence between John and him, Hongbing felt like he was suffocating.

John led him to an old study room. He looked sideways and noticed it had an electronic lock. With its high ceiling and old-styled, rather gothic interior, the study anchored the house with an authority, pressing to Hongbing. He held his breath in anticipation, praying that John wouldn't turn his back on him.

'Take a seat,' John pointed to a fancy but mismatched steel chair before a wide, wooden table placed in the middle of the study. A smaller desk with two drawers on one side sat against one side of the wall. John's face appeared somewhat devoid of emotions, making it hard for Hongbing to decipher whether he was welcome or not. John sat down across the table from him, looking at his visitor caustically.

Click.

Hongbing jumped as the sound of the electronic door lock went off behind him. Glancing over his shoulder, there were two others—a man and a woman—who had just entered the room from nowhere. In horror, he turned his head back to John.

Clang!

Before he could open his mouth, the ground beneath his chair let out a loud blast and the wooden floor below him simply gave way. Without any forewarning, together with the chair, he sank onto a lower floor, or rather, a pit. His hands clutched tightly onto the armrests as he pressed hard to stay seated while gravity took its force.

Thump!

As the chair's legs landed heavily and neatly on the lower floor, his upper body tumbled forward. Quickly steadying himself and using all his strength, Hongbing pulled himself back against the seat, firmly planting his feet on the ground to regain his balance. The moment he regained stability, restraining straps were released from the chair's front legs, tying his legs tightly to the legs of the chair. Simultaneously, chains from the floor wrapped around the back legs of the chair, securing it, and him, firmly to the ground. A woman—one of the two who later appeared in the study—jumped down into the pit. She pulled both his arms to the back of the chair and tied them tightly together at the wrists; so tight that Hongbing yelped out. Then, gripping the edges of the opening, she hauled herself up and out of the pit. It was then Hongbing saw John staring at him, menacingly.

'What's all this for?' Hongbing shouted at him. Instead of responding, John pulled out a remote controller from his pocket and pressed a button, which tilted Hongbing's chair backwards to a forty-five-degree angle. His eyes met John's, and they were dark and cold, making a sinister chill creep up over Hongbing. He opened his mouth to talk, but no words emerged.

'I won't gag you,' John said coldly, 'if that was what you are wondering. We need you to speak.'

Crossing his arms, John circled above him. When he completed a lap, he looked down at Hongbing and furrowed his eyebrows. His moves were intimidating, and his seemingly larger-than-life frame was overbearing, obstructing any light that might slip through. Hongbing felt oppressively suffocated. Clearly, this was an interrogation.

'Why are you here?' grilled John.

'I wanted to talk to you about something important,' Hongbing sputtered, as desperation crept in. 'Li Wei said you could help me.'

'Who do you work for?'

'What do you mean?'

'You heard me.'

'I don't . . . work for anyone.'

John narrowed his eyes and Hongbing sensed that his answer raised more suspicions than not. 'We know you turned against us, Mister Party Hero, a.k.a. subject 4201.'

Hongbing's heart stopped, and his face whitened. His eyes were wide open, yet he did not dare utter another word.

Is this it? Li Wei turned his back on me?

'I'll ask you again. Who do you work for? The US?'

'No.'

'Your actions indicate that you are working for a foreign power.'

'Not true.'

'Now, tell me where Li Wei now lives. Is he the point of contact?'

Hongbing was somewhat relieved. *Okay, they're actively searching for Li . . . meaning I have the information they're desperate for. Maybe, just maybe, they won't be so quick to get rid of me.* 'No idea what you're talking about,' he shouted back. He was still shaking but was less fearful, as he thought he had figured them out a bit better. He hadn't seen any mind-reading equipment in the house, like those he had seen in Unitas. This realization sparked a strange sense of confidence in him and, perhaps, he thought, *I could manoeuvre my way out of this situation by engaging in a mind game with them.*

'You won't walk out alive unless you give us what we want,' John said fiercely. 'You of all people should know well that the Party doesn't take kindly to traitors. This is your last chance to return as a loyal servant for the Party.'

By this point, Hongbing was certain that John was lying. The actions he had taken were unforgivable in the eyes of the Party, and he knew all too well that they did not grant second chances, especially not to those they defined as traitors. The Party he knew showed no leniency to those who it claimed showed betrayal. This led to a nagging question in his mind: *If not the Party, then who are these people?*

Hongbing's prolonged silence seemed to have frustrated John. 'I think you're seriously mistaken here,' John torpedoed him. 'You think you've got leverage, don't you? Let me show you that you don't.'

As John disappeared from his sight for a while, he felt a breath of fresh air and some light streamed through. He breathed easier. From the sound of his footsteps, John must have walked to the wooden desk by the wall. Hongbing heard him pulled open a drawer, followed by the sound of metal scraping against the wooden surface. When he was back, he was holding a gun.

'This is your last chance. Where is Li Wei?' The gun—with a silencer—was pointed at Hongbing.

'I'll give you three seconds. Three, Two—'

'Oh please, no, no, no!'

'One.'

Bang!

The loud, deafening sound snapped Hongbing's ears. He had never imagined that his life would end this way. Tears streamed down his face at the misery and regret of living a life fooled by the Party, and existing as its tool.

A few seconds later, Hongbing realized he was still alive. The bullet had deliberately missed him. Given the close range, a miss would have been impossible. John's expertise with a gun was enough to direct the bullet closely past his face without even grazing it. The sound of the bullet slicing sharply through the air was still resonating in Hongbing's right ear, sending vibrations directly to his brain.

'So . . . where is Li Wei,' John continued, but Hongbing couldn't hear him clearly, as his ears were still ringing from the sound of the gunshot.

'Confess, and you will live.'

'I've got nothing to confess, I swear.'

'Consider yourself a dead man, then. Don't test me.' *This must be a test,* Hongbing thought. Although they claimed to be affiliated with the Party, their language clearly implied otherwise. Trusting his instincts, Hongbing took a gamble. It was his last-ditch effort, a carefully calculated move aimed at maximizing his survival chance. 'I really don't know,' Hongbing rolled his dice.

Bang!

John was merciless. The deafeningly loud sound filled the room. The second bullet came from the gun and pierced the air between them.

And Hongbing was still breathing.

The bullet had missed him again.

Then, the sound of giggling and clapping gradually increased in volume as Hongbing's hearing slowly came back. The other two were now behind John, peering through the opening, smiling.

'Passed,' John gave his verdict and pressed the button on his remote-control and Hongbing's chair gradually came back to an upright position. 'Li will be impressed too, I must say.'

'Julie, the floor,' John added, as the floor beneath his feet slowly rose up. Hongbing was soon back in the study.

'Dan, his hands, please.'

'Can any of you tell me what on earth is going on here?' Hongbing reprimanded, relieved but irritated. He stood up, shaking his hands and legs.

'It's the Resistance,' Dan winked.

'The Resistance?'

'Well . . . call it a civil society . . . aimed at creating awareness about the Party's oppression,' John answered.

The Resistance had begun in the capital city, John explained, with more than a hundred founding members working together towards the common goal; Li Wei had been one of them. Their mission was to gradually foster awareness in Unitas, to plant the seeds of independent thought among the general public, and ultimately build a substantial following. They had only contacted people who questioned the Party's ruling and gathered like-minded people in local communities. After assembling a group of people, the Resistance initiated 'Discussion Sessions' focused on the importance of freedom and the necessity of collective action to safeguard their fundamental rights. The group also used 'Cultural Expressions' to subtly communicate with the general public. Through paintings, music and lyrics, it embedded messages to challenge the Party's propaganda.

But the ambition was short-lived. With the Party rapidly implementing its surveillance equipment throughout the city, almost every member of the Resistance in Unitas was tracked down and taken into custody. The captured individuals were then sent to re-education camps or, as they had recently discovered, some form of high-tech detention facilities and never returned. Eventually, there were only four of them who remained uncaptured as of now, those in the study and Li Wei; thanks to Li's order to flee Unitas years earlier when they had got wind that the Party was planning to implement its new control system in the capital. So, Li Wei went to Fengshou, and the three of them to Tenfeng.

'Why did you abandon Li Wei and flee here?' It was now Hongbing's turn to ask questions.

'Abandon? We didn't abandon him. We have our purpose here,' Dan said.

'And that is?'

'Before that, let me ask you something,' John intervened. 'I heard, in detail, what you've been through, so I have a quite good grasp of where you're coming from. But I'd like to hear it from you directly. Why do you want to fight the Party?'

'People are being deceived, coerced to forfeit their rights, and being raised as the Party's wolf warriors without realizing it.'

'Yes, we are all aware of that, a.k.a. the great cause,' John frowned. 'But what drives you personally?'

'How is that any relevant?'

'Because it reveals who you truly are. We all have our own stories here,' John said, with a clear voice, but Hongbing could detect a subtle quiver in his tone. 'For me, my kids were arrested by the Party agents, just for reading a book deemed improper, and they never returned.' Shocked, Hongbing was confronted with a reality he never wanted to face. This indicated that after all these years, this man was still unable to reunite with his family. This hit Hongbing hard, stirring a deep sense of empathy and concern. 'I don't seek your sympathy,' John said. 'All I want is to hear your story.'

'Well . . . my friend, wife, and daughter got detained without any explanation, and they completely exiled me, leading to my current predicament. I'm still in the dark about the real reasons. After everything I've been through, I've now realized I can't live like this any more. Not like this! In the palm of the almighty Party, which was dictating every aspect of my life. So, here I am, part of this fight.'

'Selfish.'

'Selfish?'

'Nothing wrong with being selfish, it's human nature,' John defended. 'It can reinforce your dedication towards your goal, if conditions are right. Please, continue.'

'So, as I said, I tried to flee Utopia and found that it was impossible. Now the only way for me to live is to change the way things are in Utopia.'

'Now that's a hell of a cause,' Juile said, grinning.

'Fair enough,' Dan nodded.

'If you guys approve,' John's lips twitched, 'come along,' he said as he headed out from the study. This was clearly another pass. 'We'll show you what we're doing. Get ready to play your part.'

* * *

Hongbing was led to a spacious bedroom located in the basement. The dimly lit bedroom looked like it hadn't been used for ages. Except for a queen-sized bed in the middle, there was nothing else. The wallpaper looked mouldy and was peeling. On one side of the room, a heavy wooden door was embedded in the wall.

'Shall we?' Dan said as he slid it open, leading the Resistance to a small dressing room, stacked with piles of clothes. Julie closed the door behind her after the group was ushered into the tiny space. Dan stepped further in and shoved his arms into the clothes pile.

Click!

The tiny room shook, causing everyone to wobble. Hongbing felt his body lift as the entire room began to descend. Realizing it was an elevator, he quickly grabbed onto a hanger attached to one of the walls to maintain his balance. About two floors down, the lift came to a stop. Juile pushed aside another pile of clothes stacked on the opposite side to where they walked in to reveal a keypad. Entering a four-digit code, she slid the wall open, slowly.

A secret basement came into view—a large room filled with tech equipment. High CPU usage computers and shelves of servers somewhat reminded Hongbing of his office at UF-Clanta. 'My babies,' Dan said, calling himself the resident programmer.

The lights in the room were dim, probably intended to reduce eye strain. All monitors—there were eight of them—were on night mode, hardly providing any source of lighting. As Hongbing walked towards the centre of the room, it dawned on him that he could be standing in a *hacking hub*.

'Are you here to carry out. . . hacking activities?' Hongbing asked Dan, quite assertively. 'What is it you are doing?'

'We're not black hackers,' Dan retorted. 'Not engaged in any malicious hacking here.'

'If not, what's all these for?'

'Creating a new system,' John interjected, 'aimed at uniting people with similar values online.'

'But that seems quite impossible,' Hongbing countered. 'Especially when the authorities can block access to the internet, no?'

'Well, we're working on an online platform that can spread information without being blocked by the Party authorities,' John explained.

'Is that really possible?'

'In theory, yes. We just need to constantly move our servers to avoid detection. Our aim is to ensure that any communication we release stays online for at least a day before it's taken down.'

'So, you're recruiting people who share our cause, using this method?' Hongbing asked, piecing together the strategy.

'Yes.'

'Then what?'

'We'll start from there. The key for us right now is to create awareness,' John stated firmly.

'And what role do I have in all of this? I might have experience in the semiconductor business, but I'm no computer programmer,' Hongbing asked again, trying to understand his fit into this plan.

'You can help us with creating materials that we will use for recruiting members.'

'Let's delve into the specifics, shall we?' Hongbing said, his voice carrying a renewed sense of purpose, invigorated by the hope of reuniting with his family, and the possibility of restoring Utopia.

The four began to put their heads together in the hacking hub. It made Hongbing think of the numerous—and what now seem ridiculous—meetings he had hosted at both UFITC and UF-Clanta. Unlike the Party meetings, however, he listened respectfully to what others said, and when he spoke, it was reciprocated with respect. They sat in the room and talked for hours.

'Okay. Next Sunday it is,' John declared after hours of discussion. 'Seven days from today.'

* * *

Ring!

The alarm clock went off in a fury. Hongbing jumped up from his bed, leaned over the bedside table and slammed it off with his palm. It was six in the morning, but Hongbing was already wide awake. He had been turning and tossing for quite a while. Exhilarated yet worried about what would transpire the coming day, his efforts to get a good night's sleep had failed miserably. His heart pounded rapidly throughout the night as though he had been injected with a free flow of caffeine. He opened the tiny window of the room he had been sleeping in, which had become his morning ritual in the last six days. Looking out to the distant mountains, as the cool autumn wind blew gently, and hearing the birds sing helped calm his nerves, he prepared himself for each new day in this mysterious new home. The chilly air this morning slapped Hongbing's cheek and cleared his head to prepare him for operation D-day.

In the shower, he saw himself in the mirror. Unhealed scars and bruises on his body were marks of small successes in his fight against the Party's hard-handed tactics and proved that he was no longer the loyal bureaucrat sheltered in a sterile office. He saw a rebel in his eyes, filled with bitterness and remorse for having unquestioningly played his part in the state's oppressive programme.

'Morning,' Dan greeted him as he walked into the hub. The programmer was already at his desk, biting into his second sandwich of the morning. John and Julie were also nibbling on sandwiches before computer screens, looking at the display panel that showed a digital timer.

27:42

'Twenty-seven minutes to action,' Julie said, looking at Hongbing sideways. 'Hurry, take a seat.'

'Now that we're all here, let me quickly run through our plan again,' John said, turning to face them. 'Dan's responsible for hacking into the OneAll platform for this region to create a link that will lead onto the foreign social media platform. Our goal is to get as many Fengshou and Tenfeng people as possible to read our encrypted message.'

'And that's when I intervene,' Julie said. 'And automatically provide encrypted VPNs for those who click the link that will directly transport the users to the foreign platform.'

'And I will then upload the message onto that foreign platform,' Hongbing finished.

'We have an approximate one-hour window before the Party catches up,' John continued. 'They'll probably counteract pretty much immediately once they find out what we're doing. Dan and Julie will try to disrupt and shut them down in cyberspace.'

'But even if they intercepted the message,' Dan said, 'they probably won't be able to decipher what it means.

'The message is full of jargon that only locals will understand. We'll only expose the corrupt practices of the Party when we see the people in person. And that's when the mascot of the Party will appear and expose the true nature of Utopia's reality,' Dan continued, looking at Hongbing.

The four sat before the screens and watched the timer descend fast. No one spoke. The risks were stacked high, and they had consciously refrained from delving too much into the consequences but chose only to skim through what could befall the group. Hongbing's hands were wet with sweat and his pulse was fired up. With the see-saw fluctuations in his emotions and pulse over the past weeks, he wouldn't be surprised if he wasn't prone to cardiac arrests soon. He hid his uneasiness and heaved in deep breaths.

'Counting down,' John said.

'Three'

'Two'

'One'

'Action.'

Dan's fingers flew across the keyboard as he worked his way through the Arcade's complex network of IT security systems. He was entering codes tirelessly for about five minutes, when suddenly his eyes glowed—he'd found a loophole in the system. He grinned as he typed even faster. After about another minute of furious typing, he looked up, smugly. 'Done. We're in.'

That was the cue for Julie and Hongbing to begin typing. Clearing his throat, Hongbing posted the message on the foreign platform.

> **Come to the well when the moon shines the dell,**
> **And leave behind the shadows of the quell.**
> **Drink the waters of the hallow,**
> **And let light lead your way to tomorrow.**
>
> **Emerge from your gloom,**
> **Let the light of hope bloom.**
> **Join the comrades of the glade,**
> **And slay the shadow with the new blade.**
>
> **So come to the well, and drink your fill,**
> **And let its drop guide you to the moor of heal.**
> **Let the moon fill your heart and blind you from the fears,**
> **And find the courage to persevere.**

The poem was written by the four—mainly by Hongbing—by picking up lines from anecdotes and old wives' tales specific to the town, that they had collated over the past few days. It was encrypted so only the villagers would figure out its meaning.

The well they were referring to in the message was a village library on the outskirts of Tenfeng town. During the Cultural Revolution, thousands had perished there to ascertain the Party's version of diversity decades ago. The people of Tenfeng were widely affected. The town was home to multiple prominent 'opponents' of the Party. They were cornered, pursued, and forced to jump into the well. To erase its record of brutality against civilians in this dark period of its history, the Party sealed up and subsequently demolished the well. A few years later, a library named after the first Party Leader was built on the site, for the 'welfare of the people', encouraging them to read and learn about the Party's core principles. Young people might not have even known the bloody period of the town's history, but the elders, and even Hongbing's generation, had some recollection. Ironically, it became a known venue among the local people. Communities met there to honour the memory of those who had suffered and died at the hands of the authoritative unfairness of the Party. But as time went by, the villagers began using the venue for casual purposes—to meet others for a cup of tea—transforming it into a sort of community centre of the town.

The posting also hinted that the gathering would take place in five days. The villagers would install stalls around the dell located in the centre of the town every fortnight, where they held a flea market to sell and exchange homemade goods and antiques. It had been a town tradition for the longest time, and it was called the Moon Market, as it usually ended up taking place when the new moon arose. The phrase, 'When the moon shines the dell' told villagers of the time of the gathering—as the Moon Market always opened at three o'clock in the afternoon, with the next market set to take place in five days.

'Okay, we're done posting,' John said as he glanced over Hongbing's shoulders at the screen where the post had successfully been uploaded. 'Julie, show me the number of viewers.' Julie nodded before filling the room with the clatter of her keyboard as she typed furiously. Her screen showed a tally of the users who had accessed the post. After about the first ten minutes, the tally started rising slowly.

'Well . . . that was a piece of cake,' Dan said with a smirk.

'Can't call it the great firewall any more,' Julie added.

The post stayed up longer than expected: for more than two hours. And the final tally showed that more than two thousand people had seen the post.

'Is that enough?' Dan asked John.

'Better than expected,' John muttered. It was hard to read him, Hongbing realized.

'We'll recruit more in the second phase of the mission starting from tomorrow,' John said as he stood up to leave the room.

'So . . . that's it?' Hongbing asked. 'That wasn't too dramatic. I was expecting us to shoot a movie.'

'Were we tracked?' Ignoring Hongbing, John turned to Dan and asked.

'No. Pretty sure we're clear,' Dan replied, lacing his hands behind his head and leaning back in his chair. 'Hope this makes a difference.'

* * *

Small, misty clouds of his breath ballooned before Hongbing as he walked briskly to the grocery store at the centre of the town. His body was crouched, head nudged in the upturned collar of his overcoat, taking cover from the morning chill. This had also become a recent default posture for him to escape the prying cameras even though surveillance was less intense in backward Tenfeng; he had learned to be highly vigilant regardless. His hands were shoved deep into the pockets of his outer coat. A thick roll of A4-sized flyers, tightly rolled up and secured by a sturdy yellow rubber band was peeping through his right pocket.

Two days had passed since the Resistance embarked on the operation that began in cyberspace. Since then, Hongbing and the three members had discretely gone around the nearby villages to put up flyers with similarly encrypted messages, hinting at the gathering that would take place when the Moon Market opened. Hongbing seldom thought of Li's role in this whole operation. Surprisingly, Li's name never came up during the planning or execution phases—perhaps it was intended that way. Hongbing just assumed that Li was overseeing everything, as he understood that important figures like Li needed to be kept safe in case of failure, to ensure the continuation of future operations. Recognizing this, Hongbing decided not to ask any questions to express his respect for Li.

The flyers were the second phase of the plan—a guerrilla tactic to spread awareness about the gathering, targeting the older generation, who were less inclined to use the internet.

There hadn't been a whiff of reaction from the authorities. He was relieved and somewhat emboldened by the possibility that the Party had yet to establish a full surveillance system in the town. The fact that he was still alive and able to move around freely was proof of this. He had been able to put up the flyers at several bus stops and community centre bulletin boards yesterday without any drama. Probably because the streets were quiet with hardly a soul around. This morning, he had checked the flyers and found them still on the boards, undamaged. *Maybe Tenfeng is the closest thing to a real utopia,* Hongbing thought. *Let's see if it will be as easy putting up flyers in the grocery store.* The chance of strangers seeing him putting up the flyers would be higher as would the risk of being caught. But it didn't seem to bother him as much, his motivation to complete the mission blunted his fear.

The grocery store was a single storey building with a pointy red roof. On one side of the shop front was a large window so people could see straight through. The parking lot in front of the entrance was small and empty with just a few cars scattered around. People greeted one another in the lot before walking up to the store. In this small town, everyone seemed to know each other. Next to the shop window was a large notice board, freely available for use by the townsfolk.

The notice board had only a few small service advertisements, leaving it mostly bare, with enough space for six flyers to be pinned side by side across two rows. He took out the rolled-up flyers from his coat pocket and pulled out about half a dozen pieces. He shook them out to straighten them, and the flyers fluttered gently in the breeze. Then, he straightened another ten pieces and folded each of them into half. Once he was done, he went into the grocery store. A few customers were there, choosing what produce to buy while keeping an eye on the short line at the checkout counter. He could hear the beeping of the cash register and the humming of display fridges. Looking around, he went straight to the shelf where cereal was stocked, a morning staple. He slipped a few flyers between the stacked cereal boxes before he moved on to the next aisle, where the sanitary products were stocked, and did the same. Quickly and effectively, he managed to distribute all the flyers he had throughout the store.

As he stepped out of the grocery store, he noticed a young man looking at one of the flyers on the notice board. The man was clean-shaven and bespectacled. He was reading the verses, probably trying to make out what was behind the words. His eyebrows furrowed and he stepped back in frustration, seemingly ready to give up the guessing game.

'Are you all right?' Hongbing couldn't help asking.

'Er . . . hello,' the man replied, not taking his eyes off the flyer. 'I'm just a bit confused here. You read this too?'

'Ah . . . What's this about? Let me give it a read,' Hongbing pretended. He intentionally furrowed his brow to give the impression that he was just as perplexed by its contents.

'Do you even get this?' the young man quizzed as he observed a baffled-looking Hongbing.

'Ah . . . It's a little confusing, I must admit,' Hongbing replied, scratching his forehead.

'When I first came across it at a bus stop night, I thought it was random poetry. Reading it again today it seems like there might be some message.'.'

'Oh, there's one at a bus stop too?'

'Yes, which made me think there could some meaning behind it.'

'Why do you say so?' Hongbing ramped up his acting skills. 'I mean, it could just be a poem.'

'A gut feeling,' the man said plainly, returning his gaze to the flyer. 'Otherwise, why would someone be spreading it all over the town?'

'Beats me. Could be just some kind of prank, I suppose.'

'Well, yes and no,' the man narrowed his eyes. 'This town is relatively surveillance-free. I'm sure whoever's putting this up is well aware of that.'

'So, you're suggesting that the person, behind the posters intends to communicate with us without being detected by the authorities? Why would they do that?'

'No idea. Maybe they want to do something under the table?'

'Do what?'

'Some activism of some sort?'

Hongbing stopped talking. The young man was perceptive, and it was impressive. But he had yet to get the juice—when and where the meeting was taking place.

'Hey, don't think I've seen you in this town,' the man said, offering his right hand to shake. 'I'm Brett. I am also quite new here. Just moved here three months ago.'

His newcomer status pricked Hongbing's interest.

'Oh, so you're new to here too?' Hongbing asked, his demeanour instantly becoming friendlier. However, he made sure not to disclose his name and pulled his cap down a bit further to avoid being recognized as a Party Hero. 'I'm also relatively new to the town. Nice to meet you,' he added. 'Hmm. . . I'm not entirely sure about the meaning of the verse, but . . .'

'You have some idea about it? Please share!' Brett said, his interest piquing. He didn't seem interested in knowing Hongbing's identity, with him not even bothering to ask for Hongbing's name as if he already knew him, or simply didn't care. His main focus appeared to be on figuring out the message. Watching Brett's struggle to decipher the message, Hongbing felt a surge of frustration. He started wondering what would happen if everyone in town found themselves similarly perplexed and chose not to attend the gathering. *That would mean failure.*

'I was just thinking . . .' Hongbing opened his pandora box, giving away some hints, 'Perhaps it's referring to the Moon Market? Just a wild guess of mine.'

Brett looked at the flyer again and fell silent. After a while, his eyes sparkled, and his mouth curled into a big grin.

'You're quite astute!' Brett said. 'I have lived in this town longer than you, yet I would never have made that connection!'

'It's just a guess. I may be mistaken.'

'Thanks! We'll meet again in a couple of days then,' Brett winked and slipped away into the shadows.

* * *

Finally, D-day arrived.

Hongbing woke up well before the first ray of sunlight hit his bed, feeling restless and lost in a whirlwind of conflicting emotions and thoughts. He was determined to make some changes in Utopia, but he also just couldn't help worrying about the possible consequences—for both him and his family—should the mission fail. He looked out of the window as he tried to soothe his nerves. The quiet of the mountains, the red and orange hues of the rising sun, and fallen leaves brought him that sense of calmness. Just like the trees that had shed their leaves with the passing season, he too had changed. Still, fear had penetrated deeply into his bones, like the leafless trees facing the brutality of icy winds. He shook his head to rid himself of his fear and jumped out of bed to layer himself with warm clothing. It was a big day and keeping himself warm was a sensible move.

Sealing off the fear, he rehearsed in his head what he had to say to the group of local people later in the day. He had meticulously planned every detail, down to writing out a full-text speech so that no issue, however insignificant, would be overlooked.

When Hongbing went downstairs, the members of the Resistance were already sitting in the living area, chatting. They kept the conversation light and casual, in spite of the heaviness surrounding them. Each one understood the gravity of the journey that they had embarked on, and nobody needed to express their uneasiness.

'Morning,' Julie greeted him. 'Ready for the big day?'

'Can't wait,' Hongbing replied, grinning, before he sat on a brown armchair to join them. On the table were a bunch of newly printed hand-outs that the group would distribute to the local people at the meeting. The handout detailed the Party's espionage activities on foreign entities and how it was using the people's personal data for stricter surveillance. Dan and Julie were busy folding the A4-sized hand-outs into half. John, looking over the two, did not speak a word.

'A little too serious there, John?' Hongbing tried to lighten up the mood. 'You look like someone on death row. Don't be too serious. Come, let's help them fold the hand-outs.'

'Oh . . .' John muttered as he quickly erased the anxiety—he had unconsciously expressed—from his face. 'Of course.'

'Nicely done, Hongbing,' Dan said. Hongbing winked at him.

As they folded the hand-outs together in the living room, they also went over the plan one last time—who was going to say what and how they were going to guide the people in the library. A feeling of solidarity and fraternity warmed up the house.

'So . . .' John said, wearing a determined face. 'I received a note from Li this morning.'

Before Hongbing was Li's handwriting on a piece of paper:

Go set a fire in their stronghold of control.

* * *

There was one more hour to go before the meeting. Hongbing was already making his way to town. The library was a short, fifteen-minute walk away, but he couldn't bear sitting and waiting in the house. The weight on his shoulders was simply unbearable. Not wanting to show his nervousness to others, he decided to take a walk before the meeting and told the others he'd meet them at the venue. *What happens if I get caught?* The constant fear of consequences lingered in his mind, bringing back memories of his days as a Party bureaucrat at UF-Clanta. He couldn't forget the expressions on his colleagues' faces when they blindly praised the Party and its leaders. If the Resistance didn't step in and protect the people, he worried that the people in Tenfeng would also one day be subjected to the same kind of indoctrination. The thought of more people being entrapped in the Party's quagmire fired him up. He would do whatever it took to stop that. It was his duty to speak out, to expose the lies that the Party brainwashed the people with. He needed to at least give people the right information so that they could choose based on their free will.

Taking a deep breath, Hongbing walked into an old pub at the corner of the street. The gentle lighting and weathered walls inside offered him with a sense of strange comfort. Embracing the scent of beer, mingled with cooked potato chips that was wafting through the pub, he ordered a glass of beer, before settling at a table near the fireplace. He then spaced out, watching the dancing flames cast flickering shadows on the walls. Only a handful of people were inside, creating just enough background chatter and giving the pub a comforting human touch. This was his moment.

He let comfort clear his mind for about half an hour. When he looked at his watch, he realized that the meeting was about to begin in fifteen minutes. He drained his glass, paid his tab and left the pub. As he turned the corner of the road that led to the library, he saw a familiar face standing in a narrow alley—Brett. He was facing the wall and smoking a cigarette. For some strange reason, he appeared nervous. *He's probably undecided about whether or not he should go to the meeting*, Hongbing assumed. *I should take him with me.* He raised his right arm to get Brett's attention and was just about to call his name when Brett spoke up. But he was facing the other end of the alley, his back towards Hongbing.

'Ma'am, this way,' Brett called nervously. He flicked the end of his cigarette to the ground and snuffed it out with his foot as a woman walked towards him. The shadowy figure passed him a thick brown envelope.

'Thank you. Thank you.' Brett replied, bowing his head, as he opened up the envelope that was filled with cash. His eyes glittered.

'I hope your information is accurate,' the woman whispered softly. 'We have all of our regional resources prepared for action.'

'You can count on me, ma'am,' Brett said with a sly grin on his face as he tucked away the envelope into his pocket. 'Several people confirmed that I've correctly deciphered the message.'

'Total number of contaminants joining today?'

'Not entirely sure, but I got it confirmed from more than twenty.'

'Good. Move back to the safe house and await further instructions.'

'Yes, ma'am'

No way. Hongbing sweated. He didn't have any time to waste. He turned back immediately to get back on the road to the library.

Crack!

A sharp noise filled the air. He had carelessly stepped on a discarded soft drink can. The flattened can made a sharp metallic noise, which reverberated through the dark alley. It reached Brett's ears, who turned around and saw him. Hongbing froze as Brett glared fiercely at him.

Brett slid his body towards Hongbing, growling as he threw a punch that cut through the chilly air between them. Hongbing's head jerked to the side as Brett's fist landed on his jawline. Falling to the ground, Hongbing briefly lost his vision as his head collided against the brick wall before landing on the pavement. A trickle of blood started to flow from the spot that had been injured previously, from when he'd fallen on the moving escalator at the station. As Hongbing opened his eyes he let out a groan of pain. Droplets of blood ominously dripped to the ground.

I don't have time for this, I must run and let them know we're exposed. But before Hongbing could turn his body towards the library, Brett's second attack came. A foot in a heavy boot was raised over Hongbing's forehead. In a burst of energy, Hongbing rolled to his left quickly to dodge. He also countered the attack by grabbing the agent's standing leg with his hands and then giving it a tug. Brett lost his balance, his body wobbling before stumbling sideways and collapsing to the ground with a loud thud. Both men grunted in pain but neither of them had time to be disoriented. Breathing heavily, they grappled and continued to throw punches at each other. Brett's body coiled like a spring around Hongbing, choking him. Brett's eyes were glowing with a sense of triumph as Hongbing beat his back furiously, gasping for breath. Hongbing wriggled as hard as he could to free his head from Brett's hands, which were around his neck. But his whole body was neutralized, as Brett was sitting, bearing down on him. He could not move his arms as his opponent's knees were pressing against them with force, pinning them to the ground. Brett was pressing against his hands with so much force that Hongbing could no longer feel them. That was when everything around him blurred, and his vision faded. He couldn't see that Brett was struggling as well, squeezing out the little energy he had left just to finish him off. Just before Hongbing lost complete consciousness, the glint of a metal cudgel lying in the corner of the alley caught his eye. Squeezing out his remaining energy, Hongbing stretched his arm, as hard as he could, towards the metal cudgel.

Thud!

Hongbing felt his neck being freed as the hands around it released their grip. As he swung the cudgel on Brett's head with all his remaining strength, the sickening sound of the cudgel striking Brett's scalp echoed through the narrow alley. Brett's head spun wildly before his entire body collapsed. Motionless, Brett lay unconscious, and a bright red pool of blood slowly spread and stained the ground.

Catching his breath between coughs, Hongbing stretched his body, lifting his head to breathe in the cool air as he pushed his hands against the ground to stand up. He stood still for a bit to regain some stability, as his head felt woozy, making him feel like he was floating in mid-air. *I don't have time for this.* Steady or not, he had to get moving, as there was no time to lose.

Hongbing sprinted as fast as he could to the library. His heart was racing, and he was feeling short of breath, but he dragged his heavy and sore body along—he must warn the Resistance members and people who might have come before the agents reached the library. Glancing at his watch he saw that it was already three o'clock, and he desperately hoped that he wouldn't arrive late. Sweat dripped down from his forehead, blurring his eyes but he had no time to wipe it off.

That overwhelming fear of putting the lives of his friends and others in danger weighed heavily on him. And when the library came into view, he knew he was there.

Boom!

Massive clouds of black smoke blanketed the sky before him, casting long, dark shadows over the library building, or what used to be it, as well as the surrounding areas. The structure was burning and crumbling as debris flew in all directions. Though he was at a safe distance from the sudden disaster, Hongbing lost his footing as the force of shock knocked him down backwards. Then, he heard people screaming.

* * *

Petrified, Hongbing dashed to the Resistance house and hid himself in the hacking hub. He was trembling so hard that it was like he had lost control of his body. Scenes of the massive clouds of smoke replayed endlessly in his head, overlaid by the sound of people screaming. The smell of ashes still remained in his nostrils, burning his heart from within. *This is all on me. It all began with a simple, careless mistake of mine.* Tears welled in his eyes as regret turned into fear and then to despair. Hongbing now realized that there was no way out. The Party was too powerful and almighty—truly unescapable. Feeling powerless, Hongbing hollered in despair. In front of him, eight computer screens said:

'You must come in to talk to us before it's too late.'

Chapter 8

Defiance

The green light on top of the multiple screens lit up. Hongbing perked up. He was certain that the Resistance members would have been careful to not leave any gaps for the enemy to infiltrate the network when they left the house. Obviously, their security was inadequate, and they were no match for the Party's capabilities—both physically and in cyberspace. All the Party needed was for an agent to slip into the house when they were at the library to lay the bugs. He shuddered, fearful and lost.

'Who are you? What do you want?' He asked defiantly, trying to fake courage in the face of his vulnerability. He had barely recovered from the shock of the fire. His pulse quickened from fear and anger.

'You don't need to know.'

The words appeared, letter by letter, with each click of the keyboard typing echoing across the silent room.

'The hell I don't! What have you done at the library?'

Silence.

'You need to come in now.'

The words appeared on the screen.

'Why?'

'Don't be stupid, Hongbing. Do as you're told.'

The typing accelerated in pace.

**'You're playing with fire. Don't tempt fate.
You know the drill and consequences.'**

Hongbing burst into a torrent of profanity, but the screens went blank and the room fell into darkness.

He simmered down soon, exhausted. He closed his eyes. Just days ago, this hub had been a perfect hideout and more. He had met and bonded with like-minded Utopians, regained confidence, and cemented his new calling. Their plan had been bullet-proof. But in his complacency, he had ruined a painstakingly built-up, resilient force and, worst of all, caused the lives of those who had bravely fought to end. All because of his folly. Tears rolled down his face. He wiped them off with the back of his hand. He would never know the extent of the damage. The Party would never reveal the truth. The Resistance, albeit quelled, was still a blemish. At a personal level, shame overtook him. He came from the system, a senior Party member who knew how it operated. He had carelessly let his guard down. The Resistance's technological expertise was impressive but how could he have forgotten the Party's ability to throw all of the state's resources behind whatever it set to achieve? The fact that Tenfeng wasn't as heavily surveilled as other cities and towns didn't mean the Party's reach was any lesser. Only days, if not weeks earlier, Hongbing had been the purveyor of such behaviour, which he had hardly considered wrong. He, of all people, should have smelled a rat, having adopted similar tactics to do his job at UF-Clanta. *It is as though the heavens are playing a prank on me*, he thought mournfully. What's more, the Party's strategy was deceptively simple and old-school. It preyed on what Hongbing coveted most at the time—soliciting like-minded warriors to fight the institution. All it had to do was deploy Brett, a spy. The fact that Brett could move easily despite Utopia's residence restrictions also meant that he had means that ordinary citizens didn't. Instead, he only saw what he wanted to see. Because of his presupposition, he now had blood on his hands and would carry the weight of this unforgivable sin for the rest of his life.

Flickering light from the screens brought him back to the present, putting a stop to the maelstrom of thoughts swirling in his head. Two of the screens flashed to a room set up with a podium with Utopia

State Information Council logo on the front. The camera then pulled back to capture reporters with their backs towards the camera entering the room. When everyone was seated and had settled down, the camera zoomed in to the podium where a council spokesman, whom he knew, had taken his place.

'Good evening, ladies and gentlemen, thank you for attending this briefing at such short notice. As such, this is an unexpected emergency. A fire broke out this evening in Tenfeng, a township in Fengshou town. We believe this was no accidental fire but the act of an arsonist. We have a person of interest who can shed light on the matter.

'In light of Utopian spirit where every citizen, every person, is assured their rights, we urge this individual to step forward as soon as possible.'

The spokesman looked intently into the camera. Hongbing could feel his eyes on him. They were cold and determined. *That's what you get when you turn against the Party*. But he was more taken aback by the Party's determination to nail him down, even at the risk of tarnishing its own reputation. The wrath of senior officials must have overpowered their reluctance to admit that they had picked the wrong hero. It was an unpredictable change of tack to coerce him.

'I don't need to remind you of the consequences of not acceding to our request. Party Hero or not, you'd be treated equally.'

'I will now take two questions,' the spokesman's cold eyes turned back to the floor where a sea of raised hands dominated the screen. 'Yes, Utopian TV.'

'Why did the arsonist set fire to a library? What people were there at the time of the fire? How many casualties?' asked the broadcast reporter.

'The matter is still under investigation. As far as we know, there were about twenty people gathered at the library. Most of them didn't make it; about five or six have been severely burned and are in critical condition. The doctors are doing their best. The next twelve hours will be critical for these good people and will decide whether they survive.'

He then pointed to another reporter at the far end of the room.

'I'm from Utopian Times, sir. Is the person of interest you mentioned a Party Hero? We have a credible source telling us that.'

'There should not be any speculation at this point. We urge the person of interest to come forward and help in our investigation.'

With that, the spokesman left the podium, and the screens went blank once more. Although the spokesman had refrained from revealing his identity, it was clear all hands were now on deck to find him. The scariest bit about the United Front strategy was that you could never be certain of the extensiveness and expansiveness of the covert network. It straddled the line between the white and black territories, between the ones that upheld the law and the ones that didn't. Additionally, they had millions of sympathisers who acted as the eyes and ears of the Party.

About ten seconds later, all the screens lit up again, as well as the cameras.

'You need to come in as soon as possible.'

'Why are you doing this to me? I did not start the fire!'

'All the more reason for you to come in so that we can clear this up.'

'How can I trust you? You already maligned me at that briefing.'

'No identification was made. Unless you are guilty . . .'

But Hongbing knew the Party didn't have to explicitly drag his name through the mud; his reputation was already crushed. He stood no chance with Utopia's propaganda machine at work.

'What do you want from me? You've already taken my best friend and my family!'

'Are you sure you'd call him your best friend? And your wife?'

'What do you mean?' Hongbing screamed. He was clearly exhausted by the process of obtaining information.

The screens didn't respond to his last question.

'Turn yourself in within twenty-four hours or you'll regret it.'

He felt dejected and hopeless. Yet, another part of his mind refused to give up. *What can I do? What other options do I have?*

And then, the most incredible thing happened. The screens began playing a video. Rather, it was a badly pieced montage of surveillance videos that had been rudimentarily edited and joined together.

As he watched, his jaw dropped. He was the star of the video. It opened with him waiting for his train at the Link and the dreaded conversation with Jane, and his look of disdain at her state of being. He noticed the stark contrast in expression he had after he was out of Jane's orbit. He was smiling and jostling down the Kilgate, his feet never touching the ground. He could only see a bright future then. He now cringed with shame. The video continued, showing his meetings with Lan and Yuan. There was no other interpretation—he was all but the submissive subordinate, frantic with worry when attempts to find out about Yiping were abruptly repudiated. *The replayed scenes amplify how enslaved I was to the Party*, he thought miserably. The person he was viewing was a stranger. Then came a jump cut. It was a scene of a meeting with his assets, and he was reprimanding their work.

In it, he was bellowing at his subordinates, and just short of a torrent outburst of profanity.

'What do you mean you can't get deeper intel about Clanta? There are countless ways, and you have all done it before!' He went on to list the tactics used: bugging the Korean partner's offices and planting microcameras, deploying spies in the offices and households of senior Korean executives, paying off individuals within the Korean community to rat on the executives and so on. Almost everything was achievable as long as one was willing to pay. And Utopians were never stingy on this front. By the same token, Hongbing also never left any stone unturned. It had been the norm to him, even with friends. He surrounded Jay Kang with his people so that he could keep things in order and be informed of the very minuscule details. He was unabashed about it too. He took comfort in the assumption that Jay acted likewise.

Now that he was on the receiving end, it certainly didn't feel normal or acceptable. He regretted that he could not turn back the hands of time. Henceforth, he would always carry this inglorious past with him and, one day the sheer weight of the guilt might bury him. In his soul, there'd always be a furious debate that would rage till the end of his time.

The video shifted to a haggard and unsettled Hongbing on the run in Fengshou. Face pale, eyes tired and bracketed with dark circles, he was seen walking up Li's front porch. The scene meant Li was probably implicated. His heart sank. 'There's a theory that goes, a Party member is never alone,' Li told him as they bade farewell, urging him to be careful.

Another jump cut in the video transformed the scene to a dimly lit bar, where the silhouettes of the backs of a man and a woman came into focus. The camera panned towards the front of the couple. The woman's head was resting on the man's shoulder, her arm snuggling into his. They were intimate and looking at each other, laughing. As Yiping bent his head towards Sara, the camera cut away to another scene, mercifully sparing him another bout of pain. Or not. He was made aware of Sara's betrayal when the United Front Prosecution officials came to pick her up at their flat, but to see her infidelity with his own eyes was not something any spouse would be emotionally prepared for. Worse still, her lover was his long-time buddy. He felt deflated, beaten and weary; the footage he had seen so far was like a sharp knife twisting his stomach.

Before he had sufficient time to digest his wife's extramarital affair, the video moved to another scene. In an abandoned warehouse, Yiping was seen meeting the Chief Research and Development Officer of the US's biggest semiconductor maker, where he handed the American engineer a USB flash drive.

His mind was now swirling, and his pulse quickening. He was overwhelmed by the leverage the Party had on him, truth or otherwise. The leverage was carefully nuanced, as it did not rely on direct action or evidence against Hongbing, but rather on the personal and moral ties to Yiping. But he knew better than anyone that the Party could manipulate these ties to destroy everything—his name and his family. It dawned on him that the content could have been fake, as the scale of disinformation—if it was so—was modest and could easily be produced with deepfake applications and AI technology. But would the Party pour so much of their resources into breaking him? He wasn't sure any more. All he knew was that the technology—which he had once been immensely proud of—had become his biggest threat.

The video finally ended with the screen flashing with the following words:

'You need to come in immediately. You have twenty-four hours.'

As if on cue, Hongbing forced himself out of whatever emotional turmoil he was experiencing. He must move quickly or face captivity. The truth was he was at wit's end. He gritted his teeth and tried his utmost to figure out the next step. A plan was out of the question; the next shelter was more probable and pressing. He ran his eyes around the room, desperately searching for inspiration. All he saw were screens, filled with warnings for him. The green light on the centre screen remained on, which meant he was still being watched. It was alarming how technology controlled one's life. Without a mobile phone, he felt lost and stumbling. There was no way out except to turn back and retrace his path. Ideally, he would like to see Li again. The wise professor might just have another solution. Realistically, however, it was a risk as Li was in the video, which meant the Party would have tracked him down. And all because of him. Tears welled up and he rubbed them off his eyes with the back of his palm. As apologetic as he was, he would have to seek out Qian and Ai-hua again for an interim shelter.

With the state's eyes still on him, he crawled towards the side of the room, in the hope that sucked into the darkness, his movement would be captured less precisely. He grabbed a baseball cap left on one corner of the desk along the way. With his back firmly against the wall, he crab-walked slowly towards the door.

* * *

The image of a smiling and kind Li dominated his mind on the way back to Qian and Ai-hua's place. The journey seemed much longer than it actually was, stretched psychologically by Hongbing's heavy heart. The night was long and there were moments when his mind was blank; when he kept walking but his legs didn't feel like they belonged to him. The scenery along the way was also different. A cool autumn breeze was blowing, and a full moon illuminated the path ahead. Alas, he saw only darkness, without any light at the end of the passage. He only hoped Qian and Ai-hua wouldn't be implicated, that they would be saved.

Several hours later, he turned onto the gravel pathway leading to Qian's house. A small porch light was lit up, but the house was dark. Except for the occasional chirp of crickets, the small estate was eerily quiet. He reached the porch and knocked softly on the door, and waited. The master bedroom windows at the far end were open, which meant Qian and Ai-hua should be home. But thirty seconds passed, then fifty, and there were no signs of life. Nor did anyone answer the door. He circled the exterior of the house and peered through the bedroom windows. In the moonlight, he saw no one in the room and the bed looked untouched, neatly covered by the bedspread. He moved back to the living room window. In spite of the darkness, he noticed that the mugs on the coffee table were toppled, and books and files were scattered on the floor as if there had been a scuffle. Suddenly, the worst thought seized Hongbing. He dashed back to the front door, and this time, he pounded on it, hard. He called out the couple's names and reached for the doorknob. He was surprised when the door opened. He fumbled for the light switch by the door. Lit up, he surveyed the living and dining area, where books and papers were splayed across the floor. Photo frames were cracked and swept to the corner of the living room. He was too late. *The Party took them*, he thought miserably as he slumped down onto the floor. His very existence was an affront to the Party. And it had been made crystal clear to him. Everyone who had helped him had disappeared, vaporized into thin air.

This time, he was totally deflated. It was either he gave himself up or forever be on the run. Reluctant to compromise his newfound values, the latter would be a preferred route but without money or means, it meant relying on the kindness of communities he would come across. It also meant implicating more innocent people. He cupped his head, ruffled his hair in utter frustration and agony while grieving, silently. If he went back to the origins, this was all the doing of the chip, a double-edged sword. For all that technology could achieve in propelling societal advancement, it can equally raze the goodness of humanity when put in the wrong hands. Like it or not, he was part of that enabling system of destruction. *But what is humanity?* If the video was authentic, Yiping clearly showed there wasn't much. Gradually, curled up in the corner of Qian's living room, between the bookshelf and a windowed low wall where the moon's rays beamed through, his body was pulled to the ground by gravity, and he fell asleep.

It wasn't until the next morning that Hongbing recalled his conversation with Qian. 'Ai-hua, we should put your toast and jam in the Store,' the old man had said, pointing at a drawer in the kitchen. He told Hongbing that it's where the couple kept their valuables, as they didn't trust the Party, thus didn't use banks. Rushing to the kitchen, Hongbing opened up all the drawers in the kitchen. An enormous stash of cash, likely the accumulation of the wealth of the couple's entire lives, laid before him—perhaps enough for what the fisherman at Eastport Harbour wanted for smuggling.

* * *

He was at the pier in Eastport Harbour. He was pacing up and down with impatience, but stopped as a diesel-powered vessel came into sight. His eyes steadily followed the vessel, which came to a temporary stop. He handed a black duffel bag to the fisherman, who was now the boat's captain. As Hongbing jumped on board, he unzipped the bag and scrutinized the contents, before nodding cunningly at his customer. He walked back to the bridge, swerved the vessel around, and sailed off. The sea breeze caressed Hongbing's face as the vessel motored towards the open sea. He experienced a tremendous gush of relief as he sat on the damp deck, and his eyes felt heavy.

He was suddenly awakened by commanding orders blasted from a loudspeaker. 'Vessel 889, stop where you are!' His glazed eyes travelled choppily towards a bright light from an approaching vessel.

'I repeat, Vessel 889, turn off your engine immediately. This is Utopia Coast Guard.'

Two officials jumped onto the vessel's deck and made their way towards Hongbing, swiftly holding him down on his front. One of them twisted his arms around his back and handcuffed him while the other went to the wheelhouse to cuff the fisherman.

'Get off me!' he shrieked at the top of his voice, forgetting that no one would hear his plea in the middle of the ocean. 'You have no right to arrest me! Turning to the fisherman, 'Tell them, we are just going out to fish, right?'

'Bah, you've caused me enough trouble,' his accomplice retorted.

'I did nothing wrong!' Hongbing continued to protest, struggling to shake off his captor's hold on his shoulders and kicking his legs in the air. 'I'm a Party Hero!'

'I don't care who you are,' the Coast Guard told him firmly. 'We are just acting on orders from the above. Keep quiet or we'd add on with the charge of obstructing the police from performing our duty.'

In terror, Hongbing woke up, screaming, twisting, and turning his body forcibly. His head was heavy and spinning, and he broke out in cold sweat. He laid still for a moment, staring at the ceiling, trying to catch his breath. As he was taken to the Coast Guard's ship, it all came back to him. He sat up, his face ashen with fear. Outside, the wind was blowing gently in the darkness. The moon was still up. He guessed he must have dozed off for about two hours at the most, as his body had now been conditioned to sleep light.

'Good morning, my Party Hero,' a woman's high-pitched voice called out from the pier as the ship began to embark. He glanced out of the window, and it was still dark. He turned to look at his watch— five o'clock in the morning.

The woman emerged from the shadows and stood in front of him. In her super high-heeled shoes, she towered over his defeated frame. Only his eyes could move up as his head and neck were sore and heavy. It was the woman agent he'd seen paying money to Brett. *That's it. I'm done.*

'What do you want? How can I be of service?' he gnashed at her.

'No different from the first instance. We just need you to come with us to sort out some queries we have.'

'Like I've told your people umpteenth times, no! Unless you show me the papers that you're formally charging me with.'

'Don't be silly! How can we be laying charges on our Party Hero?' she told him snidely. 'We would just like you to help with our investigation. Come with us and it'll be over soon,' she said and broke into laughter.

'No!'

'Don't make this more difficult for yourself, and the good people of Tenfeng. If you had been cooperative when we extended the invitation to your home in Unitas, none of what ensued after that would have happened. The Central Station, Qian and Ai-hua, and the Library,' the woman worked on his guilt. 'And oh, dear old Professor Li.'

'Argh!' Hongbing screamed. 'Haven't you done enough? What did you do to Professor Li?'

The female agent broke into a fit of conniving laughter. She stopped, her eyes glowering at him. 'Will you come or not?'

He shut his eyes and turned his face away in defiance. He figured that he couldn't repair the damage caused, and there was no basis for the Party to act out against more people—strangers he had no prior engagements with.

She nodded to a young male agent who had accompanied her. The young man retrieved a syringe and a vial of medicine from a metal case he was carrying. He stuck the needle into the vial and pulled the plunger to draw the medicine as Hongbing watched in horror. He was completely helpless, alone in this dark house in the middle of nowhere. His vision became hazy. His senses numbed, the woman's face blurring until all he could see were her crimson lips, and the noise of everything receding until all he could hear was her demonic laugh, echoing within the four walls.

Then, darkness dawned.

Chapter 9

The Ultimate Utopia

With his limbs restrained and eyes covered, Hongbing walked along the corridor of the detention centre. Each step sent a stab through his ankles as the tight chains dug into his skin. At times the pain was so intense that it numbed his senses.

His captors couldn't care less. 'Pick up the pace!' the guard next to him yelled, prodding him roughly with the tip of a baton, which he swung menacingly in the air as a show of his power over the fallen Party Hero. As the baton swung to and forth, it crushed one of Hongbing's shoulder blades as he raised his head to stretch his stiff neck. He yelped in agony. He rubbed his shoulder and felt a nano piece of metal that had been embedded under a bumpy piece of skin.

'What's that under my shoulder?' he shouted and stopped in his tracks, infuriating the guard even more.

'Those who betray their country shall not dare to look upon its sky! Move!' roared the guard. Hongbing resisted and stood still, grounded his feet firmly with some support from the heavy tight chains around them. 'What is under my skin?'

Exasperated, the guard reluctantly said, 'That's a chip, okay. Like the ones humans injected into their pet dogs to keep track of them. Satisfied?'

'What kind of chip is this?' he pressed.

'How would I know? You are the semiconductor company's big boss, you would know what UF-Clanta chips do. Now, quit asking and get moving. We're almost there.' With that, the guard gave him a hard push forward. He almost tripped as his mind was occupied by the pathetic irony that the chip whose production he oversaw was now forcibly inserted in his body—his fate forever linked with UF-Clanta.

'Stop there!' After about twenty steps forward under excruciating torment of body and soul, he was abruptly ordered to halt. The guard tore off his face hood and he found himself in front of a heavy iron door, wide enough for one person to enter at a time. He gulped, and a shiver ran down his spine as goosebumps prickled his skin. This could be it, the end. Execution.

Click.

The door opened.

Then, another click went off, like one of a gun being cocked.

'Come in,' an authoritative voice commanded from the room. He was too frightened to move. But the guard gave him a big push and then shut the door behind Hongbing.

A man in his forties, dressed in a suit, whose face was covered by a cloud of cigarette smoke, sat at a table. Another chair was placed on the opposite side of where the man sat. He paid no attention to Hongbing as his eyes were on the documents laid out across the table.

'Come forward,' he ordered Hongbing towards the table. He then tossed a piece of paper in front of him, followed by a black pen. 'Sign it,' the man demanded.

'Just for the sake of formality,' continued the man. 'In case the Village's existence is ever revealed. You don't have a say in this. Let's get it done quickly.'

Hongbing slowly pulled the document towards him.

MEMORANDUM OF UNDERSTANDING
SURVEILLANCE AND USAGE OF STATE DATA

Effective immediately

Between

Shan Hongbing (referred to as the 'Participant')

and

Utopian Government (referred to as the 'State')

---

1. SURVEILLANCE SCOPE

The Participant willingly relinquishes all rights to their data regarding their behaviours, locations, communications, and interactions (detailed in Appendix I) to the State. The Participant agrees to the State's implementation of a surveillance programme within the United Front Village surveillance zone. This scope remains valid indefinitely or until death.

2. DATA UTILIZATION

The Participant consents to the State's collection, storage, analysis, and utilization of gathered data for advancement and control. This is not limited to security measures, scientific research, policy making, and law enforcement, but also extends to other State interests, defined at the discretion of the State.

3. PRIVACY WAIVER

By entering into this Agreement, the Participant explicitly waives any national or international privacy claims concerning their data. This waiver also encompasses the waiving of any privacy protections that would otherwise be granted to the Participant.

4. TERMINATION

Termination of this Agreement can only occur through a written document signed by both parties involved—the State and the Participant.

Participant   Government Representative

_____   _____

[Please fill in your name or   [Please fill in the name or title of
identifier]   the government representative]

* * *

It, at its first glance, looked no different to other regular villages in Utopia.

The houses and roads on the street somewhat resembled those in Tenfeng, sadly reminding Hongbing of the one he temporarily called *home* a few days ago, a place that was probably burned and had now turned to ashes. The sound of chatter and laughter echoed through his head as he slowly walked around this eerily familiar-looking terrain— the Village. The air was thick with nostalgia, as though the very atmosphere held fragments of his past. Time seemed to have stood still in this idyllic corner of the world.

No. This is only an illusion.

As Hongbing explored his surroundings further and became more acquainted with them, he noticed the stark contrasts between this place and his *home* outside. The level of surveillance was a different level, something he had never experienced before. The sights, sounds and everything he experienced in the Village was like a thick pervasive fog, hanging in the air that refused to dissipate.

The rooftops of the townhouses lining the streets displayed a uniform splash of red. Actually, to be fair, they ranged from the deepest crimson to the most vibrant orange, representing the maximum extent of diversity approved by the Party. The range of reds and oranges emphasized how this artificial community took pride in embracing differences—a display of diversity within a sense of unity.

A few people were shuffling down the streets. No uniforms of any type like the UniDress to monitor emotions and thoughts were required. Everyone could wear what they wanted. But there was an air of detachment; people maintained blank looks. Each step that was taken appeared as though it was driven by an invisible force; an automation following a predetermined path. They didn't know their destination, but went on, without a purpose or intention. Their homogenous silence screamed hideously at Hongbing.

The deafening silence became even more overwhelming as he turned the corner and entered a main boulevard, a busy street, in the Village. Many people were walking quietly along both sides of the road, with their faces looking somewhat gloomy. Each person seemed lost in their own world; many walked alone. What surprised him was the sheer number of individuals who had been exiled to the Village. He guessed that there could be hundreds of people like him, victims from all over Utopia, trapped in this place. The realization that he could have had more allies in his fight was just too painful to accept.

He reached the end of the main boulevard and turned into a narrow lane lined with small houses, which gently sloped upwards, before descending just as gradually. He walked all the way to the last house with a red pointy roof, his designated dwelling for, probably, the rest of his life.

Whirr!

A mechanical clatter-sounding object approached him as he unlatched the tiny gate leading into the small garden in front of the one-storey house. Hongbing stopped to look for the source of that rather irritating noise. A small, futuristic-looking ball had rolled close to his right foot, with a red blinking light, just like the one in most CCTVs. It was sleek and minimalist in design. *This orb-shaped object is probably packed with multiple sensors and cameras*, he thought, knowing the Party. It would be menacing and intrusive, but he would have to live with it. His every movement would be monitored, recorded, and fed into the central database on human behaviour. Just the thought of his data contributing to sharpening the system's artificial intelligence technology, amplifying the state's capacity for autonomous surveillance and therefore stricter control of Utopian society, sickened him to the core.

'I see that you've met your Sphere,' cackled an old man with a wrinkled face, leaning over from his side of the garden fence. *A nosy neighbour. As though my life isn't scrutinized enough.* He ignored the old man, who went on.

'Even when you're sitting on the toilet bowl or washing your back in the shower, it's going to be your shadow, mate. Prepare to adapt!' The old man's enthusiasm was seriously annoying, but Hongbing was curious about how he remained sane and energetic in this claustrophobic environment. He was about to open his mouth, but the old man beat him to it.

'Oi, fresh meat! What juicy state secret did you spill to land yourself in this paradise?'

'Didn't do a bloody thing wrong,' Hongbing shot back.

'Ha! That's a familiar joke! In this crazed asylum, everyone is a helpless bunny!' He laughed heartily at his own joke. Hongbing didn't respond.

'I bet you're dying to know where in the heck you are right now,' The man went on. 'Welcome to the Party's brand-new laboratory for studying human behaviour! Just so you know, I'm Aron.'

'It's like . . . the future of Utopia, you know?' Aron went on. 'It's all about the progress they've made in surveillance and behavioural analysis.' Then, pointing to the Sphere, the man continued, 'And this thing will totally capture every little detail of your life, like absolutely every tiny nuance. You should just totally get used to having it around.'

'And how do you manage that?' Hongbing asked bitterly, he just couldn't resist.

'Manage what?'

'You seem . . . not like the others . . . I mean, you seem to be keeping your individuality quite intact. That's odd.'

'Oh, that? It's a piece of cake!' Aron exclaimed again with his trademark grin. 'You just need to keep in mind that the Spheres are here to analyse your every idiosyncrasy, including your ability to form an alliance and fight back. The Party is relying on the Village to provide all the information to suppress any uprisings in the outside world.'

Confused, Hongbing just stared at him in silence. He didn't really answer Hongbing's question. Aron simply stared back intently at Hongbing. After a little pause, Aron broke the silence, 'Dingdong! That's right, that means you just have to act naturally and can do whatever the hell you want! The more freedom you give yourself, the more information the Party has to control people's actions outside! So, in the end you're freer here!'

'You're quite chuffed about it all, aren't you?'

'Of course, I am! Why wouldn't I be? Think about it, greenhorn! As a Party experiment, you will enjoy greater autonomy here than everywhere else. Oh, by the way, you're not completely free though, bear in mind. Sometimes the Spheres go all disco on you, flashing red lights before the guards swoop in and clip your wings. I've seen people pushing their limits here several times. Still trying to figure out what's acceptable and what's not.'

'You're completely out of your mind.'

'Ah . . . a rebel here, huh? Take a look around, greenhorn. Everyone is trying to hold themselves in check, and it shows. Can you imagine being under continual surveillance for good? That's why they're all looking so miserable! Before I had this epiphany, I had been one of them for several years. You owe me one for sharing this pearl of wisdom!'

'Several years?' Hongbing was stunned. Now he understood that the Party had planned for everything. It also clarified why Aron had initially failed to recognize him. Aron was already a guinea pig in this lab before he became a Party Hero. At that moment, his mind flashed back to his discussion with Li about the high-tech detention centre. The realization hit him—he was indeed in that very place. A flicker of unexpected hope ignited within him. This could mean that Sara and his daughter might be held here too.

'Have you met a woman named Sara around here?' he asked.

'Sara . . . who?' returned the puzzling response.

'Sara, is it?' A third person appeared from the lane, her Sphere following her like an obedient little pet.

Hongbing's pupils dilated. 'Do you know her? Is she in the Village? Have you also seen a young girl with her?'

'No no,' the woman murmured. 'I've only heard the name a couple of times in the past.'

'So, they're not here? Where did you hear about Sara?'

'I used to work for the UF's espionage investigation division. My coworker was looking into a case and that person's name came up.'

'That was before our Phoebe here decided to peddle Utopia's top state secrets to foreign buggers, wasn't it?' Aron added, smiling smugly.

'Oi!' Phoebe shot back at Aron, 'Hold your horses. He was a scholar, not a foreign agent.'

'Yes, sweetheart, take that explanation to your next trial. Oh, just for your information, those aren't available in the Village, are they?' Aron broke into a fit of laughter.

'Stop talking nonsense!' Phoebe's tone was no longer playful as she raised her voice. 'I didn't betray any of you. All the professor cared about was how Utopia's bureaucracy works. I only gave him a high-level overview. Simply said, it's a beginner's guide to Utopian society, which could be found on bloody Wikipedia!'

'Blimey! Urgh, the Anti-Spying Act, eh?' Aron's voice was tinged with cynicism.

'So, what's the word in the office about her?' Hongbing interjected. 'I'm her husband, by the way.'

'Ah, umm . . .' Phoebe hesitated.

'I already know about her fling,' he assured her. 'I am past the point of being surprised. Just give it to me straight.'

Phoebe murmured, biting her bottom lip, 'Well, word around town is . . . she's been rubbing shoulders with the Shi camp.'

'Shi? You mean *the* Shi?' Hongbing's brows furrowed in surprise.

'Yep, mate,' Aron cut in, not wanting to be left out of the gossip conversation. 'The Party Leader's biggest political rival!'

Phoebe reclaimed the narrative and continued, 'They claimed that she was feeding insider information on Clanta to Shi's top political aides. Apparently, the intel was dug up by her husband. You.

'My colleague was given the greenlight from the Top Office to investigate. The Top Office suspected that Shi was trying to sell the Korean blueprint to the highest bidder to raise money and support the Party Leader's political rival.'

'How long was your colleague involved in this case?' Hongbing probed, his gaze fixed on Phoebe the entire while.

'Yiping was deeply immersed in that project for years collaborating closely with Sara.'

'Wait, who now?'

Hongbing was stunned to hear that name. If what Phoebe was relaying were true, Sara could have been manipulated and strung along like a worthless puppet.

It was becoming clear that the affair was not a coincidence. Rather, it sounded like a carefully planned UF operation, targeting those opposing the Party Leader's internal power grip. He was all too familiar with these tactics of the Party. He just never anticipated that these same tactics would be turned against him and his family. And like a bolt of lightning, his rage surged back, blazing like a storm within him. He had imagined himself to have been among the best, a key player in the game, one of the ruling elites, but in reality, he was nothing more than a silly pawn, who only needed a little flattery to feed his small ego enough to jump into the fire for the Party. He was only a puppet.

'Who was pulling the strings?' Hongbing asked, quivering in anger.

'What, now you expect me to start rattling off the names of the bigwigs? A bit too much, don't you think?' Phoebe responded, frowning.

'Just tell me. Why the hell do I have to be caught in the middle of some sort of power play between the high and the almighty?'

'What . . . You want the name of the person who greenlit this operation?'

'Yes.'

'And what can you possibly do? Roast that person alive?' Aron mocked.

'Come on, let it all out. I need to know,' Hongbing wailed.

'Well, I'm stumped, but if we're talking about authority,' Phoebe said thoughtfully. 'Wouldn't it be up to . . . the Party Leader?'

Beep. Beep.

A sharp, piercing noise thundered through Hongbing's eardrums. Red beams burst out from the centre of all three Spheres, muting the three. The beams targeted their heads, chests, and legs, like snipers zeroing in on their fields. All three froze, unsure and fearful of what could transpire.

Nee-naw!

They heard a piercing siren, and a police car of sorts, likely from the Village's law enforcement body, drove to a stop in front of them. Two burgundy-uniformed men jumped out of the car, their faces flushed with misguided passion and enthusiasm, with a smug look as keepers of the villagers. He felt an impulsive urge to shout at them, but he was wary of the red beam pointed at his forehead. He kept his mouth shut, as he watched the two men approach their small group. 'Social Ideology Management', the emblems on their clothing read. He gasped when he saw their faces. One of them was a familiar face. Hongbing felt like he was looking at a ghost of the past.

'Hello there,' Muchen from the car rental shop greeted, smirking at him.

Hongbing's heart skipped a beat as the name burned in his mind. *Muchen. Why is he even here?*

'Looks like you remember me?' Muchen's voice brought him back from space.

Hongbing went silent.

'All are free to do whatever you want here,' Muchen proclaimed loudly. 'Everything you do will be analyzed, and the Party will use the results to improve our social well-being. Thanks a lot for your service.'

He paused a bit to check Hongbing's reaction, before continuing, 'But . . . there are rules,' Muchen's eyes glowed intensely. 'Never, ever speak ill of the Party Leader. If you don't follow the rules, you will lose your chance to serve the people. Trust me, you don't want to find out where disobedience will lead you.'

The threat was crystal clear.

'There will be three warnings before you are kicked out. You have just been served one each,' Muchen continued, with an evil grin. The sleepy and blurred-looking face he wore at the car rental store was simply to cover the real him.

Muchen then knelt down and slid his badge across the three Spheres. The sensors picked up the data and retracted the threatening red beams.

'Okay. Behave well guys. You better hope not to see us again!'

'Wait,' Hongbing shouted, spurred by an unexplained wave of courage, surprising Muchen who stopped short and turned around. 'How did you . . . end up here?'

'Oh, don't you know, Party Hero?' Muchen grinned crookedly.

'From the moment I saw you, I knew you had turned against us. I did what any upright citizen in Utopia would do.'

'What happened to Jin?' Hongbing fumed as the weight of remorse forced his voice to crack.

'Gee, what do you think?' He giggled evilly.

'Jin was a real tough guy. He wouldn't break, or tell us where you were, not even under all that interrogation. He was thoroughly brainwashed by you.'

'That's because he truly had no idea where I was!' Hongbing shot back, his cheeks flushed with rage. 'Are you serious about wanting to be a part of this system?' He jeered. 'You're wasting your time trying to be a player here. You'll never make it.'

'What an uplifting speech!'

'Where is Jin now?'

'He's gone.'

Gone? Those words powerfully knocked him out.

'Thanks to you, criminal. You also gave me this chance, a chance to serve the people.' Muchen waved goodbye and the police car drove off.

* * *

The following few days were a living nightmare. Hongbing had already seen enough unnecessary deaths, but swallowing another was still unbearable, especially when it was a direct consequence of his action. He holed himself in the new fancy cage he was now forced to call home for the rest of his life. He didn't eat and could not sleep. He had manipulated Jin, in fact, he consciously, shamelessly strategized at the time on how to do so. In hindsight, he never considered anyone else but himself, never thought about the consequences that might befall Jin. He was also arrogant, to the point where he fully believed he wouldn't get caught. And for his part, Jin was oblivious to his agenda and believed him until his final moments. Every time he closed his eyes, he could hear Jin's sobs, his cries for help echoing in his ears. The young man had been a faithful and model Utopian citizen, a paragon of the common folk who never questioned the authorities, but the Party didn't even afford him a second chance. Such was the value of people's lives. He stayed sequestered in this thought prison, punishing himself relentlessly.

Hongbing found himself spiralling deeper into a complex tapestry of the very nature of these political charades of Utopia. The more he delved in, however, the simpler it turned out to be: the Party's hypocrisy. No other places symbolized the Party's hypocrisy better than the Village. It was the only place he knew in Utopia that was bereft of those mind-numbing slogans. You could typically spot 'Uniformity is Diversity,

Conformity is Harmony, Prosperity is Freedom' emblazoned on every street corner, and in every public building in the country, but not here, not in this peculiar freedom zoo. Aron was correct. For all its monitored existence, the Village was paradoxically the freest space in Utopia, except for the Spheres' incessant vigilance curtailing liberties to some extent. It was laughably ironic—freedom afforded only to let the Party study its criminals, or rather, people with questions whom it considered strayed from Utopian ideology and values, unhindered, collecting a rich harvest of behavioural data. Diverse behaviours, including the rebellious ones, were valuable assets to the empirical research that served to justify its cause to tighten its grip more on its citizens. But the fun stopped at challenging the Party Leader and his supremacy. The minions, in their misplaced allegiance, must have set this parameter to display their loyalty. A true empirical study for comprehensive societal control would have necessitated total freedom to capture the broadest spectrum of behavioural data.

The blatant contradictions were not just confined to the Village alone. Even the Party, which unceasingly advocated the virtues of uniformity was, in fact, a diverse entity within, filled with factional political infighting. The existence of Shi's political faction, overlaid with constant power struggles conflicted starkly with the Party's claims on unity. This boded the question—how can it enforce conformity when the Party leaders were discordant among themselves? *How can such convoluted politics serve the people's glory?* It was all an elaborate game, where bureaucrats and key political figures were the masters of that game. There was only one winner in the journey to build the New Utopia and bring glory to the people, that was the Party which claimed its complete representation of all Utopians. The Utopian dream was all but a smokescreen masking the top Party echelons' selfish ambitions.

Knock! Knock! Knock!

A persistent knocking disrupted Hongbing's solitude. From that light and cheery rhythm, he had no doubt it was Aron. Besides, neither did he have any friends in the Village nor would anyone know or care where he lived. Wanting to rest, he felt reluctant to open the door.

All he wanted now was to be left alone and wallow in self-pity, which he reckoned was a necessary stage to face himself going forward.

But the knocking wouldn't stop, and then Aron's voice came booming through, 'Hey Hongbing, time to get some sun. Open the door and let me in.'

It's either he got up to open the door or lived with that endless knocking.

'Hello, neighbour!' Aron greeted him cheerfully as he came to the door. His accompanying Sphere turned its camera lens towards Hongbing, tilting slightly, like a curious dog meeting its master's friend.

'Good to see you're still alive!' Aron exclaimed. 'Well, I knew for sure you weren't dead, 'cause these little guys' job is to make sure we don't kick the bucket ourselves! Unless, of course, they are the ones terminating us!' He pointed to the two Spheres and laughed at his own humour.

'You have to take these into your house,' he continued, indicating to him the stacks of boxes piled up outside of Hongbing's house.

'What in the world is this?' Hongbing asked.

'It's your weekly food distribution from the state!'

'They even distribute food to us?'

'Indeed! It's a true Utopia! Didn't I tell you, you're freer here?' Aron cackled. 'These have been piling up outside your house since yesterday. I thought I might give you a hand!'

Hongbing merely stood there, processing the situation.

'Are you going to invite me in or what?' Aron probed.

'Ah . . . sure, come in.'

Aron entered the house eagerly and walked into the living room as his eyes ran across the space. But he didn't help Hongbing bring in a single box packed outside.

'Wow, your place has some really good furnishings. I'm a bit jealous, I must say!'

'Huh? I would have imagined all the houses here to be identical.'

Hongbing hadn't paid close attention to his new dwelling, since he was wallowing in misery. He didn't need to step out of his bedroom, which had an attached bathroom, as he had no energy to do anything else.

He only went two or three times to the kitchen for water when he really needed it and had a couple of slices of stale bread to avoid fainting.

Aron was right. The interior was surprisingly well-furnished, with everything one would need—from a sofa, coffee table, a TV, bookshelves to a chest of drawers—all of them looking brand new, perhaps creating an illusion meant to make the inmates forget their life-long sentence. The portrait of the Party Leader hung prominently on one wall, serving as a constant reminder of their entrapment.

'The Party's goal is to make the Village as real, as authentic as possible. The only difference is that we don't have to spend our hard-earned money to buy these things. A true liberation from labour! Didn't I tell you, we're freer here?'

'Oi, can you just not?' Hongbing snapped. 'Cut that freedom crap. We're doomed for life, okay? This is it. The end. Freedom? I was set up by UF agents and now I've lost my job, status and my entire family. I don't even know if they're still alive. You call this freedom?'

'Calm down, mate,' Aron said, his tone suddenly serious. 'I think we might need to talk. Is there anything you want to talk about?'

'Can't even talk freely here. Did you forget what happened just a few days ago?' Hongbing retorted.

'We *can* talk,' Aron replied. 'Provided we do not refer to *our-mutual-acquaintance* in an inappropriate manner, I do not believe the Party AI would detect any seditious undertones in our conversation. Besides, we have two more strikes before eviction-slash-possible-execution. We could potentially explore the limits!'

Hongbing paused for a second. *Is Aron another puppet of the Party?* Hongbing had none left in his trust. But the bitter solitude and the isolation were also chipping away at his sanity. *How could the Party possibly let people have such a free reign here?*

'Do you reckon Utopians could ever rally up and throw some punches back at the Party? Like, as a united front or something?' Hongbing asked.

In a rare moment of seriousness, the friendly neighbour paused for a long while before he spoke, minus his usual silliness and goof. 'The odds are slim. I mean . . . Utopians are likely to revolt *only* when the Party blatantly infringes on their interests, mostly material interests. Until now, the Party hasn't implemented any measures that can sufficiently provoke a considerable portion of Utopians to trigger a significant protest here.'

'So, they are skilled players?'

'Yeah, of course. They are well aware of Utopians' inherent materialistic self-centeredness.'

'I suppose they are not entirely selfish then,' Hongbing rationalized.

'Far from it. They implement policies that would protect the interest of the *majority*, to avoid sparking a major rebellion. If they wish to experiment, they do so incrementally, meticulously formulating policies to minimize the number of affected individuals. As long as these measures do not impact them directly, they won't bat an eye! By the time the policy evolves to impact them personally, there would be nobody left to fight with them.'

'What a utopia,' Hongbing grunted, sarcastically. 'What if ... just what if ... there's a massive protest due to a policy blunder ... an accidental effect on a large population at once? Something they didn't foresee?'

'That hasn't transpired in the past, but I would wager the Party would back down.'

'And show its weakness? No way. That's unlikely.'

'Consider this, time is on their side. It would seem as though they are accommodating the demands. Yet they can come back with their slow, steady approach to reintroduce whatever the policy piece by piece. I doubt such a move will inflict any lasting damage on the Party.'

'I still don't fully agree. How can it possibly not harm the Party when they back down? Outward appearances are of *paramount* importance to the Party Le—I mean to our mutual acquaintance.'

'Woo, that was close! Well, I think it depends on whether these protests endure. Do you think Utopians would persist in the fight once their immediate complaints are addressed? I bet not. As long as the Party eases the immediate issues and ensures no direct effects linger, the people will retreat to their comfort zones. That's the Utopian way. Would they form a civil society? Would they fight for a greater cause? Absolutely not.'

'So, in the end, we stand no chance unless we become one of them?'

'Exactly. The ones who chose not to fight should have realized that anyone can end up in a place like this. Under the Party Leader's rule, anyone can be labelled a criminal, provided the circumstances align.'

Beep!

A piercing sound filled the room, followed by red beams targeting the foreheads of the two, and the appearance of Muchen.

* * *

Once Aron had left, Hongbing sunk into his Party-distributed couch, which probably was collecting every bit of his biodata, and blankly gazed at the unlit TV screen before him. His own reflection on the black screen appeared somewhat distorted, but his radiating fear was all too clear. After everything that he had been through, he was surprised to find himself still scared of death—actually, not really death per se, but the uncertainty that came with it. He had wasted his first two opportunities, and now the Party would either execute him or subject him to an experiment considerably worse than this one. He just told Aron that he hated this place, but he realized that he was also afraid to leave. Perhaps, deep down in his heart, he yearned to remain. His conversation with Aron did little to improve his mood. His insight hit too close to reality—something that Hongbing wanted to overlook on purpose—that Utopians wouldn't revolt against the system.

It was, clearly, game over.

This renewed enlightenment made him as listless as everyone else sauntering on the streets. When he did venture outside, it was for brief periods at most, his eyes were glued to the ground, like everyone else. The homogenous colours of red rooftops and the blank expressions on the streets were the last things he wanted to look at. Trudging along like an android, he began to blend in with the mob, like one of those model citizens he had first spotted on the street—an ideal subject for the Party's ruling.

Today was another regular day, and six months into his new de facto vegetated life in the Village. The scene of a crowd congregating in front of the Village Centre lay before Hongbing. The scenario stupefied him. It was the first time since his arrival that he had ever seen total strangers talking to one another on the street. For a change, people looked alive. Strangely, though, they weren't looking at each other when they talked. Instead, everyone's gaze seemed to have been fixed on the same object. Following their gaze, Hongbing stopped at a hologram being projected from the Village Centre.

Announcement

Unleash Your True Self: The Return Game

The Objective: To kindle Utopian spirit of uniformity

The Challenge: Mingle with your fellow Villagers, pull out your detective glasses, and uncover any hint of dissent simmering beneath those neighbourly smiles. We're looking for those brave or foolish enough to harbour rebellious thoughts against our beloved Party.

The Method: Gather shiny nuggets of evidence—careless whispers, curious behaviours, any sizzling titbits that build a rock-solid case. Submit your treasure trove to our vigilant UF Security Officer in the Village division. Your identity will be locked up tighter than a drum until the guilty one is unveiled!

The Intrigue: Permission to bluff, bamboozle, and coax the truth out of your friends granted! Can you outwit your neighbours? Does your best friend harbour secrets? The thrill of the chase awaits you!

The Big Reveal: Once the rogue element is unveiled, your exciting pursuit, captured in every minute detail by our friendly Spheres, will make its grand premiere on national television. Ready to bask in your well-deserved fame?

> The Prize: For our victorious Villager, a golden ticket to not only reclaim your original esteemed position in the Party but also the chance for an express elevator ride up the Party ladder! You're also granted the power to pardon one person, irrespective of the crime they've been convicted of.
>
> Remember Villagers, the game is about unity and harmony, but a little bit of friendly betrayal can be the spice of life!
>
> The thrilling game starts today.

Here comes another dirty Party trick, Hongbing thought. But his pupils dilated wide, and his heart raced fast.

The game was repulsive . . . yet captivating.

* * *

Over the next ten days Hongbing confined himself to his house. During that self-imposed isolation, he reflected on all that he had witnessed and experienced from his time as a Party official to being an outcast in society. Faces of individuals replayed in his mind, evoking a range of emotions from sympathy and anger to guilt. As he sorted through it all without the burden of trying to do things, he began delving into his own thoughts; his deepest desires—his name and his family. The fog of confusion gradually lifted—relieving months of built-up stress and resentment that had weighed him down—and, for the first time in months, Hongbing's eyes sparkled with newfound clarity.

* * *

On the tenth day, Hongbing emerged from his *home*. Stepping out into the world with brand new confidence and, inner joy, whistling with pride. Filling his lungs with the fresh air outside, he began to walk. Every stride filled with determination and strength.

He held his head up and looked around him, as he walked around the town. The sea of rooftops, once dull and lifeless, now glimmered in a vibrant array of red hues—a delightful blend of crimsons, oranges, and pinks. The previously expressionless faces of those in the Village began to shine with a mix of fear, caution, and weariness—showcasing a sense of unique diversity of his country. Here was everything he needed to carve out a niche in this dystopia. This would be his new sanctuary, his refuge, his Utopia.